Bonk on the Head

BONK
ON THE
HEAD

John-James Ford

NIGHTWOOD EDITIONS
ROBERTS CREEK, BC
2005

Published by Nightwood Editions
R.R. #22, 3692 Beach Ave.
Roberts Creek, BC, Canada V0N 2W2
www.nightwoodeditions.com

Cover design by Silas White
Edited for the house by Silas White
Copy editing by Adrienne Weiss
Typesetting by Kathy Sinclair

Printed and bound in Canada

Nightwood Editions acknowledges financial support from the Government of Canada through the Canada Council for the Arts and the Book Publishing Industry Development Program, and from the Province of British Columbia through the British Columbia Arts Council, for its publishing activities.

THE CANADA COUNCIL | LE CONSEIL DES ARTS
FOR THE ARTS | DU CANADA
SINCE 1957 | DEPUIS 1957

BRITISH
COLUMBIA
ARTS COUNCIL
Supported by the Province of British Columbia

LIBRARY AND ARCHIVES CANADA CATALOGUING IN PUBLICATION

Ford, John-James, 1972-
     Bonk on the head / John-James Ford.

ISBN 0-88971-204-2

     I. Title.

PS8611.O73B65 2005   C813'.6   C2005-901392-3

For Karie

Book 1

Book 1

Ah, mon cher, for anyone who is alone,
without God and without a master,
the weight of days is dreadful. Hence one
must choose a master, God being out of style.

–Albert Camus

Buttercup

Gertie was the reprobate. She had her own methods, and as her brother I understood that she'd been gone for too long now— long enough to know that she wasn't coming back.

"Could be she just needs time," Mom said during breakfast. Nobody was eating because the postcard had just arrived in the mail.

"She needs a swift kick in the ass is what she needs," Dad muttered.

"Every family has one, I guess," Mom said.

"One what?" I asked.

"A menace," Dad said. "She's a goddamn menace." Gertie had really put a spoke in his wheel. For an infantry colonel, it must have been a hard blow to experience powerlessness over one's own daughter.

"Well, she's gone anyway," I said. "Gone but not forgotten, right Ailish?"

"Don't antagonize your little sister, you!" the Colonel spat.

"Whewis Gewty?" Ailish whispered.

"She's gone on a holiday," said Mom. "She'll be home soon, baby."

"Don't hold your breath," said the Colonel. "She'll never set foot in this house again while I'm alive."

"Who's that?" shouted Gramps. Gramps squeezed his toast in panic, spilling marmalade on his trousers.

"Gertie, Gramps," I said.

"Who's that?"

"Chrissakes Dad," the Colonel said. "Put in your goddamn hearing aid if you want to join the goddamn conversation!"

We sat around the table like uninvited guests, meditating upon the postcard as if conjuring it to speak. Only the Colonel wouldn't allow it to interfere with his meal, feeding himself forkfuls of breakfast links. The sunshiny otherness of the waxy beach photo made me hungry for adventure—to be anywhere but here, at this table, in the Kempt family breakfast nook. My runny eggs got cold.

"Someday, her gutsy attitude might pay off for her," I said.

"Could happen. You never know," Mom said. The Colonel snorted.

"Gondam gondam meniss," Ailish whispered. She banged her fork against her tray.

"Who's that?" Gramps pulled the oxygen tube from his nose, as if it helped his hearing. He tapped his wooden leg. "The toes itch," he said.

Gertie vanished at approximately 11:45 on the night of her seventeenth birthday—a day I like to refer to as the "August 17 Chicken Killing." That was over seven months ago, and since then the only word of her whereabouts was this dog-eared, patchouli-scented postcard of Wreck Beach, British Columbia.

"She's just testing the waters," Mom said. She stared at the wide-angle photo of the nude beach and frowned. "She's just fallen in with the wrong sort."

"No doubt her present company are people whose moral fibre is suspect," Dad said. "But I have to wonder who is influencing whom."

According to her message, Gertie had joined a commune:

Word to the muthaship, Herbie! Don't need clothes. Every-body works for the growth of the soil: yesterday my friend from Vancouver Island spent the morning weeding the tomato patch wearing nothing but a tampon. I know you're blushing but the body is beautiful and nothing to be ashamed of. You should get out this way if you ever get your nose out of your dusty books. We need an adventure Herb and you could use some of this California sun. Give Ailish a big wet kiss and a tight one from me, and tell Mom I miss her. Tell the Kernel I'm sorry about Buttercup. Love G.

"Is that Gertie home?" Gramps shouted, struggling to his feet. He leaned on his shillelagh for support, and smacked at the gobs of HP sauce around his lips. "Got sauce on my cakehole, what." He leaned over, trying to focus on the postcard. "That's pornargerphy!"

"A postcard from Gertie, Gramps," I said. He looked hurt, and shuffled off to the family room.

"The *Kernel!*" Dad said. "She'll fry her brains in no time with those hippie throwback ingrates!" He wiped spittle from his lips and twisted up the red tips of his mustache.

I struggled with the visual of the naked female body with a string dangling between tanned thighs. "I thought hippies were against tampons."

"That's enough crass talk out of you!" Dad said.

"Gondam meniss," Ailish said.

Buttercup had been the Colonel's honey pot: a street-rod kit car with a feather-light body. Bright orange and yellow flames exploded off the grill, licked at the cherry-red paint job and wrapped around the hood, which housed a 350 4-barrel.

Above our mantle hung Dad's favourite photo: he looked almost boyish next to Buttercup in a soft white polo shirt and shorts, beaming. It would be hard to guess he was a soldier.

I am a year older than Gertie. I always have been. Still, I have yet to feel that way because Gertie has the exact brand of confidence I've been seeking since forever. I have tried to muster the same kind of guts many times, but it doesn't work like that—you can't make that stuff up on the spot. Even the Colonel used to say she had a pair.

Presumably, Gertie had hitched across Canada and the northwestern states without reservation, without a whiff of concern for her own well-being. Or, she might say it was concern for her well-being that prompted her to leave. She's the type that you just know would come through a car crash, or a war, unscathed. Anybody who's met Gertie feels safe around her.

After she vanished, I got in the habit of studying the atlas, guessing at her whereabouts. I followed her, measuring her movements in centimetres. Every time I converted the distances according to the map legend, the mere thought of covering that much ground without your own car, or money, gave me the heebie-jeebies. The atlas stretched out in faded, inky colours, blurring my field of vision, defying me to jump in.

"I've got to get out of Basseville," Gertie said once. "*We've* got to get out of Basseville, Herbie." We were fishing off the Main Street bridge. It was a catch-and-release competition to see who could haul in the most deformed bugger in the river, and Gertie was winning. I'd hauled up a bass that had started to divide but never fully split—on the belly was an area where the head of the second fish was forming. It was gross, but no match for Gertie's prize: she'd hauled up a pike that had two bodies with one head. It was amazing this guy was alive, he was such a terrible swimmer. When we let him go, his two bodies smacked against each other again and again, working against each other and the current.

"I like Basseville," I said. "It's not really rural, and it's not the suburbs either. It's quiet and safe, and we're only a twenty-five-minute drive to Ottawa. I like Basseville—why shouldn't I?"

"You don't like Basseville, moron," Gertie said. "You're just comfortable in our boring house, with our satellite TV. The problem is you've never stopped to ask yourself *what* you like. You're too happy to let real life pass by unnoticed. You can't even describe Basseville."

"I just did!"

"That wasn't a description, that was a sales pitch. This place chaps my ass."

"So leave if you want to leave then." She must have known I didn't mean it, but now Gertie was living in a commune—

somewhere far away in the land of milk and honey, where there's pot and naked tits all day long.

Almost a year to the day before Gertie left, she had coerced me into taking Buttercup for a joyride. Mom and the Colonel were at the cottage, and as I had just turned seventeen, it was the first year that Gertie and I weren't required by standing orders to join them on the shores of Round Lake.

"We need to celebrate!" Gertie said. I had finally obtained my driver's licence after the third attempt. Gertie was sixteen, but hadn't been allowed to go for her learner's permit because the Colonel was still waiting for an apology from her for coming home from school drunk one afternoon. Gertie wouldn't apologize because she was upset with Dad over what he said after I failed my test the second time:

"Hey Gomer! That'll be your new name, since only a goddamn gomer could fail a driver's test, eh?"

"Gomer'd be a better goddamn name than goddamn Herbert!" Gertie said. "Or goddamn Gertrude, for that goddamn matter. Why would you do something like that to your own goddamn children?" Dad cuffed her a good one on the ear for that.

"To mark our first step towards freedom," Gertie declared, "we are going to liberate this over-cared-for, underused vehicle."

"I won't do it Gertie, there's no way." She'd let Buttercup's roof down and the smell of Armor All was playing with my head. It occurred to me that there might be surveillance cameras in the garage. Every few minutes I thought I could hear Dad's Datsun coming up the drive, even though I knew they weren't supposed to be back for another week.

"Just think of it, Herbie—"

"Think of it? It's retarded, is what it is. It's preposterous. What if something happens?"

"What if, what if, what if? What if we might have some fun for once? Show some balls, Herb."

"What about Gramps?" I was stalling. I knew I couldn't argue with her for long.

"I don't think he'd be interested in coming," she said.

"He'll tell."

"Are you kidding? I put *Patton* on for him. He'll be rubbing his wooden leg and crying until the movie is over—and by then, he'll probably be back in Normandy," she said, tapping her head.

"Don't play with me, man—you know full well we've got all afternoon."

"I don't know, Gertie," I said.

"Suit yourself." Gertie slid behind the wheel, caressed the leather bench seat, and engaged the clutch. Buttercup coasted easily out of the garage.

"Gertie! Dammit Gertie! You can't drive without a licence!"

"Case of beer says I can drive better than you," she said, turning the ignition. Buttercup's engine growled awake. Even the idling engine indicated the power it contained, and it penetrated me like someone had shoved a fistful of bumblebees into my spine. Gertie looked over her shoulder: "You coming or not?"

Gertie rode the clutch and drove like a bandit, but even when she bunnyhopped it, she looked comfortable with what she was doing. We made it into the city without incident, and crossed the Champlain Bridge into Quebec, where we spent our grocery allowance on Labatt 50 at the first depanneur we came across. The beer fit snug into Buttercup's rumble seat.

"Jesus H. Christ!" said Gertie. "The old man made this seat just for a two-four! I don't know about you, Herbie, but I feel all growed up."

We got lost in Hull and ended up on the MacDonald-Cartier Bridge, following the signs for Ottawa. Buttercup hummed. She seemed well-oiled and impatient. The wind flapped Gertie's red hair into tangles that went in her face—she looked like a woman with her head on fire.

"Bet she doesn't get to run like this with the Kernel!" she screamed.

"What?" I clutched the tiny dashboard as we picked up speed.

"She doesn't—never mind!" Gertie braked suddenly and swerved into the right lane, sending Buttercup into a stall. We made the Sussex-Dalhousie exit with inches to spare and shot down the off-ramp in high-speed silence.

"We should get her home." My knuckles were white and numb on the dash.

"We can go right now if you're willing to drive," Gertie said as we coasted into the ByWard Market.

"Not a chance. Forget it. No way am I driving this thing."

"C'mon Herbie—she drives like a dream."

"This is crazy, what we're doing…"

"It's a car, Herbert. It's just a fucking car."

Gertie restarted the engine at a stoplight, and we puttered around the market. In slow degrees I took interest in my surroundings, forgetting from time to time that we were fugitives. Row after row of fruit stands and vegetable stands stood among the crowds, and ladies with apron pouches grabbed bills and doled out change, and old guys with cigarettes hanging off their bottom lips—with ashes you'd swear were about to fall any minute but didn't—bagged a bushel of cukes here, a basket of peaches there. There were big smells of hot dog and Polish sausage vendors mixing with the hotsweet and sticky sidewalks. Some good old boys spilled out of the Chateau Lafayette and stumbled through the litter of stale butts and a hundred years of pissy draft.

There were buskers at every corner, bracketing the quiet and almost invisible blemishes of the city: cracked-lipped winos and soiled panhandlers. Above this litter and around it were the Gap-clad pedestrians lugging satchels of fresh produce, grande iced mocha frappucinos, frozen yogurt and large bouquets wrapped in waxed paper. Variety abounded: BluBlockers and Gucci sunglasses, Tilley hats and silk headscarves, Reeboks, Birkenstocks and Italian leather shoes—many accessories covering both tanned flesh and white flab.

"Look at all these people," said Gertie. "They're beautiful!"

We peered out of the flaming hot rod at what, for us, seemed a huge slice of the big world.

"This is a long way from Basseville," Gertie said. We cruised down York Street, and an oncoming patrol car slowed its approach. The officer scrutinized Buttercup from behind his aviator sunglasses.

"Cops!" I said, ducking.

"Nice one, Herb. That'll throw him off our tail." Gertie squinted into the rearview. "Ahhh, *fuck!* He's turning around!"

She stomped on the accelerator and squealed through a stale yellow, making a hard left onto Dalhousie. She cut the engine and coasted into a no-parking zone.

"SWITCH!" she screamed. I reacted immediately to her tone of voice—it was the same as the Colonel's—and crawled over Gertie as she squirmed beneath me to the passenger side. As I sat in the driver's seat, I felt more beneath the wheel than behind it.

"I don't have my licence!" I patted my empty pockets.

"Here—I brought it. Wipe off the dust."

The cop cruised around the corner with his cherries flashing, and we made eye contact as I peered over my shoulder. I whipped my head around as the cruiser pulled up behind.

"Dammit Gertie!" We were done for.

"Relax man—okay? Just relax. You're legit, right? This is perfectly legal, as long as he doesn't insist that it was me driving."

The cop got out and hitched up his belt, then strolled over. He looked Buttercup up and down before coming to my door.

"Nice ride," the officer said, taking my licence.

"Thanks."

"This your car?"

"Yes. Well—no … I mean it's my father's."

"Right. Registration?"

Gertie took it from the glovebox and handed it over.

"Are you aware you went through a red back there?"

"Oh, I'm sorry sir. I thought it was yellow."

"Yellow still means slow down, not speed up. Especially to a new driver."

"Yessir. Still getting used to the clutch, sir."

The officer took a look at the rims and the grill, whistling in admiration. "That's some custom paint," he said. He walked slowly to the back of the car.

"The beer!" I hissed. Gertie tensed.

In the rearview I saw the cop look sideways at the case of beer in the rumble seat. He tapped his notepad against the palm of his hand, then ambled back to his cruiser to run the plates.

"See Herb? No problem."

"Gertie please, shh!"

The officer came back and smiled at us. "Your old man would be none too happy if you brought home a citation for a moving violation, am I right?"

"Yessir," I said.

"And that case of 50 in the back belongs to your old man, am I right?"

"A hundred percent, officer," Gertie said. She gave him a sweet smile.

"Traffic lights are there for your safety. I don't want to be picking you kids out of any wreckage, hear? Get this beauty home in one piece."

"Yessir," I said.

"Thank you officer," Gertie said.

I started the engine, signalled, checked my mirrors, and pulled into traffic. Neither of us said a word as we left the market and steered south down Highway 16 for Basseville. After the run-in with the cop, I felt like I now had a right to the car. Between Gertie and me there was something sinister, like we were both criminals, untouchables.

"Give 'er gas Herb!" Gertie screamed. I floored it and was sucked back into my seat as Buttercup shot forward, eating up the highway. I eased off and shook my head to get rid of the giddiness; there were volumes and volumes of unread power beneath the flaming hood. I beat my hand against the wheel, laughing.

"Well, Gertie, I think I've chipped a piece off the cornerstone of manliness."

"WHAT?" she said. I waved her off and smiled. My glad heart was no longer shivering at the image of us smashing the street-rod to bits or being pinched in the act by the Colonel.

It was pre-dusk but the air was warm and the sky was a heavy crimson.

"RED SKY AT NIGHT, SAILOR'S DELIGHT!" I screamed.

"YOU'RE A NATURAL DRIVER, HERBIE," Gertie said. I could barely hear her over the wind. She said something else and I just nodded.

The temperature dropped and the air was cool as we followed the Rideau River south. Barely perceptible beneath the noise of the engine was the humming of grasshoppers. The buzz rose from the grassy ditches as thousands of tiny legs rubbed in a rhythmic and sustained chirping. I had fleeting thoughts about sound, frequency, emotion—I wanted to make up a theory about life and prove it in my own heart and share it. I sniffed at the country air and stared at the bulrushes, remembering how we used to pick them years ago.

That had been in Petawawa. Or Borden. Could have been Wainwright—one of the Colonel's early postings, anyway. In those days there were less shadows. Mom and Dad would ritually stop the car on lazy, sunny afternoons and follow hand-in-hand as Gertie and I scrambled ahead to cut down velvet-brown bulrushes, tug at soft cattails. Gertie would lead me on, showing me where to pick and how many and why. Every so often we would look back, always keeping within shouting distance.

I downshifted and accelerated, just to feel the pull and to live through another satisfactory moment of shifting. Gertie had her feet on the dash, and let her hand rise and fall with the wind. For the moment, Buttercup belonged to us. The earth and our movement over it seemed impeccable.

12

I daydreamed that someday I would learn to explain about the bulrushes, to talk about the grasshoppers of late summer. And the crickets singing from the ditches and culverts that seemed to go as far as you wanted to drive. Someday, I would communicate the same essence as the moist air and the smell of warm, sun-drenched earth. I wanted to write a poem, or sing or something. I couldn't remember the last time I'd been conscious of being so outside, so out-of-doors and alive. It was as if I'd forgotten something important. Or it was like something important was happening to me, but I couldn't say what. It felt good—it was like what being drunk should feel like, but doesn't.

I imagined my face projected worldwide, in live coverage, as my parents and Gramps and Gertie and Ailish watched from home, jockeying for positions on the couch. Ailish would stop talking and point at the screen. Gertie would shush Gramps and turn up the volume. Mom would clasp her hands together in anticipation. The Colonel would wipe his misty eyes, waiting for me to speak.

The Kernel

After Gertie left, school just didn't fit right. School hung around me like a cheap wool suit: it itched, it chafed, it got in the way. "I wonder if Gertie's going to finish school out there," I said. "Don't hold your breath, you," the Colonel said. "Your sister was expelled, remember? She'll get a few hard lessons in the School of Life." I wanted to ask what the hell the School of Life was, but I checked myself. Whatever it was, it had to be better than Holy Name of Jesus High.

At the end of every day I climbed on the yellow short bus and found a seat. I could always feel dried sweat on my forehead and grime on my hands by this time. I looked forward to washing up at home, and having a snack, and lying in my bed and listening to music. On the bus, math formulas and Shakespeare's greatest hits jockeyed for position in my head. Too many loose ends in my mind.

The school bus was small relief, since we had Betty, the union-protected driver. Big Betty's grey eyes were as cold as the Colonel's, and her nicotine-stained lips puckered into a permanent, fleshy pout. To avoid eye contact, I usually stared at the polished silver handle before Big Betty's man-hands grappled it—her arm lunging out, bingo wings flapping, to pull the doors shut. She had kankles; her big butt was a keel in her spring-cushioned seat. Betty was always armed with a box of glazed chocolate Timbits by her side.

I was in the habit of sitting at the back, alone. I kept my knapsack over my lap as camouflage for stray farts and intermittent hard-ons. It was dead easy to get a woody on the school bus, due to the motion. I usually clicked my window panel down a few notches, even in winter, hoping for a fresh breeze to displace the stale air of bus—air thick with the smells of sodden stale-mustard sandwiches and sugary drink boxes. There was always something sticky beneath the soles of my sneakers. The bus is a cesspool of teen spirit.

With Gertie gone, there was no one worth speaking to on the loser-cruiser. Isaac Kotlarsky lived five blocks from Holy Name of Jesus and walked home, taking his whole existence at his own pace. Isaac, a.k.a. Icky, was self-indulgent to the point of cool, in a sinister, Dorian Gray kind of way. I am sure Icky will end as a junkie or a rock star, or maybe both. And my friend Won-ton worked two part-time jobs. "For something to do," Won-ton said, though we all knew it was to help his mom make rent each month. Icky's dad was the deadbeat kind—gone but not forgotten, and Won-ton's dad was a myth, a drifter who'd never laid eyes on his son. I had no end of speculation as to what life would be like in a house with no father.

So ever since Gertie left I was mule-dumb on the bus, staring out at the farmers' fields compressed between Ottawa and Basseville. I watched for cattle, or anything else I could count. I hitched my knees against the seat-back, and opened a book to avoid conversation, though I was generally too hungry and tired to concentrate. And every day Betty blared soulless AM radio. It was generally at this time of day that my mouth would go chalky, and I'd plan.

One thing having a father in the army taught me is that there is Intelligence, and there is Counter-Intelligence. I speculated in black ops. Time now: 3:47. Time of arrival at home: 4:16. Assets: in the fridge, the breadbox, the freezer. The Colonel's ETA from National Defence Headquarters: 4:32. Situation: perpetual hunger. Mission: clandestine snack. Execution: microwave. Support: Ailish, possibly Mom. Communications: subtlety, nuance, stolen glances. Enemy Forces: one Colonel, grumpy.

I gave myself pep talks: "Move in and move out fast. Speed is the key, Herb. Like clockwork—don't waste any movements. Learn your timings, stay in the shadows."

Sometimes the mission would be a success. Sometimes it would be as simple as Melba toast with butter, or cheddar on pumpernickel, or rye toast and honey, or a bowl of ice cream. Sometimes I'd nuke a J. Kwinter gourmet hot dog, adrenalin pumping through my heart the whole eternal minute the microwave was on.

"Watch your six!" I'd say to myself. "He could be home any minute." I'd make straight for my room with a blistering wiener in my hand. No time for ketchup or mustard or relish or bun. There was always a twitch at my temple: I wasn't safe until my door was shut and the wiener was in my belly. I left no evidence, not even a dirty plate, except for the dissipating aroma in the kitchen and the meat on my breath.

I'd throw something on my turntable—say, *The Best of Bread*. But nothing would block out the sound of the Colonel's Datsun gearing down to turn into the laneway. I cringed. I waited for the front door to slam. I could close my eyes and see his perfectly formed green beret still on his head, briefcase in his left hand. He would pause at the door in mid-stride, right hand clenched, head up, shoulders back, eyes alert, ears cocked, and nose trying to distinguish the nature of the smell originating from the grease-splattered microwave.

"Davey!" yelled Gramps, his oxygen machine gurgling away happily. "Where'd that remote get to? This bloody show is the pits. The shits, what!"

And the Colonel, this time, was thrown off my scent. I could breathe deep, breathe easy. Mother Freedom.

Since Gertie left, we still had dinner together even though each of us would have rather slapped a plate on a TV tray and watched *Entertainment Tonight* or *Jeopardy* or whatever Gramps was into.

Sometimes I watched Mom run the family show—she wasn't obvious about it, she was more like a soft-shoed black-clad stagehand in the wings. She'd try to coerce Ailish into eating a token amount of peas or carrots, then she'd talk to Dad for a bit then me for a bit then Dad for a bit more, walking this tightrope of tension, balancing the entire household on her head and smiling as if it were no big thing. Sometimes I'd try to talk to Ailish, but at dinnertime it was useless. She'd just babble. On her second birthday Ailish was speaking in full, grammatically correct sentences. But by the age of three she had reverted to baby talk. It was awful, like she'd disappeared. The remarkable thing was that nobody considered this remarkable. Come to think of it, I'm not so sure my parents ever noticed. After a while, I got used to it.

If Mom was the stagehand, she had her job cut out for her because the family drama was mostly a silent one. I felt more uncomfortable around the Colonel every day. When Gertie was here, there was spinach as well as salad when Mom overcooked a mess of pork chops. There were nutburgers and soy milk in the fridge. There were card tricks or a game of dominoes after dessert. There were clandestine smokes behind the woodpile. There wasn't so much silence, that's for sure. Our hub was missing, and it was all the more unbearable because nobody would admit it.

One night I couldn't take the dead quiet anymore.

"So I got a role in the school play, a speaking role." I tried to sound offhanded.

"That's wonderful," Mom said, patting Dad's hand. She looked worried, as if I'd just told them I was gay. "What's the name of the play?"

"*Inherit the Wind*," I said.

"Pass the bread please Paula," said the Colonel. He cleared his throat.

"It's a smart play," I said. "It's about a teacher who teaches Darwinism in some hick school and has to go to court to defend himself from Bible-thumpers."

"The Scopes Monkey Trial," Mom said. It wasn't a surprise that she knew it. She'd grown up with Bible-thumpers.

"That's it," I said. "Gertie would get a kick out of it. I'm going to play Meeker, the bailiff."

"I'll have the butter if you're about done with it, Herbert," said the Colonel. I passed it to him. I hadn't even used the goddamn butter.

"Hi Hewbie," said Ailish.

"So Dad, how was your day?" I said. There was a big pause. He didn't answer but he stopped chewing and put his fork down. "How's work?" I asked again. Mom shot me a look, like I was speaking someone else's lines. After a moment Dad answered.

"Busy," he said. He picked up his fork and started chewing again.

I often guessed at what went on within the walls of National Defence Headquarters, and more specifically, what military intelligence was supposed to mean. The one time I asked him he told me that it was an oxymoron, which was a word I had to look up. Dad had medals on his chest when he wore his dress uniform but never spoke of them.

Dad always sat, whether at home or in public, with his back to the wall. No prying eyes behind him—no one to sneak up on his six. Reams of intelligence passed by him every day. He wasn't born until after Gramps' war and had been too young for Korea, and he was now too old and too specialized to stand on the battlefield in any war to come.

"I'm a celebrated—*celebrated*—fucking combat soldier," he said to me once when he was drunk. "And I'm destined to never fire a weapon in combat." We were sitting on the couch and I'd just mixed him a stiff gin and tonic, and he had his arm around me. His hot and clammy weight pressed against me—I'd tried to detach and get to my room several times, but he kept hanging on.

"My rifle is a flaccid cock!" he said. His gin breath wafted all over my face. "I want to go to war!" he whined. "I'm destined to die in war."

Always with his back to the wall, watching the front for snipers. I watched him at dinner—he was always Colonel Grumpy Pants right up until he had a drink in his hand. I often wondered why he didn't just have a drink as soon as he walked in the door.

I regretted talking about the stupid play. Standard operating procedures were to keep mum. I poured another glass of milk and pushed my plate away to make room for dessert. Mom had baked my favourite dessert, apple dumplings, and Ailish had managed to smear enough peas around her tray to warrant a dumpling. They were still warm from the oven.

"Yum-mee!" I winked at Ailish and chugged back my milk.

"Any reason you have to drink like a horse?" the Colonel said.

"Sorry." I felt my face flush. It was suddenly hot in the room.

"Nothing like a cold glass of milk to wash down a sticky dumpling," Mom said from the wings. She was like a fearless bomb squad, trying to diffuse the situation with a smile and a nod. She passed Dad the brandy sauce for his dumpling. "I made it special," she said.

"If you're thirsty, drink water," Dad said. He gave me the Eye.

"Okay. Sorry. I won't have any tomorrow."

"That's not the bloody point, you! When are you going to start thinking of others? How much is left? Enough for coffee in the morning? Enough for Ailish's cereal?"

"Fwoot Noops?" said Ailish.

"You've had two glasses so far, and Christ knows how many after school. Do I need to start buying milk every bloody day on my way home from the office?"

I stared at my saucy little dumpling, and resolved not to eat it no matter how much I wanted to.

"THERE IS ABSOLUTELY NO REASON YOU NEED TO USE SO MUCH MILK ON A DAILY BASIS. PERIOD." Then his voice got real quiet: "I'm always at the ready, but you just don't get that do you? I can see through the bullcrap, my son. I can see right through, to the cut and dried." He pushed his plate away and went to the sideboard to mix a drink.

Yeah, mix your own bloody drinks, I wanted to say. I made the resolution not to fetch a single beer for the Colonel. I wouldn't mix him one ounce of his lousy gin.

It didn't last, though. I knew he'd had a hard day. After he'd had a few, he called me down and all was forgotten, and he asked me to open a bottle of scotch from the basement. I did it—I wanted to do it.

In my room I turned my music down low and listened for the hum of oxygen—I pictured Gramps shuffling aimlessly downstairs, the plastic tube clinging diligently to his old nostrils. At this time of day Gramps would mumble vague references to Normandy while sniffing out the keys to the liquor cabinet, or whining to my old man for just a shot of whiskey, and if not whiskey, brandy then.

Dad always said that Gramps was an old-type soldier who would never lie down. He wouldn't surrender to a thing, even as he held onto his turbulent, torn mind with kite string.

I felt another headache creeping behind my pupils, and shut the music off. In silence I plodded through several calculus problems, then wrestled with the periodic table until I couldn't fathom how all these elements could really be captured. None of it made sense. Eventually, the headache overran me.

Ailish splashed in the tub down the hall. The bathroom door was wide open, and she sang a song Gertie had taught her about bare bums. At that moment, when I recognized her voice and what she was singing, I had what I think is called a panic attack. I clearly understood my life was heading in the wrong direction, and I wasn't doing a damn thing about it. I got up to walk around, but there was no place to walk in my room. I pressed my pillow over my face until I couldn't breathe. When I took the pillow off, I really couldn't breathe, and started hyperventilating. I threw my sorry self on the ground twisted to and fro, and played up a coughing and gasping and choking fit just for my own amusement.

Then I got the idea that I was on stage—just like at dinner, but now Gertie was somewhere in the rafters, watching my choices play out and checking them against the program in her hand.

"I'm having heart palpitations," I groaned, as if she were there. I lay on the floor and repeated her name. I half expected her to swoop down from the sky and take me out of the house. At the very least she'd send me a telepathic message. I pressed the rounded corner of Gertie's postcard against my forehead and moved it in a small radius until I found the spot, my third eye, midway between my eyebrows. A slow tingle seeped through the postcard and into my skin, spreading outward as I lay motionless, eyes shut. I waited for her message. I forgot about my panic attack as it subsided, and I remembered the details of the day we stole Buttercup, convinced there was a hidden meaning in Gertie's actions. I sorted through the memories slowly and carefully, as if they were made of glass.

I remember we arrived home when day had ended and night had not yet come. Cast in half-light, Buttercup seemed illusory, as if she was more of a friend than a vehicle. The expedition was already dreamlike. What had been accomplished felt nothing short of genius, as if we'd taken part in a masterwork of art.

I had tried to reverse Buttercup into her spot, but couldn't manage the steering quite right and clipped the fender against the garage. I could still hear the scratch. Gertie assumed command immediately.

"We need a few pints," she decided. "To focus." We drank some, then she scrounged an old can of red latex from the loft and did a touch-up.

The initial application was too light—more of a beacon to the scratch than a cover-up, so she mixed in some blue and practised on a piece of plywood until she was satisfied. After the second coat, Buttercup's cut was hardly noticeable. "You'd have to be looking for it specifically," Gertie said, but by that time we were drunk and working under moonlight.

We went to the gazebo to get drunker. Gramps was watching *Hollywood Squares* and sneaking snorts from the bourbon Gertie had left out for him with instructions not to drink it. Gramps was totally oblivious to the fact that we were still technically in his charge, and that we'd disappeared in the hot rod for the better part of the afternoon and were now getting pissed in the backyard.

"Isn't it weird," I said, "how, no matter what is on TV, the blue light always looks exactly the same from outside?"

"You read that in a book," Gertie said.

Fonz

The day the package arrived was the same day Ruth McBride asked me to work on the English project with her. We had to present a group of poems to the class in an interesting way— a challenging project. The package arrived anonymously, but I immediately sensed Gertie in the wrapping. I waited until I was at school to open it. No letter, no return address, and this time it was postmarked Big Sur. Under the brown-bag packaging was a journal wrapped in tissue. It was hard-covered, with hemp paper and sewn binding. For a journal, it seemed quite exquisite. There was also a bud of sticky weed wrapped in tinfoil. I had no idea why Gertie would send me a journal, even less so when I read the inside cover.

To my brother, the poet.

I have written one thing in my life that could be described, loosely, as a poem. It was more of an emotional outburst scrawled onto a piece of birchbark that I'd ripped off of a stick of fire-wood when I couldn't find paper. Also, Gertie knew I didn't much like smoking dope. But if Gertie thought I should write some poems, I couldn't help but give the idea some thought.

I opened the journal to the first crisp page, but couldn't think of anything to put down, so after a while I closed it. Later, on the late bus home from play practice, I wrote down the birch-bark poem. I figured it was as good a place as any to start, it being my first and only poem to date. It wasn't hard to remember, being only three lines long.

I fly with life
as fast as age
will carry me

I read it several times. Then I added one more line:

what a lie!

I closed the journal in disgust and stuffed it in my knapsack. Poet, my arse. I'd be better off as a soldier.

And then an odd coincidence as Betty blared Majic 100: "In today's world, life skills are as important as professional qualifications. The Royal Military College of Canada lays the foundation for personal and professional skills necessary to meet the unique challenges of a career as a Canadian Forces Officer. If you are a good student, if you enjoy physical activity and if you are not afraid of hard work, perhaps RMC is for you."

I imagined coming home from pilot training for a little R&R. I'd unzip my flight suit, casually, and lay my helmet on the kitchen table and joke with the Colonel in MilSpeak—nobody else would understand our sophisticated humour. Maybe Gertie would come home, and I'd take off my aviator glasses and give her a long look, and she would try to take the piss out of both of us for being so goddamn *military*. But we, father and son, officers each, would just laugh and grin, brushing off her childish adversity and her girlish poetic ideals with our own private, heroic confidence.

I climbed through the crisp blue sky in an F-18. I was niner-zero-bogey for vector on the tail of three MiGs. What was my call sign? Unfortunately, Maverick was used up by Tom Cruise—Maverick was a good one. Talk to me Goose!

Then it came to me: Fonz.

The three MiGs were sweeping right ... but wait! Something was wrong with engine number four! I paused, trying to remember if F-18s had two engines or four, and then I couldn't remember if it was F-18s or F-15s that Canadian pilots were flying. It didn't matter. Fonz had no time for these questions as he was thrown into a flat spin. The tower screamed into my headset: Fonz! *Pull out!* You're way too low! *Pull up!* I didn't know if the tower would be shouting *Pull out* or *Pull up*, so it shouted both.

My navigator, Potsie, said: "Fonz, gee whiz, you'll get us out of this crazy mess, won't you?"

"Correctamundo," I said, even though I was now in danger of losing consciousness from excessive g-forces. Still, I calmly pressed red flashing buttons and grappled with the stick, fighting my way out of it.

The tower screamed: *Eject! Fonz, Eject! Eject!*

"Whoa!" I said. They were pissing me off, messing with my concentration. I yanked the headset off. The tower could sit on it. The Fonz does not eject. I'd pull out of this one, or thunder in with my plane. My dad was on the ground watching me fly, his teeth clenched.

I could hear Potsie whimpering.

"Hold on Pots!" I yelled. "The Fonz'll get us outta this!"

I felt for the sweet spot on the control board, and then gave it a solid thump with my fist. I touched the stick with one finger and we pulled out, or up, at three hundred feet. No—one hundred feet. Expertly, I regained altitude, defying the unfriendly sky with steel-blue eyes—eyes with the same confident severity that the Colonel had—and I positioned myself on the tail of one of the MiGs, zeroing in for the first kill.

"Herb," somebody said. "Herb?" The fools! The tower wasn't using my call sign! Then I remembered that Fonz wasn't wearing his headset.

"Herbert!" Nicotine-starved Betty leered at me in the rearview mirror. She was dying for a smoke, and I was her last stop.

I looked out the window at our house, and was momentarily reluctant to get off the bus until I saw Ailish waiting for me on the porch.

While she was only four years old, Ailish was smarter than most people I knew. She was a quiet girl, and her capacity for stillness was uncanny. She had this skinny little body and a quirky way about her.

In Ailish I had found what Gertie liked to call a "kindred spirit." As an infant, she had already guessed at the same connection with me: when she was fussy with Mom and Gertie, I could quiet her by softly telling her about my day. I'd sit with her in the rocking chair and if we were alone I'd tell her how nobody understood things, how my teachers and Mom and Dad expected way too much. I told her how I had no idea what, or who, I was supposed to be. She would coo softly with these big, wide eyes, and though I know she didn't understand English then, she understood me, and agreed.

I knelt beside Ailish on the porch and she clasped her tiny arms around me. "Hewbie I made cookies!"

"What? Cookies? Again? All by yourself?"

"I put dem inna oven aw by mysewf!"

"I'm going to eat them *all* right now!" I boomed in a deep voice. I picked her up and threw her over my shoulder as I opened the screen door. The heavy smell of peanut butter swirled from the oven into the entranceway.

I made a beeline for the kitchen, jammed two of the cookies cooling on a rack into my mouth and propped Ailish on her feet.

"Mmmm!" I moaned, rolling my eyes back before closing them. Ailish giggled and put her hands over her mouth. I sank to the floor, rolling about in playful ecstasy, happy with Ailish's belly-laughter. I hadn't heard her laugh like that since before Gertie left. I jumped suddenly to my feet and swept her into my arms, kissing her cheeks and neck, and goosing her sides.

Ailish stopped laughing abruptly and stiffened. I cocked my head, listening intently as I set her down. We heard the Datsun gear down to make the turn into our driveway. We were silent. The slam of the car door indicated what kind of a mood the Colonel was in, and when I heard it, I snatched three cookies from the cooling rack, kissed Ailish on the forehead, and booked.

"That you Herb?" Mom said as I passed the washroom.

"Uh-huh."

"How's school?"

"Mgood," I managed through a mouthful of warm cookie. I took the stairs three at a time and slid into my room. I closed the door quietly and leaned against it, chewing and catching my breath.

26

When my heart rate slowed, I put Ween's *Pure Guava* in the stereo, and thought a bit about Ruth McBride. I had been considering for some time asking her to work on the poetry project with me, and today she had just come and asked me out of the blue. It was significant, but I couldn't make out why.

I opened the atlas and tried to pinpoint Gertie's exact whereabouts. I imagined her right now with big-breasted women—blonde, raven-haired and chestnut-haired beauties with colourful braids, and bangles, wearing tie-dyed pieces of almost-nothing, fondling each other to the Grateful Dead. Gertie was no doubt smoking a big joint, and I imagined her getting homesick and telling her horny half-naked companions about her big brother. She would show them the poem on the worn birchbark—they would sigh, and giggle and gather round to ask questions about me. Later they would think over what she had said, and touch themselves.

I decided that it couldn't hurt to start working on a poem. I couldn't think of a title just yet, or a subject, but I imagined that as far as poems are concerned, you can use anything as a title—even a punctuation mark. Poems don't need a subject for that matter—and judging from the poems I'd read, they don't even need to make sense. It would be a long poem. Pages and pages—impressive! While thinking about the poem I thought of Ruth again, and when I thought about Ruth I thought about the army, and eventually I got around to thinking about my old man, who was sitting one floor directly beneath me in his worn easy chair, sipping a dry martini.

In the Basement

The day we stole Buttercup, neither Gertie nor I had given any thought to the telling evidence we left on the odometer. It was a pretty foolish oversight, considering we had both seen *Ferris Bueller's Day Off* at least half a dozen times.

"Gertrude! Herbert!" Dad screamed. "Outside, you! Both of you!"

The Colonel pointed at the figures in his mileage book, then at the odometer. He glared at both of us, defying us to explain the discrepancy. His face was blotchy, and his mustache twitched like it had its own brain.

"I did it," Gertie said.

"WHAT?" the Colonel roared.

"What are you doing?" I whispered.

"Yeah. Sorry," Gertie said. "Just a little spin on the back roads. I wanted to see what she had in her. She runs great, Daddy."

"You, YOU! This is *not* your bloody car, you! You know you are expressly forbidden to sit in this car, let alone drive it. And you don't even have a licence! Have you *any* idea how much parts cost for this machine?"

"I didn't drive *fast*, Dad."

Her quick confession threw me for a minute. It phased the Colonel too, I think, because he didn't seem to know what to do.

"Get up to your room," he said, finally.

"Oh wow. Some punishment. Like that's not where I want to be anyway," Gertie said.

Then I understood. Gertie was surfing the Big One on the Colonel's sea of blind rage. She knew that if she pissed him off enough, I would be left outside his narrow focus. To my credit, I was about to step in and ante up when our father went non-linear.

"Up to your fucking room you insolent little bitch!" he screamed. "I'll deal with you *later*. And you don't come down until I've come up to let you out!"

The Colonel fumed all through dinner, then tromped upstairs. Nobody said anything. We heard him scream her name as he barged into her room, but instead of Gertie, he discovered an open window, a broken eavestrough, and a note:

I've gone away to think about how bad I've been. Mom don't worry I packed lots of clean underwear. Kernel sorry about Buttercup and the scratch I put on her. Herbert tried to stop me but I snuck out. Tell Herbie I'm sorry too since he is my elder and I shouldn't have disobeyed him. Love Gertrude Kempt, your loving daughter.

Mom sobbed: "As if I don't have enough to worry about. Look at this dinner. It's ruined."

"She crossed the line this time," the Colonel said.

"Kids today, Jaysus!" Gramps said.

I wanted to scream out that I was part of it, but I bit my tongue. It was torment—I considered admitting everything, but something in the flippant tone of Gertie's letter stopped me. It was evident that she was up to something grandiose, and I had stayed silent for too long to speak up now. The Colonel would call me a low-life coward, or worse.

Dad mixed stiffer and stiffer drinks, and sat in the dark living room. He hadn't had a cigarette in years, but after she disappeared I spied him smoking by the woodpile. Mom called Gertie's friends and spoke with all their parents. She phoned the police, who said that she'd most likely show up in the morning. She had left a note. There was nothing they could do, they said. Dad took three days off work and drove around the city looking for her. The police were called again on the third day, and reports were filled out. An officer came to the house. He looked at the window, the eavestrough and the letter, and he concluded that she had run away.

"Stick by the phone," the officer said. "Gertrude will probably turn up in a few days or weeks, when she starts missing the comforts of home. Generally, it happens like this. The big thing is that she left a letter, so we know it was her intent."

"What do you mean, her intent?" Mom said.

"Any trouble in the home lately?" the officer asked. He pulled out his pad and flipped it open.

"She's a teenage girl," said the Colonel. "What do you think?"

"You know anything about where your sister is, son?" the officer looked at me. His pen was poised to take notes.

"No." I was dizzy and had to sit down on the couch.

Mom put her hand to my head. "He has a fever. He's sick with worry," she said to the cop. She sent me to bed and brought me aspirin and apple juice, like I was a little kid.

"She'll come home, Herbie." Mom rubbed my back for a few minutes. I felt like a big fake. When I woke up it was night and I tossed about, kicking at the sheets and sweating. I hated myself for letting her take the fall.

After several days of no sleep, I went to the basement to watch TV. I couldn't watch upstairs, on account of Gramps, who had taken over the family room. After he was diagnosed with emphysema, Gramps had, at Dad's urging, sold the old homestead in Renfrew to come live with us. The office was refurbished into a bedroom so that he could stay on the main floor with his clunky oxygen machine. The clear plastic tubes reached the family room easily, so he could lap up cable-access game show coverage every day. There was now a dent in Gramps' favourite side of the couch where he screamed at the television and fumbled with the remote. He had learned how to tape his game shows so he could watch them over and over. If he managed to sneak a drink or two, he'd become a madman.

"What the fuck Jesus fuck!" he'd yell during *Final Jeopardy*, convinced the whole show was rigged by Alex Trebek. And while he liked Bob Barker's suits, Gramps loathed the contestants on *The Price is Right*.

"Too high, numbnuts!" Gramps would scream during Showcase Showdown. "Goddamn rotten shit-arse, too bloody high!"

The recluse-friendly basement was more comfortable anyhow. There was an old worn quilt and the tacky red leather couch that Mom and Dad had received as a wedding gift. My stomach was perpetually sour over so much worry about Gertie. I sipped ginger ale and watched *Kids in the Hall*. The way I saw it, Gertie could have at least warned me that she'd planned on leaving. She could have stashed another note for me, at least so I'd be in the loop.

"Shift it!" Gramps yelled upstairs. "Move yer fat arse Vanna so we can see the bloody puzzle!"

I muted the TV and looked through my father's vinyl collection. It was all either military stuff or big band or country music. I slid a recording of Tchaikovsky's 1812 Overture onto the pristine Dual turntable.

I lay back on the couch and listened to the hiss and crackle with anticipation. The music gained momentum slowly, and by the time it was galloping, I was no longer Ottawa Valley Irish, but came from hard Russian stock. True passion for the Motherland flowed through my veins, a passion which overcame the greatest of hardships: the fact that I was starving, my feet black with frostbite. I had no time to stop for my fallen comrades, but lamented for them, weeping openly as I pressed on to push back the dark forces of the French. For food I would suck on a heel of moldy bread, or boil a patch of leather from my boot. I gained ground, and came across a figure of a woman in such distress that I wept openly at the sight of her. There was Gertie, waiting for me, torn and ravaged and ragged, but weeping with tears of her own—tears of joy at this reunion with her brother, her comrade, the poet-warrior. The crescendo of bells, whistles and cannons washed over me, just as Gertie opened her lips to speak ...

"Hey dumbass," she whispered. "Quit your blubbering. I'm starving."

The Overture halted with a scratch. I opened my eyes to see Gertie standing by the stereo, needle in hand.

"Jesus Christ!" I said, leaping up. "We've been looking—Mom and Dad, the police, *everybody's* been looking all week! The cops have been here twice now!"

"I know I know," she said. "What the fuck do you do with your time? Don't you watch TV, ever? I've been waiting to nab you for days."

"What? Where the hell have you been, Gertie?"

"Here," she said. "I never left." She pointed to the open half-door to the crawlspace beneath the stairs. I inspected, noting a sleeping bag, pop cans, a pizza box, a flashlight and a pile of my books.

"It smells like stale farts in here," I said.

"It's not so bad at night," she said. "I can usually get enough out of the fridge to last me through the day at least, but I've got pits like a lumberjack. I need a fucking shower. I never knew Mom spent so much time at home. Do you know she cries when she's alone? Man, she has got to get out more."

"You're lucky she hasn't decided to clean the crawlspace," I said. I felt a sense of peace, having her back. "I tried to tell them—I wanted to tell them it was me, too. I started to say something so many times, but I couldn't."

"Horseshit. Forget about it, Herbie. I need some fucking food. Gramps has been wandering around at night lately. You know I can't afford to get caught on this one."

I dashed upstairs to fix a cheese, lettuce, and tomato sandwich on rye. I also grabbed a bag of chips and a ginger beer and returned to the den.

"I'm going to eat the shit out of this," Gertie said. She gave me instructions with her mouth full: "I need you to bring me food every night. Some vegetables would be nice. See if Mom has any of that Swiss chard. An apple maybe—a mango if there's any. You could take a loaf of twelve-grain bread out of the freezer and sneak it down. Some unpasteurized honey. Maybe a dish of butter. Some cheese."

"Shouldn't you come home now?"

"I am home."

"I mean come out of the closet ... You know what I mean!"

"I have to make sure the Kernel's not still pissed."

"He's not, he's not. I swear he's not! He's pretty miserable actually. He's smoking again. I never thought he cared about you that much."

"That's heartwarming."

"Why don't you just come upstairs now?"

"I mailed a letter and envelope to a friend in Calgary. She's going to mail it back here so it looks like I've been halfway across the country. It should be here any day. If I've duped them into feeling sorry and worried for me, how do you think they'd react if they find out I've been in *here* the whole time?" Gertie said, pointing at the crawlspace.

"Who do you know in Calgary?"

"Circle gets the square me arse!" yelled Gramps. Gertie looked at the ceiling.

"How does he manage to find the booze?" she said. "Speaking of which—bring a few snorts of Scotch. And that bottle of sherry that's been in the cabinet forever. The Kernel won't miss it."

"What do you want the sherry for?"

"Cuz I'm bored as shit is what for."

"Fine." I turned to go.

"Herbie!"

"What?"

"Bring some fucking smokes, too. I'm out."

"What? When did you start smoking?"

Bantam Chickens

After the second time Gertie disappeared, the night of the August 17 Chicken Killing, I periodically checked under the basement stairs in case she was pulling the same stunt, but she had vanished for good.

The chicken fiasco began in late spring, shortly after Gertie's expulsion from Holy Name of Jesus High. She had no valid reason to take up studies at a new school until the autumn, so a full month was padded onto her summer. She spent her days in her self-designed home-school, alternately ripping through my books and watching daytime television in the basement. She hotboxed the crawlspace and slept most nights on the red leather couch.

"Gertie, you've been down here for over a week," I told her.

"I'm cocooning, Herbert. Even though it may seem otherwise, I'm actually growing quite rapidly beneath the surface."

"I still can't believe that Mom and Dad let you get away with doing sweet FA."

"Are you for real? They know they've never had it so good. I'm at home, but I'm out of the way and not throwing parties. I'm not out in the big bad world, so they know I'm staying out of trouble. They're on vacation from me, as far as they're concerned. And you're just jealous."

One day her home-school syllabus incorporated a few intriguing hours of the Learning Channel. I came home from a final exam to find Gertie with eyelids at half-mast after smoking a football-team-sized joint. She was tuned into a documentary about livestock. Whether it was the marijuana or the plight of farm animals, she experienced a crystal-ball vision of her crusade. Her *raison d'être*, she called it. Gertie lectured the whole family for a week, expounding on her half-baked philosophy that meat eaters were innately immoral.

"Veal parm? You've got to be kidding, Mom!" Gertie said one night.

"You do not have to eat it if you so choose, Miss Muffet," Mom said. "And besides, it's not *red* meat. Before you became a vegetarian you used to love veal."

"Time to take the blinders off, folks," Gertie said, eyeing our dinner plates hatefully. "Do any of you care to know how veal is raised?"

"Nope," said the Colonel.

"No thank you," I said.

"From infancy they're kept in aluminum boxes and fed a strict diet of milk," she said. "They don't get exercise or sunlight so their flesh won't toughen up or darken, and eventually they'll start gnawing on their metal prisons in a pathetic attempt to get roughage! All this so we can chew white, tender carcass."

"Suit yourself," Dad said. "Have some more pasta, and I'll eat your meat. In fact, you can have my salad. But be careful! The stuff in tomatoes isn't juice—it's tears."

"What's the point of technology?" Gertie said. "You are cave dwellers—all of you."

"Carcass carcass carcass," said Ailish.

"Meat. Cook. Yum. Eat," said the Colonel. He was in a rare mood.

I twirled my linguini and listened to Gertie, who had moved onto the topic of chickens.

"They clip their wings, and then singe their poor beaks so they can't peck at each other. It's fucking brutal!"

"Language, please," Mom said.

Ailish looked up from her bowl: "Fucky fucky."

"They chuck them down chutes onto huge conveyor belts where they're picked at and have dye squirted into their eyes. And the growth hormones—no thanks. I'm now officially off eggs."

"How will you get enough protein?" I said. I wanted to ask her if there was any protein in the drugs she'd been smoking.

"Nuts, cheese, beans, lentils, yogurt, tempeh, miso, whole grains," she said.

"Oh we're going to buy all that health junk now, is that it?" said the Colonel.

"I'll pay the extra out of my allowance."

"Maybe you can get a job now that you've got free time," I offered. Gertie shot me a hard look.

"I'm a victim of politics," she said.

"You still haven't paid for Buttercup's scratch," Mom reminded her.

"Well *I'm* going to take affirmative action," Gertie said.

"Atta-go, boy—you get 'em!" Gramps yelled, shuffling into the kitchen with his empty plate. "Paula Sweetie. Great chow, but ya don't gotta skimp on the gravy next time, what?"

"I'm a girl, Gramps. A *girl*," Gertie said.

"There was no gravy," said the Colonel. "Was there?"

On my last day of exams, I came home to find Ailish sitting on Gramps' lap in the family room, tugging at his oxygen tube. Gertie was out somewhere and Gramps was enlightening Ailish on trench warfare.

"Hadda piss 'n' shit in yer helmet and throw it over the lip. Can't have piss 'n' shit floatin' 'round in yer bed. That's the only time you can take yer helmet off."

"Piss inna hewmet, Hewbie!" Ailish said.

"You're not supposed to tell her those stories, remember Gramps?" I said.

"Who's that?"

"Where's Gertie, Gramps?"

"Nap time!" he shouted, throwing Ailish off his lap.

Gertie came home late that night with thirty baby chicks in a cardboard box. She showed them off in the kitchen.

"Where in blazes did you get these?" Dad asked her.

"I'll never tell."

"Well I know you didn't pay for them, wherever you got them," Mom said.

"They are not stolen," Gertie said. "They are liberated."

She wouldn't even let me in on the plan. Eventually Mom gave up on telling her to return the chicks. Gertie got a full-time job packing groceries at the Basseville IGA to pay for the pen that had to be built in the backyard, and I lent her cash for feed. The rapidly growing chicks demanded her constant care and attention.

But there was a problem with Gertie's chickens.

Her error was exposed in July, when they suddenly stopped growing. At about half the size of normal chickens, they stubbornly refused to get bigger. Gertie increased their feedings, but they only got fatter. More and more they would cluck madly in the pen, running helter-skelter and then leaping into the air, flapping their wings. They seemed foolish and angry.

Gramps, having grown up on the old farm in Renfrew, spotted the problem one day as we sat outside eating dinner. The oxygen machine, attached to a power source in the garage by a series of extension cords, gurgled away happily beneath the picnic table.

"Them there're BANTAM chickens!" Gramps said. We turned to witness a small, fat chicken take a running jump at the mesh wire and rise clumsily in the air, flapping furiously. It sailed drunkenly over the fence and, after a short flight, dropped heavily to the ground. Freed, pecking at fresh grass, it clucked happily.

Gertie went after it, unsuccessfully, and returned to the table flushed, panting.

"Freakin' chickens are fast," she wheezed.

By the time we were onto dessert, seven more chickens had escaped. They were quite happy outside of the pen. Gertie caught two eventually, but they sailed over the fence again while she went after a third.

"Well, I guess those chickens are liberated after all," Dad said.

It only took a few days until every chicken was able to fly, albeit in a lazy, clumsy manner. They scattered all over the yard, yet not one of them went missing: they never left the property, but took to roosting in the trees and in the garage, fumbling awkwardly back to earth for feedings.

It was comical until the hot rod caught a few loads of chicken shit. The Colonel washed her and waxed her and wrapped Buttercup in brand-new sheets. But he didn't forget.

August 17, Gertie's birthday, was a scorcher. It happened like this: first, I watched her open her gifts. I'd bought her two tickets to see the Buttless Chaps that night at Barrymore's, and the Guided by Voices box set. We pilfered the beer fridge and adjourned to Gertie's room, incense burning and smoke-eater humming, to blow a joint. With her stereo cranked we downed can after can of Old Milwaukee and batted the breeze.

Then I heard Gramps shout, but didn't make anything of it. We made some hazy plans on how we'd get into town. Gertie changed the CD—she put on *The Queen is Dead*. And that's when I heard more shouting, but it sounded like the Colonel. At the time I was half-cut and entirely unconcerned. Finally, midway into "There Is a Light That Never Goes Out," I heard shooting. We both heard it.

Later, I gathered that the Colonel had been nursing several stiff martinis for a few hours when he decided to take Gramps for a spin in Buttercup. Gramps had been in a foul mood all day, on account of the fact that he'd shit his pants en route to the washroom. I had heard Gramps talk of Normandy, of losing his comrades under fire, of losing Grandma. But the day Gramps shit his drawers was the first time I had ever seen the old soldier cry. Dad gave him a few fingers of scotch to bring him back to his old crusty self.

"What the fuck Jesus fuck can you believe I shit me goddamn pants!" Gramps yelled. This was the first yelling we heard from upstairs.

The shouts that I heard after that had most likely come from the garage, where Dad had found the sheets missing from Buttercup and a fresh layer of chicken shit all over her. Apparently they'd scratched the hood, too, with their beaks and claws.

"You hear something?" Gertie had said, squinting through the smoke of our third joint.

"You better finish that if we're ever gonna see the Chaps play."

"Wait! There it was again—you hear that?" she said.

The stereo said: "And if a double-decker bus crashes into us..."

And then we heard, distinctively, two shots.

"Well I heard *that*," I said. "*That* I could hear."

The next report was different. It was louder—impossibly loud, and it rattled the bedroom window. Gertie peered outside, but couldn't see anything. Morrissey sang: "And if a ten-ton truck kills the both of us, to die by your side, well, the pleasure, the privilege is mine!"

Another shot shook the house, followed by Gramps' shouts. He was unmistakably drunk. "Whoo-ee! That's my boy! Nice fucking luck!"

Then the Colonel hollered.

"It's Dad!" screamed Gertie, dumping the ashtray over the floor as she bolted out of her room and downstairs.

"One inna hand worth two inna bush, meboy!" Gramps shouted.

I trailed Gertie outside to where Gramps was in tears of drunken bliss, hopping on his one foot and huffing away on his puffer, waving his wooden leg in the air. The Colonel stood bare-chested in the driveway, unaware that Gertie and I were now watching him. Slung on his back was a .22 rifle with a 4X scope. In his hands was a much more ominous weapon. I recognized it immediately as the Colonel's birthright: a thirty-ought-six Belgian-made Fabrique Nationale, with a walnut stock and a step-down barrel. Reputedly one of only two in existence in Canada, it had been used against small aircraft in World War II. Gramps had pulled it out of a German bunker himself.

The Colonel was laughing. Chicken body parts, contorted in a grisly display over the yard, had been blown from the trees and out of the sky in mid-flight. The two or three chickens that the Colonel had killed with the FN had all but disappeared in a puff of feathers and a mist of blood.

At his feet writhed a chicken, clucking in mad circles, spinning around in its own innards. The Colonel looked up, recognized Gertie, and smiled.

"Dinner's ready," he said, a little woozy on his feet.

"You fuck!" Gertie said. She was about to say something else but caught herself and stopped. She walked into the garage and came back with a hatchet. She held the spinning chicken still and chopped off its head, then threw the axe across the yard and walked back into the house.

She wouldn't come out of her room for the rest of the night; she wouldn't even answer to me or Mom.

"Leave her be," the Colonel said. "She'll get over it! Fuckin' chickens shouldn't have been here in the first fucking place." He was swimming in martinis, but no longer seemed drunk. Gramps had an attack, took his puffers, and then passed out on the couch. He woke up later, shouting. "Them're bantam chickens!"

I went to my room and lay in the dark. I had the bed spins and threw up.

Gunner Kempt

Perhaps Gertie would have talked me out of it, but she was two thousand miles away. My resolve was otherwise firm, and the plan had been formulating in my mind for some time, but acting on it was thrilling and intimidating enough to make it seem spontaneous.

I cut morning classes to walk down to Dow's Lake and join the reserves. Even though Gertie didn't know about it, I knew she was somewhere on a beach, or in somebody's bathroom, or a tent trailer, freaking out. Gertie's moral code wasn't a tough one to crack. For instance, she thought her expulsion from Holy Name of Jesus High was noble. Even if it was, I'd have a hard time admitting I was expelled from high school. Not Gertie.

"I've done nothing wrong but stir up fear," she had said. "It's their shame—not mine." Her method of delivery was the infamous *Gertie's Rag*, an underground newsletter that had asked enough tender questions to be noticed by the school administration.

Gertie's Rag was the product of slow and patient work. She wrote about our culture—what she saw as a culture of consumption and greed—and did it in a way that was honest and unmerciful. The only teacher who had fought against her expulsion, Mr. Bayne, talked to me about it after Gertie had left. "It's really too bad about your sister. Gertie is just a girl who has grown too tall too fast for the short blanket of denial."

"Yes," I agreed. Mr. Bayne was sort of a nervous type, which made me nervous. He had this tick, which he said was due to malaria, but most students suspected it was from too much LSD.

"In a way she is before her time. But in a way she is too late, simply because environmental concerns have already reached the stage of irony."

"Yes," I agreed. Mr. Bayne admired how Gertie wrote about how global warming had caused a massive ice shelf to break loose from Antarctica; how Wal-Mart kills small towns; how TV kills the imagination; how scientists had bioengineered glow-in-the-dark pigs; how hormone shampoos worked; how First Nations women in the north were warned not to breast-feed their babies due to the PCBs pooling in the Arctic... her articles were well-intentioned. Her most thoughtful piece was on a three-legged frog that she'd found in suburbia: nobody was willing to take an active interest in the amphibian gene pool, she admitted, but then questioned what we'd do when someone gave birth to a three-legged baby. The masthead of *Gertie's Rag* read: ANXIETY IS A SYMPTOM. DEPRESSION IS A SYMPTOM. ADDICTION IS A SYMPTOM. CULTURE IS THE DISEASE. Her Christmas issue had a great cartoon piece of spy fiction about how Santa worked for the CIA, and the CIA was owned by Coca-Cola.

If she had stopped there—if that had been the extent of *Gertie's Rag*—the administration might have given her some kind of school credit or writing award. Even with a picture of a three-legged frog, nobody paid much attention. Gertie engineered her own expulsion as a method to create a bigger platform to speak from. She started by including persuasive arguments about the futility of a dress code at Holy Name of Jesus High. She questioned the Catholic Church's stance on birth control, homosexuality and abortion. That's all she did, but at a school like ours, it was more than enough. The principal called Mom and Dad to come pick Gertie up and told them to never bring her back.

The big scandal in our house wasn't the anti-church business, but the article Gertie had written on the military. She'd composed a well-researched and adequately documented essay, trying to prove that a career in the army was actually a process of losing honour, not gaining it. It was this article I was thinking about on my way to Dow's Lake Reserve Drill Hall, and every step I took seemed like a perfect rebuttal.

The Artillery Reserve Drill Hall occupied a massive warehouse, roughly the size of three basketball courts, and the entrance was large enough to fit a tractor-trailer. The space inside was polished and open, save for one strip by the south wall where six green cannon-like guns sat in measured formation. The drill hall smelled of Pine-Sol, old wood, diesel, gun oil, shoe polish, and a bit of dust. Uniformed soldiers milled about in twos and threes, talking in boisterous tones. I noted that not one person was standing alone. I was outnumbered on all fronts.

There were four huge doors inside, one in each corner of the building. It was difficult to tell which one was the office. Over two-tone blue and red paint jobs, each door had different letters stencilled in large white blocks: QM, BTO, HQ, GSM. I found the open space beneath the distant ceiling baffling—it somehow seemed heavy and compressed. I retraced my steps outside.

Two young-looking soldiers sat and smoked by the entrance. One of the soldiers had only a small round patch of brown fuzz on top of his head, the rest of his scalp shaved so short it lacked stubble. The other boy sported a blond crewcut, and swung his beret around on one finger like he'd been practising for a month. He looked like he was trying to look bored.

"Can you tell me where the office is?" The two smokers gave me a look like I'd just demanded spare change. "I'm looking to sign up—for the reserves. I was told on the phone to come here."

"You might wanna get a haircut," said the patch-head.

"You're looking for HQ," said the blond boy, who flipped his beret in the air like pizza dough, and caught it spinning. He continued spinning and smoking. I got the impression that spinning was this soldier's specialty.

I went back into the warehouse, and started towards the door at the far end marked HQ.

"Hey bud!" someone barked. I turned to face a stocky, middle-aged soldier with a thin mustache. He stared me up and down with his hands on his hips. "Hey Bud. You hafta walk *around* the parade square, get it? Just so's you know for next time."

I nodded and walked back to the entrance, a damp streak of heat spreading outwards from my spine. I was sure I had pits now. "You dumbass," I hissed. Only now did I notice the white line that indicated the parade square. I walked the perimeter route to HQ and knocked at the door. I had no guts left.

"What the hell was that?" someone said.

I heard movement from behind the door. I turned around and walked back the way I'd come. I'll be back in time for Physics, I thought. I shouldn't have come. No problem, we all make mistakes.

There was a click as the door was unlocked and I turned around. The top half of the door swung open and a lanky brown-haired man leaned out, sipping a drink box.

"Yes?" he said, biting into a cheese sandwich. I didn't say anything. For that brief moment I couldn't understand where I was or what I was doing there. "Well?" said the man.

"Here to sign up," I said finally.

"Here to sign up, eh? Well lucky for you we still have a spot open in Thirtieth Field Artillery."

"Okay."

"That was a joke. There's lots of room."

"Okay," I nodded.

"I'm Lieutenant Brown." He waved me inside with his sandwich and I filled out a standardized questionnaire.

"You'll have to complete and sign these PIN forms," Lt. Brown said. "Be back at HQ for 16:30 Monday, whereupon you will undergo the MSA test and fill out the remainder of the necessary paperwork."

"Okay," I said.

Lt. Brown escorted me around the parade square to show me

the cannons. "These are the guns. The 105mm Howitzer. We have six of them. I know it's not a lot but we do some great training in this unit. This is a unit with a lot of heart."

"Yes," I nodded. Lt. Brown nodded back and clucked his tongue, then walked me outside. The two boys were still smoking. When they saw the Lieutenant, they stubbed their butts out and stood up.

"You lads get your asses in gear and clean the barrel of that No.2 gun," Lt. Brown told them.

"Yes sir!" they shouted.

"We've got some great DS here," Lt. Brown said to me. "You should look forward to the weekend training."

"Oh, I am."

"It's a good year to come in, this year," Lt. Brown explained. "We have a surplus in the budget, which means more HE ammo. Not only that, but Two Battery is planning an Ex with Reg Force. Don't worry, you will be prepped for WinterEx during BTT, which will come after the successful completion of GMT. The CO will be present on Monday, so you might think of getting a haircut over the weekend, because if they pushed the ITT through you will be getting kitted out as early as 19:00 Monday, and if so you can attend dry training on the 105s. Any questions?"

I shook my head. Lt. Brown crushed my fingers in a solid handshake. "Of course a uniform is paramount. Nothing can be done without one." He pivoted on his heel and walked away.

I was still nodding after he left, trying to remember if I had to get a BTT or a GMT for Monday night, or if the CO would kit me out with one at HQ. What I understood clearly was that a process had somehow been set in motion. I marched back to school, and convinced myself that the mishap with the parade square was a silly occurrence that could have happened to anybody. I would soon have a few laughs over that one with the CO.

Jesus Christ, my old man won't believe this one! Gramps, too, would clap me on the back, congratulating me, teasing me for not joining the Cameron Highlanders. "Oh, yeah, um—by the way

Dad," I would say. "I'll need the truck at 16:30 on Monday to go meet the CO and push the ITT through, if that's all right."

By the time I returned to school grounds, I sensed that I was different. The people around me could live their lives however they wished—they could hit the road and smoke all the pot in the world if they felt it was that important—it did not matter one whit to me. They were civilians, after all, and it is difficult for a civilian mind to grasp the military sense of purpose and duty.

"Herb, my friend," Icky said after gym class. "I haven't heard you say a word in weeks."

"Yeah," said Won-ton. "You haven't exactly been verbal—that's what we should call you. Verb."

"That makes no sense," I said.

"He's being ironical," Icky snorted. "Now what do you have to say for yourself?"

"If there was war poetry, surely there can be poetry in war."

"What's that supposed to mean?" Icky said.

"Yeah, what in the hell is that supposed to mean?" Won-ton nodded his head.

In English class I carved an 'R' into my desk with the Colonel's old pocket knife. It was the first knife he'd ever owned, and he'd given it to me for Christmas. I'd never used it until today—I'd brought it with me to the armouries as a lucky piece. When I finished the 'R' I started working on an 'M', occasionally catching a glance of Ruth McBride's legs.

Ms. Jacobs wrote *What is a metaphor?* on the blackboard. It occurred to me right then that if I could go out one day and join the army, how hard could it really be to have the balls to go out and get a girl? My head was full of thoughts: if I wasn't imagining my new uniform or Dad's reaction, I was thinking about Ruth's lips, hips, ass and thighs. After class I smiled at her and went out into the quadrangle, where others lollygagged on the grass. These were once the cool students, and now they seemed simple and civil. In the span of a few hours, my whole universe had realigned.

I would learn to flip a beret in the air. I could even take up smoking, if need be. There was trouble out there somewhere on the planet calling out for someone with determination and guts.

"I can answer that call," I said out loud. I didn't care who in the quadrangle could hear me. A few students gave me a queer look but I paid them no mind. I could see Mom sobbing over my freshly dug grave, and the Colonel standing by her quietly, uniformed and honking every so often into a handkerchief. Somebody played "The Last Post" on the bugle as Icky and Wonton lowered my polished maple casket into the pit. Poor Ruth McBride threw in a handful of dirt, and then lost control and cast her grief-stricken body over the coffin, wailing shamelessly about unrequited love. It was hard on her.

Highly trained, spit-polished soldiers were at attention, alert in their sharp uniforms and ready to expertly snap the Canadian flag into a perfect triangle. They would solemnly present the folded product into Mom's trembling hands, yet her veil was not densely woven enough to hide the fresh stream of tears which stained her cheeks. She would accept the flag delicately. The Colonel would cough and blow his nose again (I made a mental note to buy Dad a handkerchief) and, after saluting my grave, would accept the Distinguished Service Order from the Governor General. And the Prime Minister. The Prime Minister *and* Her Majesty the Queen.

"Why aren't you at play practice?" Icky asked. He sat beside me in the grass.

"I was just thinking," I said, leaning back beside our tree to rest my head on a protruding root. I was tired suddenly and had an ache behind my eyes and in my shoulders.

"Don't hurt yourself."

"As long as I don't have to explain it to you," I said. Icky grunted and removed his sandals, thoughtfully picking at his toes.

"Heard from Gertie lately?" he said.

"Nope." I thought about the journal and the pot. "Screw Gertie," I said.

"What's eating you? Come on, Verb—what kind of talk is that?"

"Why aren't *you* at practice?"

"I've got a plan. I'd like to get drunk with my friend Verbal."

I closed my eyes. Icky concentrated on his feet. I could leave school and screw the play and go get drunk if that's what I wanted to do. Soon I would be a soldier. A gunner. Maybe even a lover. "Do you think Canada will ever be at war again?" I asked after some time.

"Hmm," Icky said. He thought about it. "I think aggression is for insecure half-wits with small minds and penises." He looked up from his toenails and scanned the quad for Catholic High School Girls in Trouble.

"Well here comes Won-ton," he said.

When he was three years old, Won-ton told his Mom that he hated his given name, and from then on he would only answer to *Won-ton*. Nobody had ever guessed his original name, and his mom, respecting his decision, wouldn't reveal it, living by the philosophy that you make your own mistakes in this world and live with them. Won-ton's little sister didn't even know his real name, and when he turned sixteen he made the change legal. His driver's permit said Won-ton Nugent. One time he admitted to me that he sometimes wished he had waited until he was four: "By four, I knew I could have made a wiser choice."

I watched in a daze as Ruth approached ten steps behind Won-ton. She moved purposefully, coming directly towards me. We made eye contact.

"Excuse me," I said. I went to Ruth as if we always hooked up in the quad. I spoke to her for a while and I don't remember what was said, but at one point she took out a scrap of paper and wrote her phone number down and handed it over. When she turned and left, my head felt clear and the ache behind my eyes was gone. I felt like I could join the football team, run a marathon, crush a basketball with one hand.

We went to drink at the Original Six, a sports bar/juke joint that still got away with catering to minors. It had cheap draft and everything on the menu came from a deep-fryer. We were on our third round when I finished telling them about my plans.

"But *why*, Verbal?" Icky said. "That's what I'm asking. I'm not asking how, but *why*—why the fuck would you join the army?"

Won-ton spoke softly: "I'd just be concerned that that type of experience would change you for good. I think what's alarming for us is that we don't have any friends in the military, and that maybe there's a reason for that."

"Look around this place," I said. "I'm young, and what do I know, right? But I know that I don't want to end up like this." I swept my hand around the bar to show them.

"You've lost me." Icky threw up his hands.

"See this place is already filling," I explained. "And packs of office girls are trickling in, shrugging off the controlled air of a stale workweek." I smiled at them. The sauce was doing the trick for me. Everything I wanted to express or say or feel was right there, available to me. Everything seemed to crystallize for me from one moment to the next. I felt like I could see through walls, see right into people and what moved them. "They'll have a few quick ones, and some creamy shooters before heading downtown to Stoney's or Maxwell's or Big Daddy's Crab Shack. They'll fire it up on the dance floor to shake their rigid backsides. They have stiff bums from hours spent wheeling from terminal to printer over squeaky Plexiglas in ergonomically designed chairs. The men will soften themselves with fancy booze. They'll order scotch they buy on credit and have pretended to enjoy for so long they actually can't go without it, and talk of SUVs, and software and stocks. Over the course of the evening they will decide a pecking order of alpha males—who needs condoms and who needs to download porn when they get home. And the girls will swing it, sweating their fake 'n' bake tans to wrinkly music, working in drunken seduction to the dead rhythms of Thorogood, the Bay City Rollers, Supertramp, the Boss. They will fall into drunken mystery, like they're dazed by something divine and they'll pray with titties bouncing, cellulite quivering, slipping into the post-workweek groove. They will discuss the latest vodka coolers.

"And on Sunday morning," I said, "they will make up their minds to start working out again. They'll try to forget about fast food, cigarettes and alcohol. They'll go to the Running Room in new spandex and they'll take aerobics, urban Tai Chi and spin classes. They'll wash down shark cartilage and power bars with fresh-squeezed juices filled with gingko, ginseng and spirulina. Then when they feel better they'll go get drunk and try to get laid and in the morning they'll feel shame and sadness all over again." I smiled at Won-ton and poured another draft from our pitcher. I had a glow on, and the beer was going down smooth and quick now.

"Well, I'm depressed," said Icky.

"I think it's time for another pitcher," I said. I was suddenly concerned that I'd said too much—I was afraid they were going to leave. "I'm buying. You want some snacks? I'll get some snacks," I said.

Spilled Milk

I waited for Lights Out, for my own private snack time, and wondered vaguely what the food would be like in the Army. I pictured myself in uniform, tossing my beret about listlessly. Or in parade gear, marching. Snapping to attention. Saluting. In fatigues, my dirt-covered, sweat-stained, blood-splattered combats. The dogs of war were nipping at my heels, but I seemed unconcerned as I took defensive cover in the trenches; the boys and I were covered in mud and blood and piss, because we couldn't get out to the latrines, being pinned down as we were. Some of the boys were going right there in their pissy-pants, too scared to take their helmets off. Poor lads. And the boys were out of smokes, dammit. Morale was at a new low.

One of the soldiers, a redheaded, freckle-faced fella from Winnipeg who didn't look a day over sixteen, sobbed with his helmet resting on the sight of his rifle. I happened to have a pack of Player's in my helmet band, and pulled two fresh ones out, one for myself and one for Prairie Boy. I lit the smokes, aware of snipers, keeping in mind the "only two to a match" rule. I explained the rule to the redheaded kid.

"First one, they see you," I said. The kid looked around; he was scared, all right. "Second light, they're taking aim, adjusting their sights. If you're foolish or green enough to light a third, finger's on the trigger and it's lights out, boyo."

"Gee whiz," he said. "Thanks Captain."

"Il n'y a pas de quoi," I said.

"Wow—you speak French too," he said.

"Oui," I said.

I was up from the Second Battalion Royal Canadian Horse Artillery, as liaison with the Infantry, come to see the boys have a hard go of it and gather some intel.

And now I was pinned down with them. There was a scratch on my face from when my battery got fragged, goddamn shrapnel everywhere. The scratch was bleeding again now. With the smoke between my lips, I looked at the redheaded boy and wiped at my cheek with the back of my hand.

"Oui mon ami," I said. "The bombs will stop falling someday soon. This, too, shall pass."

The field phone was ringing. It was the Arty, I was sure, ready for another fire mission. I picked it up, knowing I would have to give them coordinates.

"Roger Bravo Alpha Niner Zulu Charlie Out," I said. "What's wrong with this goddamn field phone?"

"Mommy." This Catholic Prairie Boy looks like he's gonna shit his pants. Where's your God now, Red? I want to say:

"What's wrong with the fuckin' field phone!" I said. It rang again.

"Jesus *Christ*, Herbert! Would you get that?" screamed the Colonel. The TV was off downstairs. It was late.

"Hullo?" I said. I was sleepy and I cursed my luck that I hadn't had time to save the redhead from a belly full of bullets.

"Herb? Hi, it's me. It's Ruth. Am I calling at a bad time?"

"Good God, no," I said. In an instant I was awake and the phone line was supercharged with tension, excitement, and a whiff of sex. I don't remember what we talked about, but I remember what we didn't say. And those were all the things worth saying. Like what I wanted to do to her with my tongue, for example.

We just talked and talked. We were on the phone for hours, and it got so late that it was early, and I was exhausted and so was she and even then it was hard to hang up. Eventually we did.

With my face hot from the phone, and my ear burning from Ruth's sweet voice, and my stomach rumbling, I tiptoed down the stairs. Soon, I knew—someday in the not-to-distant future—

I would get laid. In the kitchen I set to making myself a toasted tomato sandwich in celebration.

Sitting at the kitchen table, I listened to the familiar hums and groans, the well-known bumps and sighs of the house. Ailish was tucked away, the folks in bed. Gramps was sawing logs.

As long as the Colonel was in bed, I could sit at ease in the kitchen munching an evening snack, usually toast. Always toast. Nobody, not even the Colonel, counts bread slices. This was the best time to read, too—while eating.

I kept one ear cocked, though, and if I ever heard the stairs creak, I was instantly alert, calculating weight and velocity with the precise math of adrenalin. I could tell within a heartbeat whether or not it was my father. If it was, which was super rare after he'd gone to bed, there would be a mad scramble to either finish or hide whatever I was eating.

One time I got caught, and was grilled with direct questions of a suspicious nature. The Colonel gave me the cold look, the look that made him known, to both friends and enemies within the CF, as "Mad Dog," or "Snake-Eater." What a nickname! I felt like a goddamn P.O.W. when he gave me that look.

My resolve was concrete, though. It was different now that I was a soldier. Next time the situation arose I would, in the image of Gertie, face Mad Dog's gaze boldly.

I let my guard down and ate my toast and drank my Ovaltine. Then I put more bread in the toaster and poured a glass of milk and tucked into a thin volume of short stories. I didn't sense the familiar bulk of energy behind me until it was too late. Dad loomed in the doorway like a ten-ton shadow. As I turned, my fingers twitched spastically, letting go of the glass in my hand. It's crazy, but the glass didn't break. It bounced once, twice, and then rolled with a clatter beneath the table.

We both stared at the milk on the tiles, then at each other. The toast popped up, black and smoking. My mind raced for something to say, but I couldn't think. I could see the pulse beating visibly in the Colonel's retina. The blue vein bulged from his forehead—and the ever-present tension stretched into the crow's feet at the corners of his eyes.

I gave up looking at him and stooped to collect the glass from beneath the table. I was thankful that it hadn't shattered. I noticed my hands quivering, and it was strange to look at them. My movements seemed delicate when I wanted them to be strong and sure.

The silence was too thick. I stood up and stared at the toaster.

"Can I borrow the truck next week?" I said.

"Just thought you'd have some dinner, eh?" Dad said, leering. "Is this the second course that nobody else gets?"

I stammered something about needing a snack to study. I motioned to the ceiling, to indicate how serious of a student I was, that my books awaited me. I could smell gin off his breath and skin.

"Oh is that right?" There was dry white spittle at the corners of his mouth, and the blue vein bulged by his temple. "If I've told you once," he said, "I've told you a goddamn thousand times that milk is for breakfast and dinner. What the fucking Christ is your sister gonna put on her cereal! I suppose you expect your mother to start drinking her goddamn coffee black?"

"There's a full bag left," I said.

"Well I'll be," he said. "Clean that shit up and get to bed. You wouldn't have to stay up so late if you didn't spend so much time on the fucking phone."

It might have ended there. In fact, that's exactly how it would have ended if I could have just let it go.

"Yeah, but I asked you about the truck," I said. "I'd like an answer." I looked him in the eye, like I told myself I would, and I saw that he couldn't believe his ears. My words hung there for a while, sticking in the thick air, going stale. Eventually the Colonel wrapped his head around his disbelief.

"Oh," he said. "The fucking truck. Right. You won't be driving that fucking truck, you, until you've earned the responsibility."

"It's a fucking glass of milk, Dad," I said, feeling the desperation of his own temper igniting into something unnatural, something unrecognizable. "And I don't see why you have to get on my case over a few pieces of fucking *toast!* Fuck!"

Now both of us couldn't believe what I was saying. My heart raced, and I felt the blood pounding behind my own eyes, and my temple throbbed.

"You want your toast?" Dad said. He reached to the counter and grabbed a blackened slice. "You want some fucking toast?"

"Eh! Huh! And did ... agownasizer!" yelled Gramps.

"Here, have some. Eat!" the Colonel said. He held me by the back of the head and rammed a piece of toast into the general vicinity of my mouth. He crumpled the other piece and threw it at my face.

I spit out crumbs and wiped my mouth with my sleeve. "A glass of *milk!* A fucking glass of milk, Kernel, for fucksakes! Oh, what? What are you going to do—shoot me? I don't have any chickens Kernel! Jesus fucking Christ. You could have apologized to her! She didn't have to leave! She wouldn't have—you could have apologized to her, you *fucking prick!*"

A rush and a push, whirl and twirl. I didn't realize what had happened until he had released my belt and the scruff of my neck. Then everything went still.

Tick. Tock. I was sure the clock had slowed down. I understood that I was moving through the air and that I would hit the wall eventually, and that the impact would likely hurt—it might even knock me out cold. I understood that, but had plenty of time to mull it over.

I heard the drywall crack, and then give, as it absorbed my skull. I crumpled in a heap on the kitchen tile. I felt giddy, and I laughed, thinking how the old man would have to explain the skin missing from my forehead and the bruises on my face. "How come there is blood on the wall?" Mom would say.

I couldn't feel the pain yet, but my jaw was already numb. I clenched my stomach in preparation for the kick I imagined was coming. I was also trying to remember where the rags were to clean up the milk. I opened my eyes. One was full of blood and through the other I saw the old man staring at me. His skin was like boiled sausage. From where I was lying he looked old, and I noticed he had a double chin.

Then he staggered backwards and fell, sinking to his ass with a loud thud. He cracked his head against the kitchen cupboards and opened his mouth, but he didn't say anything. He put his fists up to his eyes and shook his head.

I shut my eyes because I couldn't stand seeing him like that. I heard little feet, and Ailish ran into the kitchen. "Daddy Daddy Daddy!" I opened my eyes. She hopped over me and ran to him, crowding his distorted face with her small chest. She wrapped his large head in her little arms. "Daddy Daddy Daddy," she whispered.

"Gertie…" Dad said, putting his arms around Ailish. I shut my eyes. A kick in the gut would have been more welcome than having to see the look on his face. He didn't look like a man at all.

Soon after, I heard Dad pull Ailish onto his shoulder and stand. When I heard them start heavily up the stairs, I rubbed my face with an open palm and stared at the blood. I found the rags and sopped up the mess. Drops of blood dripped from my nose into the milk as I leaned forward. There were black crumbs of toast everywhere but I got most of them with a damp Jiffy cloth.

That night I jerked off three times before I could fall asleep. I came aboard myself like a prizefighter. First I thought of Ruth but soon I was nestled in Ms. Jacobs' huge, soft English-teacher tits. I fought hard and came all over my sheets again and again. Finally I slept.

In the morning there was blood all over my pillow and my eye was swollen shut.

Listen Carefully

Gertie had refused to come out of her room the night of the August 17 Chicken Killing. Ailish woke up when Gramps started screaming. He crapped his jammies in his sleep. I put Ailish back to bed and went down to change Gramps' sheets and clean him up. Dad was passed out on the living room floor, and he stumbled to bed without a word when I woke him up. Then I went back into the hallway and listened outside of Gertie's door, but she kept mum. Not a peep.

Meanwhile, Gramps was crying downstairs and rapidly becoming a menace to himself. Our house was a goddamn freakshow. I went down to get his bottle.

"Okay Gramps, give me the stash," I said. "You know you shouldn't be drinking."

"Ahh Jaysus, huh?" he said. "Git, puppyfuck."

"Gramps, it's bad for your health."

"Health sucks shit anyhoo." He let out a loud, wet fart and looked at me, terrified. He kicked at the foot of the couch to hide the whiskey and squirmed in his seat, checking to ensure he hadn't dropped a load in his Sansabelts. I tried to reason.

"It's dangerous Gramps. Besides, you're not going to drink that whole bottle tonight."

"Says you." He coughed. Gramps seemed ripe, old. He smelled right on the edge.

"How about we have a snort. You and me. Hey? Then I'll put it away till tomorrow."

Gramps considered this, then nodded. He bent to pull the Jameson's, half-full, from beneath the chesterfield. "Git a glass, greenhorn," he said, filling his coffee mug.

"I'll get some ice too," I said, heading for the kitchen.

"No ice sonny! Not outta my fuckin' bottle!"

My palate took a moment to adjust. Fire at first, then a numbing warmth. Gramps started talking about Grandma Gertrude.

"Oh," he said. "Died before her time. A tragedy—pity you never knew her. She was a sweet young nurse you betcher life, a true Irish lass, and first time I spied her, I knew I'd propose to her—soon's I was on me feet again. Oy! That woman had a picture perfect backside! Well, I never seen the likes!" He held his mug in both hands and squeezed his eyes shut, picturing, I presume, Grandma's ass.

"Oh Gertrude!" Gramps shouted, spilling whiskey on himself. He erupted into a hacking fit, and I noticed the absence of the familiar gurgle. I grabbed the hose and stuck it under Gramps' nostrils and turned the oxygen machine on. His leather cheeks were soaked with fat, soggy tears and he blew snot bubbles into his mug. Then he told me how Grandma had died of a sucking chest wound—she had been mistaken for a doe during Dad's first hunting trip. What wasn't clear from the story was who had pulled the trigger.

I sat there until Gramps passed out. His mouth fell open and his dentures came halfway out. There was hope that Gramps was just senile. My first impulse was to tell the hunting story to Gertie—it felt like information we should do something with. Then I remembered she had locked herself in her room. I covered Gramps' legs with an afghan and turned the volume up for *Family Feud*.

"Who's that?" Gramps wheezed, coming halfway out of his stupor.

"Here, Gramps. Do your puffers and hit the sack."

"Where you off to with that bottle sonny?"

"I think you've had enough."

"I'll tell you when, snapper," he said, fully awake now.

"You're not supposed to have *any*, Gramps," I said.

He surprised me with a quick lunge, and I barely managed to

dodge him in time. I escaped the family room and bounded up the stairs with the bottle.

"I'll whoop yer scrawny arse you ungrateful cocksucker!" Gramps yelled, throwing himself into another coughing fit.

I went to the bathroom and swallowed greedily from the faucet before turning in for the night. The effects of the pot and the beer had worn off to be replaced by the warm, clear-headed buzz of whiskey.

Unable to sleep, I went to my desk and tugged intermittently at the Jameson's while composing Gertie a drunken, emotional letter. It was mushy and incoherent, so I ripped it up. Eventually I lay down and passed out into a heavy, sweaty, dreamless state of unconsciousness. Later, I would regret not slipping the letter under Gertie's door.

When the explosion woke me, the clock read 3:33. Someone must be thinking about me, I thought. I heard a loud crash outside and smelled smoke. Ailish was screaming in her bedroom.

I stumbled into the dark, groping my way along the wall towards the dim glow of Ailish's glowworm night-light. From Mom and Dad's room I heard my old man.

"Stay up here with the kids," he said. "I heard shots."

The Colonel emerged in the hallway in jeans; his broad barrel-chest was naked.

"Dad I heard a noise," I said quickly, not wanting to be mistaken for an intruder in the dim hallway, especially after I caught the silhouette of the Browning 9mm in his hand.

"Stay up here with your mother," he said. "Call 911. Do you understand?" I nodded. Dad bounded down the stairs in three leaps. When he hit the landing Gramps shouted.

"Eh? Who's that!"

"Prowler, Dad," the Colonel said. "There's a fire. Turn the oxygen off."

I heard the gurgling stop. I was afraid, but my fear was exhilarating. I imagined there were robbers outside, or killers, or terrorists. The professional and quick-thinking actions of my father indicated clearly that there was danger, yet I felt completely safe from any real harm.

Mom came out in her housecoat.

"What on earth is going on? Are you okay?" she said. Without waiting for an answer, she rushed to quiet Ailish.

I went to Gertie's door and knocked. There was no answer so I tried the door; it was unlocked. I fumbled towards her bed in the dark and felt for her feet. They weren't there. Her legs weren't there. None of her was there. Perplexed, I turned on the light to make sure. Then I remembered.

Slowly, the Chicken Killing came back to me, like small patches of land breaking through a fog. "Gertie!" I screamed, bolting downstairs. In the kitchen I passed Gramps, who doddered towards the door, holding his inhaler like a sidearm.

I was outside just as the Colonel was pulling the minivan away from the smoking inferno that used to be the garage. He parked a safe distance away and hopped out, the 9mm still in his hand.

"Dad!" I said.

"Whoever it was, they're gone now," he said, padding towards me in his bare feet.

"It was Gertie, Dad. She's not in her room."

Dad stopped and looked at the garage, then nodded, like he too was just remembering. He said nothing for what seemed like hours. We stood together, staring through the open doorway of the garage at a fiery Buttercup. There was a hole in the centre of the windshield, flames lapping over the upholstery. She was already charcoal when we heard the first sirens.

The police found the FN, one of only two in Canada, abandoned in the bushes approximately one hundred yards from the garage. They surmised that the perpetrator had placed a gas can on the hood of the hot rod then pumped three rounds into Buttercup before hitting it *and* the propane barbecue, causing the massive explosion. The fire department was there until dawn.

Before I finally got to bed, I walked in on Mom in the laundry room. Because she had rushed into the garage looking for Gertie, her face was covered in ash and dust and sweat, and she was holding Gramps' shit-stained sheets and shaking. Her face was twisted into anguish, but she made no sound. She was mute, but screaming. I went to her, to say something, and she straightened up immediately and told me to get some rest.

Book 2

The anxiety is unbearable.
I only hope it lasts forever.

–*Oscar Wilde*

Good Work!

When I was at school, I thought about sex. At home, sex. When I had to think about something else, like math or driving or food, I hurried along to get back to sex. When I was on parade, I thought of sex. I had sex alone. The best, usually, was the sex I had in my sleep. Not always, though.

"It's not really clear through Blake's poetry whether it is innocence or experience that leads one closer to the Divine, or at least which one has the upper hand in all mortal souls," I said to Ms. Jacobs in one dream. We were alone at her desk after school.

The upper hand in all mortal souls! I was pretty sure that was the most eloquent thing ever to come out of my mouth.

"These pretty petals fall so softly from your lips," Ms. Jacobs said.

"Their fragrance is for you alone."

"You know, Herbert—can I call you Verbie?" she said, taking her earrings off and putting them in her top drawer, "nothing pleases me more than a bright, young student of mine putting everything on the line like that." She sat on the edge of her desk, her sheer white cotton skirt sliding up her tanned thighs.

"What you have said," she murmured, slowly rubbing her legs, "is poetry in and of itself. Your words are stuffed with a music of their own, a music which imparts deeper meaning than the words themselves. Come here, my pet."

I approached, tractor-beam-wise, homing in to the stiff presence of her nipples, nipples that taunted me from beneath the silk of her blouse. She smelled womanly. I let her take off my shirt.

"Do you understand, baby?" Ms. Jacobs said. "You are writing poetry about poetry, and for this you should be rewarded." She reached between her thighs and my knees went soft. Two of her fingers moved inside her, and she moaned.

She came, and a geyser of her clear, honeyed nectar sprayed all over me. Then in one motion, panting, she pulled something from her vagina.

It was a stamp.

She reached up and stamped *GOOD WORK!* onto my lips. She then guided my hands up her skirt.

"Um... Ms. Jacobs, do you think I have a concrete thesis... I, ahh..."

She undid my belt, and hitched her skirt up over her waist, exposing her thick bush of brown hair, musky dew dropping, an invitation into the pink.

"Call me Jugs, baby," Ms. Jacobs said, reclining on the desk. I ripped open her blouse, buttons popping everywhere, and was stunned by the immediacy of her tits. Jugs pulled me on top of her.

"This is lovely!" I said, pecking at a nipple. She guided my erection into a squishy and electric warmth. I came instantly.

When I looked up apologetically at Jugs, I was horrified to see Gertie's face instead.

"Nice going Herbie," she said, winking. "And this concludes your lesson on the two contrary states of the human soul."

Steady-Up

A Drill Hall. TWO PLATOON *stands in formation, three ranks of ten.* MASTER-CORPORAL HOAG *enters, marching shoulder-high.* HOAG *is uber-confident, whip-smart in his movements. He is a small man, scarcely over five feet tall, but his thick black mustache and gym-hardened build raise his stature significantly. His voice is practised and confident.* TWO PLATOON *stands silently, grateful for his attention; his insults are blessings he showers over those in his care. He wheels in front of the platoon and halts, centred in front of them.* SERGEANT MADDEN *looks on, holding a pace stick at his side.*

MCPL HOAG. Steady-up, recruits. Atten-SHUN! Stand-at-EASE! Okay. Stand easy. Listen up, recruits: this class will be an intro to the fundamentals of drill. Drill! Nothing can be accomplished without it. Drill is used in the CF not only for parades, but as an important training aid to gain appreciation for timing. Timing! You must ANTICIPATE the words of command! By the end of this course you will not be conducting drill movements on your own, but will be moving in unison as Two Platoon, and Two Platoon will be moving in unison with Bravo Company. Your drill instructor this afternoon will be Sergeant Madden, Drill Sergeant Major of the finest Regiment in Ottawa, the Governor General's Foot Guards. I see we have a few Arty fags here. Perhaps you can teach Thirtieth Field a thing or two about drill when we're through with you. RECRUITS! Too slow! Too slow! Stand easy. RECRUITS! Too slow, too slow, damn you. Pay attention and anticipate the words of command! Degrandpre!

DEGRANDPRE. What one dat Master-Corpal?

MCPL HOAG. Both of you! Eyes FRONT! You look like you're going to pinch a loaf right here on the parade square. CARLOS!

CARLOS. Yes Master-Corporal!

MCPL HOAG. If I see you bear-marching like you were when we came in here, I'm going to write your mother and tell her you're a retarded fuckpot. RECRUITS! Ah, again! Too slow! Stand easy. KEMPT! Kempt, quit moving your head around! Looks like you got Parkinson's, your head bobbing all over the fucking place. RECRUITS! Atten-SHUN!

Pause.

They're ready for you Sergeant Madden.

SERGEANT MADDEN *comes to the position of attention sharply, his thigh rising ninety degrees before his super-gloss parade boot slams down beside its mate. With just millimetres between his heels, his feet open at an angle of exactly thirty degrees. The pace stick taps the drill hall floor twice, pap-pap, and is thrown up swiftly under his right arm. He steps off into quick march without a word, but his body reacts as though he'd just screamed the words of command at himself. Click click click. The clickers on his feet speak of his tightly harnessed will, the strict necessity of his professionalism. He wheels around the entire drill hall, obviously enjoying himself despite his poker face. His body loves the march, taking the long route to finally halt himself in front of* MCPL HOAG *and take over command of* TWO PLATOON. *Click click, slide, slam. Pause. Pivot, slam. Pause.*

SGT MADDEN. Thank you, Master-Corporal Hoag. RECRUITS! Stand-at-EASE! Atten-SHUN! Stand-at-EASE! Terrible! Bloody pathetic. Lift those legs up and slam them down TOGETHER. You people sound like a ten-ton centipede. There is only one motion, the SAME motion, for all of you. The timing is ONE! One bloody count! Atten-SHUN! Stand-at-EASE! Brutal! Disgusting! I'm gonna lose my lunch! Everybody is going to call the time together so you morons can't get mixed up. We can begin the lesson once you're able to come to attention together. The count is ONE. Atten-SHUN!

TWO PLATOON. ONE!

SGT MADDEN. Stand-at-EASE!

TWO PLATOON. ONE!

SGT MADDEN. Better, but still garbage. I might toss my fuckin' cookies yet. Try it without the time now. Atten-SHUN! Stand-at-EASE! Okay, stand easy. What we are going to start with today are left and right turns. To execute these turns, and for the purposes of instruction, I will be breaking each movement down into three squads. For the right turn, the first squad is executed by pivoting on the right heel and the ball of the left foot. Pay attention as I demonstrate. Move to the right by numbers, squad-ONE! As you can see, my body has pivoted exactly ninety degrees, and I am now in position for squad two. We will come to that when you have mastered squad one. RECRUITS! Steady up! Steady up! You people have to stay awake! Focused! Always anticipate the word of command. As you were. RECRUITS! Atten-SHUN! Move to the right by numbers, squad-ONE! Recruit! [*Click click click.*] Recruit Hudson!

HUDSON. Yes sir!

SGT MADDEN. Don't call me sir! I work for a living! Why are you facing Recruit Smith here? Did you want to kiss him?

HUDSON. No, Warrant!

SGT MADDEN. Well, Hudson, it seems you really want to promote me today.

HUDSON. Warrant?

SGT MADDEN. I'm a fuckin' sergeant you half-wit! And if you didn't want to kiss Smith, then it can only be you don't know your right from your left. Do you know what this is?

HUDSON. Sergeant?

SGT MADDEN. You may look.

HUDSON. A felt pen … a black Magic Marker, Sergeant?

SGT MADDEN. Impressive. It thinks. Very good Hudson, steady up. EYES FRONT! Now I'm going to put an 'L' on this cheek, and an 'R' on this cheek. If you can figure out what these letters stand for they may help you in the future. As you were, recruits! Back to the position of attention. Move to the right by numbers, squad-ONE! Not bad. Not bad. As you were. I will now demonstrate the second part of the movement. At the end of squad one I left you in this position. For the second part of the movement you will bring your left leg up—like so—ensuring that your thigh is parallel to the ground and that your knee is bent at a ninety-degree angle. Pay attention as I demonstrate. Move to the right by numbers, squad-TWO! As you can see, my thigh is parallel to the ground, my foot hangs at ninety degrees. As I was. We will now perform squads one and two in sequence. To execute this, each squad has a timing of ONE. Everybody will call out the timing. RECRUITS! As you were! RECRUITS! Atten-SHUN! Move to the right by numbers, squad-ONE!

TWO PLATOON. ONE!

SGT MADDEN. Squad-TWO!

TWO PLATOON. TWO!

SGT MADDEN. As you were! This is shit! Fuckin' pathetic! YOU! Recruit Calloway. You seem to know what you're doing. Up here to demonstrate. You! Yes, YOU, Recruit! What is your name?

DEGRANDPRE. Luc, sir!

SGT MADDEN. Don't fucking sir me, bitch-tits! Do you have a LAST name, LUKE?

DEGRANDPRE. DeGrandpre, Sergeant!

SGT MADDEN. Why isn't your name tag above your left breast to tell me this information, candy-ass?

DEGRANDPRE. Cuz it at backorder for some times Sergeant!

SGT MADDEN. Does anybody here speak DEGRANDPRE?

DEGRANDPRE 2. He mean dat we didn' get dat name tag yet Sergeant!

SGT MADDEN. *[Click click click]* Jesus! You look just like the other one!

DEGRANDPRE 2. DeGrandpre, Sergeant! We are twin Sergeant!

SGT MADDEN. Well until you get your name tags, YOU will be known as Tweedle-Dee, and your brother will be known as Tweedle-DUM.

DEGRANDPRE 2. Yes Sergeant!

SGT MADDEN. Tweedle-DUM!

DEGRANDPRE. Sergeant?

SGT MADDEN. Bite it out! Tweedle-DUM!

DEGRANDPRE. YES, SERGEANT!

SGT MADDEN. Quit waving your leg around in squad two like you're some homo looking for action. Everybody as you were! Calloway will demonstrate the last squad, squad three. I left you in this position—squad two, Calloway. The next movement is executed by slamming—SLAMMING—the left leg down so that the left heel is touching the right and the toes are open at a thirty-degree angle. Pay attention as Recruit Calloway demonstrates. Call out the time, Calloway.

CALLOWAY. Sergeant!

SGT MADDEN. As you were. Move to the right by numbers, squad-ONE!

CALLOWAY. ONE!

SGT MADDEN. Squad-TWO!

CALLOWAY. ONE!

SGT MADDEN. Squad-THREE!

CALLOWAY. ONE!

SGT MADDEN. As you were, Calloway. Back in formation. Okay. You now have fifteen minutes to practise this movement in squads on your own. I want to hear everybody calling out the time. I will be circulating to correct each of you individually on your execution. If we are lucky, we might even move on to left turns today. Steady-UP.

The Guns Are Our Colours

School wound down and was suddenly over. It was my last summer before graduation and I found myself spending it on CFB Petawawa, jumping in and out of army trucks and carrying high-explosive ammunition. Following each field exercise, my muscles seemed bigger. They were harder, anyhow. At times I couldn't remember what I was doing there. But then sometimes when I trained, was tired or hungry or bouncing around in the back of a deuce-and-a-half, or bogged down in mud and weak in the joints, eye sockets burnt with exhaustion, I thought about the Colonel. When I thought of my father, my position, my location, my duties—all of it made a bit of sense. Why not me? I was the son of a snake-eater after all.

I learned about the guns and the positions soldiers took on the guns, numbered one through seven. "Someday I will be a number one," I said to myself in the mirror, every morning before inspection.

Duties of #1
#1 commands the detachment and is responsible for the entire service of the 105 Howitzer. He acts directly on the orders of the GPO, but during the engagement of tanks he is responsible for fire control after the GPO orders "engage." #1 is certain that his equipment is, in all respects, serviceable, and that the gun is, at all times, laid at the correct bearing, gun correction and elevation, and that the fuse and charge are correct before loading. He orders the gun loaded and fired, and supervises the preparation and supply of ammunition, and reports unserviceable ammunition to the GPO. He is responsible for providing maximum protection to his detachment, consistent with the efficient service of the gun.

*During pauses in firing, he supervises the maintenance of the
equipment, and directs the clearing up of salvage. During firing,
he watches the action of the recoil mechanism, and corrects any
faults, as authorized.*

I passed the first half of the summer in the Mattawa Plains of
CFB Petawawa, tugging lanyards of the 105mm Howitzers. The
guns were older than any living soldier. The real battle was with
the mosquitoes, fought with bug nets, DEET, dirt, body odour
and foul language. I learned to swear like a true dirt-eating
motherfucker.

While I was not yet qualified as a Gunner, Thirtieth Field
Artillery was short-staffed for the joint Reserve/Reg Force
Summer Exercise. This experience gave me a leg up on the green-
green Artillery Privates-In-Training (PITS) I met at Basic Trades
Training (BTT) in late July. I was already somewhat accomplished
as a number two, operating the breech and firing mechanism. I
was also responsible for the right brake, and had to make sure it
was off before travelling. I set the elevation and gun correction
scales, and laid on for elevation.

I was a nifty number three as well. I had a knack with the
aiming posts, and I loved laying the collimator—all those little
tiny radioactive numbers that you could only see through the
sight. And I learned, in minute detail, how to clean the guns.
Always, clean and oil. Clean and oil. I smelled gun oil on myself
even after showering, and it comforted me; it wasn't unpleasant.

By the time I got through BTT, my basic training seemed
childish. General Military Training had comprised a mishmash
of infantry, artillery, logistics and medical personnel. Most of the
PITS showed up with their particular brand of esprit de corps
pounded into them from their respective units. The training had
taken place each weekend at Connaught Ranges, close to Ottawa,
and somehow I had been lumped in with a Section consisting
entirely of reserve infantry from the GGFG.

The GGFG are the ones who wear expensive black fur hats all
summer and sweat like savages under the yoke of sunshine and
humidity. On Parliament Hill they perform the Changing of the

Guard, which I suppose is an honour, despite the tourists. They must have some deep reason to be doing it; otherwise, I don't see how they could put up with the snotty children who poke them in the ribs. Sometimes bored prepubescent boys, poorly supervised and armed with bubble gum and water guns, have their way with the impassive soldiers. The Foot Guards always manage, without exception, to perform the Changing of the Guard without so much as twitching one muscle in their highly trained faces. Due to this honour, the GGFG require more emphasis on drill than on infantry tactics and weapons training. The reservists considered this something to boast about, and were given to making snide remarks about the Cameron Highlanders' poor standard of drill and the shoddy state of their parade boots. The Camerons, conversely, took pride in their scuffed gear. If they'd wanted parades they would have worked for Disney, they said. They were born to fight, they said. It was sometimes a heated rivalry, but what both units agreed on was that Artillery was the lowest of the low.

During my tour of Dow's Lake Armouries before being shipped to Connaught, I had not noticed any shiny boots at all. Moreover, I had yet to see anybody performing drill there. The concentration and effort of the part-time soldiers of Thirtieth Field seemed to revolve solely around the 105mm Howitzer. If it happened that Thirtieth Field participated in a parade, they carried no colours; instead of a flag, they trucked the Howitzers up and down the Square.

"In the Artillery," Lt. Brown had said, "the guns are the colours."

"Permission to put my gun in lockup, Master-Corporal!" I shouted once, during GMT. I held my C7 rifle smartly.

(Lesson #1: a rifle is *not* a gun.)

"Gun?" asked Master-Corporal Hoag. "So you'd call this a *gun*, Private Kempt?"

"Um."

"Don't you fucking UM me, Kempt!" He turned to a fellow GGFG: "Sergeant Madden, you think an Arty fag would at least be able to tell the difference between a gun and a rifle, wouldn't you?"

"Certainly would, Master-Corporal Hoag."

"Now why, do you think, this wannabe gunner fuck-wit has no idea what he's holding in his hands?"

"Well, Master-Corporal Hoag, I would have to guess that Private Kempt hasn't been properly introduced to his rifle. Either that or he's an inbred numbnuts cocksucker."

To prove I wasn't an inbred numbnuts cocksucker, I did push-ups over my rifle for the next fifteen minutes. At each time I let my torso down, I was required to kiss the muzzle and shout "I love you, *rifle*! I wish I was an Infantryman!"

During the gruelling morning jogs around the Mattawa barracks and up Heartbreak Hill, I could read the others and tell who was losing heart way before they started lagging behind. I would wait for them to fall back from the two-rank, double-time formation, and then move up, feeling stronger with each one I passed. At first I felt bad for them, but gradually, as I passed them, they just seemed weak, gutless, spineless. I always ended up running in the front file beside the instructor, Sergeant Cookson, my number one, with the other few Gunners who were in shape. I could get up close and keep my distance at the same time. I was close enough to be noticed and appreciated, but silent enough to avoid being labelled a suckhole. Eventually Sergeant Cookson would signal with a swift hand gesture:

"Time to pick up the trash!" We would wheel around and double back to the last straggler. One morning, at a time commonly known as Odark:30, halfway through our morning PT, Sergeant Cookson's warrior spirits were elevated enough to impart a few words of military wisdom:

"The weak don't know how to dig deep. Endurance is as much in the head and heart as it is in the muscles and lungs."

I could have run a goddamn motherfucking marathon after he told me that.

There were dreary mornings, however; mornings when the sight of the green module tents, the hastily erected field showers, the portable mess, the gravel roads, ammo dumps and the Department of National Defence signage of the Mattawa made me pause inside myself. At these times my stomach had to adjust, and there was a fear that I might have been grossly mistaken, that these things had nothing to do with me, that I was a pretender in danger, a sheep in wolf's clothing. It was then that I would remember Gertie, and think about where she was and what she might be doing. Was she strung out? Was she healthy and vibrant and living an artist's life? In my mind it could go either way.

I woke up sliding to and fro on my field cot, smelling the wet canvas of the tent, and the stench of ass and balls from my sleeping bag. I'd leap from my cot and let the pre-dawn air hit my naked body. Shivering, I'd dress quickly and fight the stiff black nylon laces of my combat boots with numb fingers.

"One foot in front of the other," I said to myself on mornings like those.

On those mornings I'd emerge from my tent to greet the smell of Mattawa's finest dust, and the stench of diesel fuel as the MLVWs (Medium Logistics Vehicles, Wheeled) roared to life. It didn't seem natural, but these things could calm me like a sunrise, warm me with renewed confidence. I would remember what I was capable of, and where I came from.

Every morning during the platoon run, we passed the mess where the smell of grease from pan after pan of bacon and sausages being broiled in their own fat hung thick and sticky in the cold morning air. It made me retch. My bowels churned fear into a brewing time bomb. I ran sometimes without awareness of what my limbs were doing.

Running was gravel and dirt and grass stains; it was sunrises, skid marks and the stench of two thousand pancakes. Running was grey and white, like concrete; it was wire and aluminum siding and the need to take a shit, and, eventually, it was the half-familiar faces of Two Platoon.

There were the lean ones, the determined ones, and then there were the white, soft, pasty ones. The flabby ones who couldn't run anymore, who twisted their faces into what they hoped looked like agony, petitioning Master-Corporal Hoag silently to ease up. I looked to these faces when I needed a boost. I would catch glimpses, small frames, of their pathetic expressions, thinking, *No self-confidence! No heart! That's your problem, fatty.*

The truly shameless would grab hold of their knees or backs and wince, trying to pass their weakness off as injury. And I'd keep running. The grey light of pre-dawn would make way for another rainy day, but I'd pass the wall of greasy carcass and buttermilk triumphantly. Somebody would stop to barf. I'd blow by another fat boy, sucking the life right out of him, putting a little more spring in my own step and looking for another slacker to pass. *The fat fucks!*

"The problem," Sgt. Cookson said once, "is that this troop is filled with pansies and split-arses."

"We have two chicks," said our number seven. "One chick is a know-it-all cunt, and the other is too fat to run a fucking mile."

During the Final Ex, we rappelled from helicopters, blew shit up in live-fire exercises, and deployed the guns to over thirty positions in one day. We were bombarded with tear gas, attacked by infantry, and at times we would only have enough time to pump off a sniping fire mission before we got the order from the command post: "PREPARE TO MOVE. CAM NETS DOWN."

At the EndEx party, I drank beers and swore and flexed and couldn't believe the summer was over and I'd come out in the top three candidates.

I went home hungover on a military bus. It wasn't long after I got off hard rations and out of the field that I started getting impromptu erections again.

I called Ruth up.

Pulled Out a Plum

I made like I was sleeping. Ruth checked under the sheets again. She kissed my lower back and then got up to go to the washroom. I opened my eyes to watch her walk away. Just beneath her ass and between her firm legs, I could make out the silhouette of her trimmed and slightly swollen pussy lips. It was a spiritual experience. That's all I can say about that.

The first few times we fucked had been clumsy. I fumbled around a bit—it was embarrassing. Then it became hilarious. After we loosened up, we connected and the first time it worked surprised both of us. We were both virgins, and I thought she was in pain, but I couldn't tell for sure. I didn't last long before I came that first time. A little while later we had sex again, and then later, again. The third time we tried out new positions and rhythms. We made stuff up, improvised and Ruth started this panting and moaning that drove me wild.

"I think I'm going to come," she said.

"Okay," I said.

"Oh my God, oh my God," she said a little while later. "I'm gonna come I'm gonna come I'm gonna come all over your cock," she said. I couldn't believe my ears. She was sixteen, and I was the one who got to do this to her. Dirty girl.

"I think I'm in love," I said. I would have said anything. She had these small, hard tits that jiggled up and down and made me dizzy. It was something special, all right.

There was that rush, the climb, that moment of blindness at the peak, and we crashed into the valley of our own sweaty, salty limbs. We couldn't look at each other for a bit. I kissed her lightly on the temple as she nestled under me, smelling the odour beneath my arm.

"That was good this time wasn't it?" I asked. She nodded with her eyes closed. My lips seemed bruised and my arms were scratched up from her nails.

I smiled and rolled onto my back. Ruth sighed, closed her eyes and rubbed her belly.

"We're not in Kansas anymore, Toto," she said.

"I really like it," I said, rolling back suddenly to touch her cheek. "I really like you."

Ruth smiled.

"I especially liked you on your hands and knees," I said. She hit me with her pillow.

"I can still feel you inside," she said. "It's starting to drip out. There's a lot of you."

"And you're sure it's okay?" I said. "I mean, to fire at will?"

"I'm still sure," she said. "Mom put me on the pill when I turned fifteen."

"I love your Mom," I said. We held each other and I dozed off.

"Listen, lazyhead," she said, waking me. "We have to go back to class. We've already missed fifth period."

"Mmm. Let's skip the afternoon."

"Can't Verbal. I wish we could, but my Mom'll be home soon."

"Ten more minutes. Just a quick nap."

She pounced on me and started tickling. Howling, I grabbed her wrists and turned her to pin her down. She strained against my hold and her tits moved up and down with each breath. She pushed against me with her hips, then caught her breath sharply. Suddenly we weren't playing. Her nipples were hard and her neck and chest were flushed. It dawned on me that it was about to happen again.

"Wait, wait," she said. "Go slow."

"Does it hurt?"

"A little, just a bit."

"Should I stop?"

"No, it's okay. Just go slow."

"Are you sure?"

"Yes it's good, just go ... ahh," she said. "Oh my god."

We moved slow, so slow. I held her waist and looked into her eyes and bit her and kissed her and smelled her and wanted to swallow her in one big bite.

"I don't know anything about women," I said. I don't know why I said that. I held her face and kissed her hard and we moved slowly until we shuddered together.

"Wow. I'm really tired," I said.

"I'm going to be sore," she said. "Really sore." She kissed me. I was about to say "We have to go," when we heard the garage door opening. I looked at Ruth and she looked at me, terrified.

We stood up on the bed at the same time, battling to unravel from the duvet furled about our waists and feet. Ruth jumped off, and I had to pause to admire her body in action, as I had never seen a naked woman jump before, and consequently I lost my balance and fell backwards. I squirmed free of one end of the duvet, which seemed to be chasing me, while Ruth buried her head beneath the other end in a frantic search for her underwear.

I rolled around and managed to hitch up my jeans, and Ruth launched my boxers at me, which I caught with my face. She flailed her arms about like some mad contortionist, fighting with the clasps of her bra. Giving up, she pulled her sundress over her head as I looked for my t-shirt. We heard the interior door open downstairs.

"Hurry!" Ruth hissed.

I shoved my face under the bed in search of my missing shirt, and then tried the bed. No luck. I wrestled with the duvet, swearing at it, wishing it would just give up this one article of clothing. It could keep my socks, but I needed that shirt.

In desperation, Ruth threw me one of her t-shirts. I pulled it on but it was way too tight and got caught up on my pumpkin. I couldn't see a thing and stubbed my toe on the bed frame. Hopping backwards on one foot, I bit my lip open to keep from screaming and thrashed my arms in search of the armholes. That's when I tripped on Ruth's knapsack and fell face first into the closet, tattooing myself with the door handle. I hit the floor like a sandbag.

Ruth helped me up and shooed me out of her bedroom window.

"My shirt!" I whispered. There was blood coming out of my nose.

"There's no time!"

I walked across the hot shingles of the roof and swung myself down by the pool. I hopped the fence into the neighbour's yard and jogged back to school, no shirt and no shoes. I felt like a warrior.

I snuck into the boys' change room off the gym, where there was a class underway, and stole a generic white cotton t-shirt off a hook and a pair of shower flip-flops.

Later, I got home and saw that Dad was already back from work and on the sauce.

Mom told me that Gramps had passed away. His liver exploded.

I was a bit numb. I tried to feel sad or upset about it, but it was no use. All I could think of was Ruth and the things we'd done all afternoon, and what I planned on doing the next time I got my hands on her.

The Head of the Home

Gramps did not go gentle into that good night; he was dragged kicking and screaming into the great unknown, that undiscovered territory called Death. He huffed madly on his puffers, screamed that he couldn't see, called out for his dead wife, called out for his mother, and shit the bed. Eventually, covered in a thick, foamy drool, he calmed himself, cooling in his ripe sweat. Mom nursed his fever. Dad sat and watched over him for brief intervals, and held his hand. After some time, the Colonel returned to the drinking chair and waited. Before he left this world, Gramps whispered something to Mom. He didn't say anything profound, and he didn't ask for Gertrude, nor did he ask for his son. He asked for a drink of whiskey.

KEMPT, Devon Andrew
Peacefully on Wednesday at home in Basseville. D-Day
Veteran with the Cameron Highlanders of Ottawa and
loving father to Colonel and Mrs. David Kempt, grandfather of
Herbert and Ailish. Relatives and friends may call
at the family home in Basseville Friday from 11 am. Funeral
mass Saturday at 1 pm in St. Patrick's Basilica. Interment
Notre Dame Cemetery. In memoriam donations to the
War Museum would be kindly appreciated.

"Peacefully my arse!" I said.

"Herbert!" Mom said. "What a way to talk! Give me a hand to clean out Gramps' room before your father gets home."

Dad was out buying alcohol for the piss-up at the wake. I had invited Icky and Won-ton for that very reason. Apparently it was going to be a traditional Irish high-profile wake, what with Gramps being one of the few veterans left.

I went through Gramps' stuff in about ten minutes. He didn't have a lot in this world. I stripped his bed, emptied his wardrobe and bagged his clothes. I turned the mattress and found a letter underneath it. It was faded and falling apart. The letter had been written by Grandma Gertie:

The head of the home is where we look for peace, justice, honesty, kindness, security, love of people, things, places. He should be a person who has consideration for others, a person who will accept us as we are. A person who will forgive another, a person who is humble who feels not greater than any of us. Because we are all creatures of God and we all have a right to be here. A person who is strong spiritually mentally and physically. A person who is radiant with happiness even in sacrifice. A person who can make every accident, misfortune, or cross into a useful way of life. Things they fall into ruin. He should be a person who can give us strength in being alive, and can give strong support as we would, if we were moulding or welding a strong bridge.

The home is not a place where we should feel afraid of doing wrong and being condemned just with the look we are given. It is not a place where we are treated with kindness today and tomorrow we are treated as if we should have never been born. One day we can have our friends in for tea and the next day we cannot. One day we should be happy to suit his temper, and the next day we should be tense, quiet, and afraid to do anything. This is when we become very frustrated, because what was right for us to do today was certainly not right for us to do the next day. This is when we become defeated, frightened. When the head of the home or school or church or country is full of hate, resentment, frustration, lies, anxiety, bitterness, jealousy. A person who rules like a false King. Who tries to deceive those of his household. Nothing strong or lasting can be built or life-moulded. On a false pretense. No matter how good it may look to the contractor or the builder of his wife and child—and a child who is not truly his.

The child who looks like other children, acts very much like other children on the surface sometimes. But he has a feeling of nothingness and emptiness. He too is very much like his master. He has very naturally moulded himself like his teacher or master and not like his true, and secret, father. The child is also full up of fears, discontent, nothingness, concern and wonderment as to will he ever know what will please the one he is supposed to love. But if we were really true to ourselves we really hate and resent the head of the home.

I am full of hostility, revenge, wanting to hurt others as I have been so hurt.

We are something like a counterfeit dollar bill. We look exactly like real money but we are only a fake, our whole life is a fake, this false head of the home a fake. Now we do not need to be like this false King. There is much help for us. We are individual. So I will give all the help I can give for truth and positive thinking and always remember that we are children of God, and secondly children of our parents. We are only obligated to follow the truth in all things and we cannot help but succeed. There are no problem children only problem parents. In any environment you can either grow or groan. We must remember proverbs.

I folded the note and put it in my pocket. "The child who looks like other children," I understood, was my father. Who was this true, and secret, father? Some questions shouldn't be answered. I'd tell Ruth about it, maybe. It was confusing to me and I preferred not to think about it. It was best to keep it to myself, I knew that much.

I brought the garbage bags out to the garage to go to the Goodwill. Two bags of clothes and an oxygen tank and a fifth of bourbon—that's what Gramps left behind. That and a mystery.

Dance for Your Daddy

It was an Ottawa Valley Irish wake, which is to say that we had it at our house to save money, and everybody was loaded. I couldn't believe that Gramps had friends, but they showed up—wrinkled, on canes, crutches and wheelchairs—the last of the Crusty Brigade from Renfrew. They had their ears to the ground, obviously. I could imagine their lips moving as they scanned the obits like Gramps used to do. They came as if they'd been waiting at the Super 8 outside of town, just waiting for Gramps to push off.

CBC Radio showed up to do a little piece on World War II veterans that they would shelve until Remembrance Day. Mom and Dad were calling the living room "the parlour" when they were interviewed.

Won-ton got blitzed tending the bar, and Icky played the spoons in accompaniment to the jigs Gramps' old Renfrew buddies scratched out on the fiddle. The casket was in the corner of the living room, open, and there was a kneeler beside it. Everywhere there was wake talk.

"They did a nice job, they did."

"He looks peaceful."

"His suffering is over."

"He's at rest, at last."

An old man came up to me. "I knew him well," he said, "and I'm glad to know he went peacefully."

"He shat himself," I said. "He screamed for his mother."

"Poor old pisser."

"What is up with the obituary?" whispered Icky. "Does your family just pretend Gertie doesn't exist?"

"I'm not supposed to talk about it. How much booze is left?"

"Enough for the fucking IRA," said Won-ton. "Did your Dad invite the whole Army?"

Behind the makeshift bar in the laundry room, there was a crate of Tullamore Dew, a crate of Knappogue Castle and a keg each of Harp and Guinness. Everyone who came said a wee prayer on the kneeler, took a peek at Gramps with his face made up and his medals polished, and then made an audible, respectable comment. Then each person would say something like, "I think I'll take some refreshment," and they'd be off to the races.

I kept going back to the coffin to stare at Gramps through different angles of drunkenness. Lips sewn shut, Gramps, or whoever he was, was dressed tidily in uniform, ready to receive the first clod of earth. No oxygen machine gurgling, no curse words or game shows.

"The Head of the Home," I said.

"What did you say?" the Colonel asked.

"And you have been small, too, Kernel. And you have been boy, too."

"You are drunk, son."

"A few sons here, but no temperance," I said.

"You ought to slow down. And lay off the hard stuff."

"Blah. We'll smooth the edges off with a drop of the dark stuff," I said. "It is the Kernel who looks drunk! And Gramps looks dead, and he's not even the real Gramps."

I started crying and Dad put his arm around my shoulder. That made me feel worse, because I wasn't crying about Gramps—I was thinking about my own funeral and Ruth throwing herself on my coffin, telling everyone I was her first lover.

Quadrant Laying

The Commanding Officer of Thirtieth Field Artillery called me into his office.

"This is an informal chat," he said.

"Yes sir."

"At ease, Kempt. Take a seat."

"Thank you, sir."

"Coffee? Something?"

"No thank you, sir."

"I've been following your progress," he said. "Balls-out, Kempt. Very good showing." The CO leafed through my file: "Topped your BTT, third in your Comms Course—tell me, Kempt, what are your plans for the future?"

"Well, sir, I've been selected for the junior leader's course this summer, but I've been thinking, sir, about an occupational transfer. Sir."

"Hmm."

"To Infantry, sir," I said.

"Right. Like your old man."

"Nothing against the Artillery, sir. Just—like you said, with my father, and my grandfather—"

"Seen, Kempt," he said.

"Though I ... haven't decided for sure yet, sir."

"How's your school, Kempt?" the CO stood up.

"Good, sir."

"How good?"

"Sir?"

"Your marks. What's your average?" he came around his desk.

"I couldn't say for sure," I said.

"Ballpark," he said.

"In the eighties, sir."

"Hmm. That's a good average."

"Thank you, sir."

"You must seriously consider your future, Kempt. You must," he said. "You need a clear objective. It seems to me that you have sustained a healthy interest in the Armed Forces. Am I correct?"

"Roger, sir."

"And you are now interested in the Infantry."

"Sir."

"Now tell me," the CO sat on his desk, "have you ever considered officer training?"

"Say again, sir?"

"I'm talking about Reg Force, Kempt. Furthering your education."

"I'm not sure I understand—"

"Have you thought of RMC, Kempt?"

"RMC?"

"BEER ESSES EMMA, TDV! WHO CAN STOP OLD RMC!" he shouted, pumping his fist in the air.

"Military College, sir?"

"A fine institution, Kempt. But don't take it from me. Just ask your old man. With your grades and with this experience," the CO said, brandishing the file, "you should have no problem getting in."

"I considered it some time ago, sir," I said. "But to be honest…"

"TDV! It's good to be honest. RMC is an experience unlike any other, Kempt. The Regular Officer Training Program is just about the only way to become an officer in the CF these days. And I'm confident you have what it takes. No duff, Kempt."

"Thank you, sir."

"And I don't mind telling you how positively this will reflect on this unit."

"I do like Thirtieth Field, sir," I said.

"Listen Kempt," his tone now confidential, "I know you like

this job, but I'm convinced you're Reg Force material. There's no life like it."

"Well, it's just that … I mean …"

"Bite it out Kempt!"

"Thank you. Sir."

"I'll write you a sterling letter of recommendation myself. I know people."

"I don't know what to say, sir."

"No need, Kempt. Don't say shit. It's my job. You deserve it."

"Thank you, sir."

"I'll have my secretary make an appointment for you at the Recruiting Centre."

"Sir?"

"She'll let you know when your interview is and what documents you will need."

"Oh."

The CO rose. I followed suit.

"Congratulations Kempt, and good luck," he offered his hand.

"Yes sir." I shook.

"That'll be all."

"Yes sir." I snapped to attention, took one pace back and saluted efficiently before dismissing myself.

No Life Like It

The clerk, her hair fixed in a tidy bun, was surfing the net. She held a blue ballpoint pen duct-taped to an inverted red pen, so that she could change colours with great efficiency. Her name tag said LAINE.

"I have an interview with Captain Ferat," I said.

LAINE stared at me, twirled her double-point pen.

"That's a high-tech pen," I said.

"You are *who*?" she said.

"The name's Kempt. Verbal—um, Herbert Kempt. What's your name?" I gave her a smile.

"Have you been made aware of the application procedure?"

"Not exactly," I said. "I brought some documents."

"Well before we start I'm going to need a birth certificate, a passport, if you have one, a valid driver's licence, a social insurance card and three letters of recommendation."

I put all of it on her desk. "I have an interview with Captain Ferat," I said. LAINE wasn't impressed.

"What are you applying for?"

"I think I'll be a pilot."

"Pardon me?"

"Well, RMC … the Regular Army. You know, to be an officer. At military college. In Kingston. You know the one?"

"That program is called ROTP," she said.

"ROTP then," I said.

"Here," she passed me some forms and a pen, "have a seat and fill these out. You'll see from the application sheet that you have to select three MOCs."

"Emmocies?" I said.

"Military Occupations. Write them in order of preference. It's pretty self-explanatory. Or it should be. If you want to be a pilot, you would write 'pilot' on the first line. You have to select three, though, in case your other choices are full."

"Pilot is full?"

"That's not what I said. The forms are self-explanatory. If you can't think of anything else, there are pamphlets on different MOCs in the waiting area."

"Okay. Do you need a transcript?"

"The forms are pretty self-explanatory."

"Okay. Thanks for your help." LAINE twirled her pen.

I selected PILOT. INFANTRY. ARTILLERY. After filling out the rest of the forms, I watched a documentary on CF-18s on the TV in the waiting room. I was suddenly sleepy.

"The Captain will see you now," LAINE said. I followed her into a small office.

"Have a seat," she said. "He'll be here shortly."

The recruiting posters on the wall promised everything. There were many possibilities. One minute I was commanding a tank as it navigated its way through a ravine, and the next I was on active peacekeeping service, saving the lives of innocent children. I had a rifle in one hand and a bowl of UN rice in the other. I was Making a Difference when Captain Ferat entered.

"So you're Mr. Kempt," he said.

"Yes sir." I stood and offered my hand. Ferat pumped it up and down.

"Got a call from your CO. It's good that you have all your paperwork in order—makes getting through all this admin easier."

"Yes sir."

"Have a seat, Mr. Kempt. Would you like a coffee? Mineral water?"

"No, thank you. Sir."

"A coke then."

"Thanks but no, sir. I'm good."

"Oh I know you're good," he said. "You've got an impressive record with the militia. And word is you're the son of the legendary Snake-Eater."

"Oh," I said. "You know my father." The light seemed bright in the room. I was getting sleepier and sleepier.

"If he's Colonel David Kempt, yes, I've met him. An outstanding asset to the Army."

"Yes sir."

"Now about you—just a chip off the old block, right?"

"Sir."

"Okay. Good. I see here that you want to go Air Force. You're certain?"

"I think I'd like to fly, sir."

"Sure sure. Great. It's demanding. But damned tempting," Captain Ferat laughed. "Sometimes I wish I'd gone pilot!"

"Sir."

"Good, then. Fair enough. We'll have to send you to Toronto for Aircrew Selection. Run some tests, put you through the simulator, that sort of thing."

"Yes sir."

"When can you do that?"

"Sir?"

"When are you available for Aircrew?"

"Oh. Anytime, I guess. Sir."

"We have a spot tomorrow. You'll take a train down tonight and be housed in transient quarters. Good enough?"

"Sir?"

"Don't worry about the tickets, they'll be waiting for you at the station. Meals will be provided. Keep a record of your expenses, taxis and whatnot, and we'll reimburse you when you get back."

"Yes sir," I said.

"Okay then. We'll get the ball rolling, and we'll be in touch when we get your results. Any questions? Okay. Is there any problem with you missing school tomorrow?"

"I don't think so, sir."

"We'll give you an official letter just in case."

"Yes sir."

"The competition is stiff, but with prior service and your marks, I don't mind telling you you're ahead of the game."

"Thank you sir."

"My pleasure, Mr. Kempt. And if you have any questions, here's my card."

"Thank you sir."

"And when you give your father the news, tell him I'm batting for you. He can call me if he has any questions."

"Yes sir."

Captain Ferat rose and shook my hand again.

"You're making a wise decision, Mr. Kempt. There's no life like it."

"So they say, sir."

The Simulator

The room was a circle. It was the only circular room I'd ever been in. It had a high ceiling and the wall was painted in a panoramic mural of a picturesque valley. Prominent landmarks dotted the mural, one being a lighthouse. It was the lighthouse that made me the most nervous.

At one point on the mural, there was an actual flight of stairs fixed to the wall, leading to a small box with windows. This box was The Tower. A plane attached to a podium attached to an intricate hydraulic system sat in the very middle of the room. The controls in the cockpit used the hydraulics to mimic a plane in flight. It was a pretty slick simulator, but when I saw it I was in no state of mind to admire it. I had a problem. A self-induced problem, but a problem nonetheless. And the problem still coursed through my bloodstream.

After leaving the Recruiting Centre, I'd called home and told Mom I was staying at Icky's due to drama guild commitments. I called Ruth and she picked me up downtown and drove me to the train station. She was driving her father's Toyota Land Rover and gave me a hummer in the parking lot before I caught my train. I borrowed money from her to cover my expenses. It was the money she needed to register for her soccer league and to buy her prom dress, but it was only just in case, and then only until I got reimbursed.

My ticket was there waiting for me, just as Captain Ferat had said it would be. I got on the train just in time. I only had the clothes I'd worn to the interview, and my dad's old leather briefcase. There was nothing in the case except for a couple of paperbacks, but it felt good to carry it all the same.

I have to admit I felt pretty fine. Here I was, wearing a silk tie and carrying a brown leather briefcase, riding the train to Toronto on official government business.

Since the ticket was free, and I was flush with the loan from Ruth, I celebrated in the bar cart with a beer. The bartender, if you could call him that, didn't even flinch. It was the tie and the briefcase, working their magic.

It was good to drink a beer—a Heineken—on the train when it was still light out. Most of the drinks I'd had in my time were in the dark. I could have been a young and successful businessman, sitting there in the bar cart. I could have been anything.

I wanted to get a good night's sleep so I had a few more Heinekens and bought a pack of Export A's. I planned to turn in early when I got my room at the base hotel. I needed to stop at a clothing store, too, to pick up something for the next day. I had Ruth's money for that.

When I got into Toronto I had a good glow on, and I was hungry, so I took a cab to the base because the wait for the bus was almost half an hour. The cab was steep, but I got a receipt. I got the key to my room and went to the hotel bar to get a sandwich or a burger.

"Something to drink?" the bartender said.

"I'll have a menu," I said, thinking I shouldn't drink any more on an empty stomach. He brought me over a menu and I went through it. The sandwiches were way overpriced, and the dinner items were too expensive. I thought getting up and leaving would be rude, so I just ordered a rum and coke before leaving. That's all I planned on having, and maybe I'd find a snack from a vending machine in the hotel.

It was a nice hotel bar—dark and cool and quiet, with thick carpet everywhere and lights going around the bar. I shot the breeze with the bartender while he polished wineglasses. When I was done my drink he poured me another, a double, on the house, which was a mighty kind thing to do. No bartender in Ottawa had ever done that for me. This was a different world. He was a student of wine, a sommelier, he said, and he told me all about different types of wine.

When I finished my rum and coke I ordered a glass of one of the red wines he told me about.

It's hazy what happened next. My room was a mess when I woke up. Thankfully I'd asked for a wake-up call. The sink was clogged with puke and the sheets were soaked with piss. There were wine stains on my shirt, and I realized with horror that I'd forgot to buy clothes.

I jumped up and down and pounded my face.

"Wake up motherfucker, wake up! Time to adapt and overcome!"

I spot-washed my shirt the best I could. The tie was gone. So was the briefcase. I checked my pants pocket: there was the cab receipt and five bucks in change. That's all that was left from Ruth's money.

I snuck onto the bus without paying, and arrived at the testing hangar at 06:30, just on time. I was sweaty and confused. I sorted through the previous night and tried to figure out what had happened after the red wine, and where I'd spent the money. My head was pounding.

The written tests started at 07:00, and after a few impromptu visits to the shitter, I felt a bit better. Better, but not ready for The Simulator.

The technician running The Simulator was a civvy, short and squat, and sported a mullet and thick black mustache. He gave the impression that his job really chapped his ass, wore his mullet like a badge of honour. I guessed he listened to Metallica. Maybe Springsteen when he was feeling mellow.

"Okay. You know the drill," he said.

"Actually, I don't," I said, aware that I could smell myself. The booze was coming out of my bones. I was suddenly self-conscious of the nicotine stains on my fingers.

"It was in the written guidelines," he said. "No matter. It's pretty basic, really. *I'm* the tower. *You* climb in *that* plane. Inside you'll find a headset. Put the headset on. Then I tell you what to do, like I'm doing right now."

"Right," I said.

The steps to the cockpit were really far apart, and I struggled for a while with my ass dangling from the door. Finally, dripping with sweat, I managed it, but I let go a huge fart when I finally pushed myself in the door. I put my headset on.

"Can you hear me?" said The Tower.

I looked through the plane's window and gave The Tower a thumbs-up. I thought of asking him for a gas mask. My own smell was nauseating.

"If you can hear me, say something into the headset. You're not going to wave at the tower from a real plane."

"I can hear you," I said.

"No static?"

"Loud and clear," I said. I wiped the sweat from my eyes. The plane was stifling. G-Forces? Head wounds? Engine failure? I was overheating. I wondered if this was a bad time to bail out, and how I could bail out.

"You'll notice a stick and two pedals in front of you," said the technician. "By moving the stick forward and aft, you control the elevators. By moving it left to right, you control the ailerons. The pedals control the rudders. This simulation will not take into account throttle, flaps, landing gear, or climate. Any questions?"

"Pardon?" I said.

"I will now unlock control on the ailerons and the ailerons only. I want you to hold the plane steady."

I heard a click, and my left wing dropped instantly. I fought with the stick, overcompensated, and dipped to the right.

"I said keep it steady," The Tower said.

I bracketed, dipping one wing and then the other, until I was holding the plane relatively steady.

"Okay. Now dip the left wing down slowly, pause for three seconds, then bring it back up to this position."

I moved the stick, and the wing swooped to the left again until the motion of the plane stopped with a thud. My headset fell off, but I could hear The Tower screaming. No time for that now. I massaged the stick, jerking the plane up slowly until I was back at the original position. I reached for his headset, knocking the stick, and swooped to the right until I heard another thud. The plane was at a sharp list and the cockpit door fell open. I put the headset on.

"...the fuck are you doing?!!"

"Sorry," I said. "I dropped the headset."

"Bring the plane back up to the original position!"

I did this, finally, and with a little less difficulty than before.

"Okay," said The Tower. "I will now lock the ailerons."

I heard the click. The stick went dead in my hand. It was like being on autopilot.

"Next I'm going to unlock the rudders. I want you to turn the plane to the left until the nose is pointing at the lighthouse."

Another click, and I was in a flat spin.

"On the lighthouse! Stop on the lighthouse!!"

I looked over my shoulders, trying to get a positive visual of the lighthouse. I saw it whiz past me a couple of times and eventually got the hang of the pedals enough to slow the spin down. My nose came up to the lighthouse, wavering. I was soaked now, and I felt supremely depressed. I wanted the autopilot back.

"Okay. Now swing it to the right until you are back at this position."

I did it. A few jerks and halts, but I did it. As a reward I was put on autopilot again.

"I will now unlock the elevators and only the elevators," said the tower. "You are required to keep the nose in place."

Click. I dropped into a steep dive. I was so far forward I was falling out of the cockpit. I pulled myself in and grappled with the stick, pulling it towards me, and quickly came out in a vertical climb.

"There's something wrong with this stick I think," I said into the headset.

The Tower wasn't talking to me. Eventually I levelled off, heading straight for the lighthouse.

"Okay. Now I'm going to unlock all three, and you are required to hold the plane steady."

A massive click. I scrambled, and fought it, even though I knew it was over. Punching the pedals, yanking the stick, I knew the game was up and I was in a world of hurt. I could barely see from the sweat in my eyes, and the headset slipped down around my nose. I'd been hit, obviously. My plane had taken a lot of punishment, and was heaving out of control.

"Fucksakes!" screamed The Tower. The plane stopped, halted in mid-spin.

I yanked his headset off, fell out of the cockpit and puked, and wondered what training would be like in Infantry.

The Medical

The medical wouldn't have been so bad if the nurse was ugly. Old, with grey hair, moles. But she wasn't. She was a like a porn star in a bad costume.

"Cough," she said. I tried to appear nonchalant, as if pretty nurses held my balls every day.

"Cough!"

"Ah-hem."

"Louder," she said. I hacked.

"You have a lump," she said.

"What!?"

"Oh. No … sorry. My mistake. But there's a scratch here."

Ruth!

"Looks like … a bite!" she said. "Is it very sore?"

"It's *fine*," I said.

"Okay. If you'll sit up I can take your blood."

"Sure."

"You can put your pants back on."

"Right." I looked away and felt the prick in my arm.

"This won't take too long."

"Oh yeah," I said.

"But I'll need to collect five vials, okay?"

Five!

"Sure thing," I said. "Not a problem. Heh." I hummed a tune, then forgot what tune. I went quiet. Five vials!

"How do you feel?" she said.

"Oh yeah," I said. "Hoo."

"Are you okay, sir?"

"Hahaha," I said.

"Almost done," the nurse cooed. "Here we go … last one."

"Wheee," I said.

"Are you sure you're all right? You sound funny."

"Of course … I … aaaahhhh," I turned my head in time to see the plasma, my plasma, separating in the neat line of vials. Then I passed out.

Three nurses brought me back around, laughing. Their faces surrounded me from all sides. One of them stuck a donut in my mouth.

"Little cutie!" she said.

"And he's joining the Infantry!" said the hot nurse.

"But he can't stand the sight of blood!" said another.

They roared.

It's a Career

I told Ruth that I had joined up.

"Full-time?" she said.

"Yeah. I'll get my degree, then I'll owe the Army five years of service."

"Five? That makes nine years, with the school." She chewed on her lip.

"If I don't get killed in the War, we could make a life for ourselves."

"I thought that was just the States."

"Don't you read the news, Ruth? We have ships out there."

"Where?" she said.

"Here, there, and everywhere," I said.

"But I thought you said you'd be in the Army."

"Right," I said. "They have special land troops on board these ships. You know... patrols, extraction teams. Special forces. Emergency Response. SWAT. That sort of thing."

"I thought you were going to be a pilot."

"Yeah. I've decided I don't want to be a hotshot flyboy. Where's the leadership in that?"

"Hmm. It seems like a long time."

"It's a career, Ruth. Careers are supposed to last a long time."

"Wow," she said. "Well, congratulations, I guess."

"You seem upset."

"I'm not upset, just... surprised. I'm happy for you."

"You are?"

"Of course I am."

"It's a good deal, Ruth. It's a guaranteed job."

"I understand. It's just that I could never picture you in the Army, is all."

"What do you mean?" I said. She was acting weird.

"I know you're in the Army, but it's hard to picture you in it," she said.

Groundhog Day

High school ended for good, and quickly seemed juvenile in retrospect. It appeared that everybody in the world was on a bender. The morning after our graduation party, Ruth cut my back to ribbons with her nails, screaming her love for me, and that afternoon, while we sat in my basement watching Bill Murray in *Groundhog Day*, she mentioned that she was leaving the country to travel Europe for a year. I had no idea what to say—up until that point I had assumed she'd move to Kingston. She stroked the back of my neck and pulled my head in close to her chest.

"It's hard to say goodbye," she said. I figured she must be in love with someone else.

"You make it look easy," I said. She missed the irony and leaned over to kiss me.

"We'll be back together," she said. "It's only a year. And besides, I'll be home for Christmas. Oh, this is so hard," she said, but I could see her mind was already on a jet plane, her hand in some Briton's pants.

It made me feel ill to know that while I was training at RMC, she'd be backpacking around Europe, getting hit on by Italians with low morals and salami breath, or by Frenchmen with black turtlenecks and no scruples. She acted like nobody had thought of travelling before her—like what she was going to do would change the world.

"Hope you have a blast," I said.

"Don't you understand?" she said. "I'm going to find myself." She was already acting more sophisticated. I asked her to go home—I said I was tired.

After she left I sat in the cool basement and had a bit of the hair of the dog that bit me. The Colonel came downstairs and had a pint with me to celebrate my acceptance to RMC. We finished all the beer in the fridge and then we finished the last couple bottles of whiskey from Gramps' wake, and Dad gave me a black Zippo lighter with 'DUCIMUS' engraved under my name.

At some point Dad passed out, and I found myself rummaging through my things in the attic. There was dust everywhere, and the light was bad, and the bulb kept flickering on and off. I packed all my school notes in boxes to be burned. I found some old two-dollar bills stuck between the pages of a 1972 *National Geographic*, and then a dusty Canadian Forces-issue duffle bag caught my eye. I pulled it under the light and unzipped it, sifting through the contents: a gun-cleaning kit, some old parade gear, a holster for a sidearm.

I folded my fingers around the worn leather and sniffed it. It seemed bigger than I imagined a holster would be, and I tried to picture what sort of handgun would be big enough to fill it. I rubbed some of the gun oil onto my fingers: it was fruity and metallic and smelled like something serious. It wasn't unpleasant.

I lifted out a musty pair of vintage combat pants and pulled them on over my jeans. They covered my feet, so I bent to roll them up. It was hot in the attic, and I was sweating bullets. The air was stale. I got to my knees and shoved my arm deep into the bag, and found an old gym shirt. I wiped my face with it, and stuffed it back into the bag. That's when my fingers came across the knife. It was black, with a black blade, housed in a black sheath. There was nothing shiny on the knife, not even the edge. I thought about it until I understood: it wasn't a hunting knife. It was a knife made specifically for killing people at night. I slid the knife out of the sheath and noted that the blade was rusted on one side. I tested the blade and instantly a prick of blood sprang up on my index finger.

I climbed down the ladder to the bathroom and looked at myself in the mirror, noting that the old-style combat pants nearly fit me. I knew they didn't make pants like that anymore. I went outside and set to work.

In the fields beyond our property, I stalked. My headache was gone. I crawled slowly through the damp, itchy grass towards a groundhog hole. In my right hand was the knife; in my left, a gas rag.

To my credit, I had hardly made a sound, even while searching out the surrounding holes and stopping them with rocks. The next hole I had left free, and I'd be there, waiting. But this hole would get the smoke.

I lit the gas rag with my new Zippo and dropped it into the opening before rolling over to the last hole. My heart pounded. I could taste salt.

The knife was poised, and I felt the sweat between my palm and the bone handle.

"One. Two. Three," I whispered.

The pants had rolled down while I was stalking. An insect crawled behind my ear. There was a drop of sweat hanging from my nose.

"Four. Five. Six," I whispered.

My knees were skinned and my pants were soaked right through; it had been a good stalk. I refused to move.

Seven. Eight—

The flash of brown fur was on its way back into the hole as soon as it appeared, but it was still too late. My arm shot out in time to catch the prairie dog square in the chin. There was a sucking noise, then a thick squish, then the soft cracking of bone as the tip reappeared in the back of the thing's neck.

I let go of the knife and jumped up, unable to stop looking. The knife was just long enough to span the diameter of the hole and keep the groundhog suspended. For a while it fought with its forepaws, clawing at the edge of the hole and then grabbing the handle of the knife, as if trying to pull it out of its throat. The thing cut its own claw off by tugging at the sharp blade. I felt sick, but eventually it ended, and I stood there, staring, wondering what had happened—where this thing had gotten to. This was death, and I might as well get used to it. My head throbbed. Ticks and fleas hopped madly all over the groundhog's fur.

The Arch

The day that I officially join the ranks of all Gentlemen Cadets, past and present, of the Royal Military College of Canada, I am aware that it is supposed to be a solemn moment, but it's kind of hard to feel solemn when you're sweating your balls off in thick wool pants.

We march smartly. A full summer of Basic Officer Training took care of that. We swing our arms shoulder-high, marching our way *through* the Arch in rank and file. This is the tradition. Heads up and swingalong.

The Arch is the key. It's the way into RMC, and it's the only way out. Hewn from large blocks of limestone, it is dedicated to all cadets who died during the Second World War.

Been here four days, waiting for this very ceremony, and I know things are about to pop. I can feel it in my stomach and between my shoulder blades. They've been too sweet to us lately. We're about to get cock, I could sense it the whole time we were supposed to be having a good time at the barbecue. They trumped up this outdoor family event like a festive reunion. All the brass was there, even the Commandant. With the balloons and burgers and cake, it looked like a church picnic, not a military school. They shouldn't have stuff like that, where family comes to visit for two hours—it just makes it harder. Especially with all the crap that's in the mail. We're Jiffy Pop on a bonfire right now.

I just want it to start. The sooner it starts, the sooner it's over with.

Mom and Dad and Ailish showed up for the barbecue. Dad wore his uniform. I didn't know if I should salute him or not.

Thankfully Ruth didn't show up. I might have quit on the spot if Ruth showed up.

"Left, right, left, right, left, right-left!" the senior cadet screams. From the corner of my eye, I see the spray of his spittle burst into the air as he calls the cadence. The others, the Cadet Squadron Training Officers (CSTO), keep calling out the time too, like we've never marched before. It's slightly embarrassing in front of this crowd, especially since we're all in step. As if we don't know the timing to a quick march.

On our approach, I sneak a look up and catch the inscription on the top of the Arch:

BLOW OVT, YOV BVGLES, OVER THE RICH DEAD
THERE'S NONE OF THESE SO LONELY AND POOR OF OLD
BVT, DYING, HAS MADE VS RARER GIFTS THAN GOLD

Somehow I'm supposed to be a part of this now. Because I'm walking under it, I'm supposed to be linked to those it was built for. I want to think solemn thoughts but instead I think I should have had another burger. I wonder: will my roommate Mack Prendergast be a solid guy under fire, will he pull his weight when it counts, or will he be a wanker?

The recruit handbook is folded in my back pocket. The information in it is vital to my survival. At any moment, I may have to explain to a senior cadet the history of the college. I might have to explain why the Arch is so important.

This is my first real parade at RMC, and the pipes and drums sound regal, confident. I'm certain, though, that the designers and tailors of the CF-issue uniforms could have found a better material for marching. My crotch itches like the devil, and I'm getting chafed. I know I've got pits already from the heat—I can smell myself. I steal a glance upwards again, and try to picture young men falling on the field of battle.

BLOW OVT, YOV BVGLES, OVER THE RICH DEAD
THERE'S NONE OF THESE SO LONELY AND POOR OF OLD
BVT, DYING, HAS MADE VS RARER GIFTS THAN GOLD

The tradition holds that we, the new recruits, must march through the Arch to join the rest of the RMC cadet wing. I try to catch a last glimpse of Ailish without moving my head from eyes-front; it's dangerous to deek on parade, but I won't see her again until Thanksgiving.

I'll be the first in line to admit that this should feel more special than it does—this is one of only two occasions where I'll be granted the privilege of marching through the Arch, as opposed to around it. The only other time is upon graduation from RMC. And for me that's four long years away.

"EYYYEEESS-RIGHT!" the CSTO screams. We look right in unison as he snaps a perfect salute.

Here's looking at you, boys.

I try to feel sad for the fallen soldiers but it doesn't wash. Death in war is a movie-of-the week for me, or a video game. In a wink we're through, marching sharply down Memorial Drive and into the heart of the college grounds.

"EYYYEEESS-FRONT!" the CSTO says. We march over the freshly paved and manicured beauty of the campus, our new home.

"Left, right, left, right, left, right-left!"

My balls need a scratch bad, which is impossible to do when marching shoulder-high.

The cover of my recruit handbook has disintegrated from sweat and friction, but the information is still intact. I have to cram a few nuggets of college trivia in whenever I get the chance so I'm prepared. There could be a pop quiz at any moment.

Be prepared. Attention to detail. Initiative and Decisiveness. These are the concepts I need to live by to make it through. They say that fifty percent of each class that rolls in here will make it out with a degree.

Past the guardhouse, we're on the college grounds proper, and in perfect formation we wheel around for our approach to the parade square.

The Wolfe Island ferry lets out a sharp blast as it leaves harbour, adrift on Lake Ontario. Seems to be getting dark quickly; Queen's

BONK ON THE HEAD

is just across the water. It can be seen clearly from the Martello Tower on Point Frederick. I can't focus. There's a slight breeze coming off the lake and I can smell dampness, like before rain. Cool air all of a sudden, a drop in atmospheric pressure. I've heard the weather in Kingston can change in a heartbeat.

Panic

I've been through enough military indoctrination to know that you've got to keep your sense of humour. To be able to laugh is the main thing. You lose that, and you're euchred. The reserves taught me that. That, and the fact that no exercise is eternal. Eventually, after all the yelling and shouting and name-calling, after all the push-ups and the running and the crawling through mud, *eventually* it will end. And if you're standing with a shred of dignity when it ends, you gain unspoken accolades from your superiors. They will respect you for making it without whining. I've been there, so I considered myself to be amply prepared for rook term.

While standing at attention outside my door, I thought it odd that the military would leave the lights off in the hallway. The CF is usually so particular about safety. There must be a rule against this somewhere, I thought.

I really should've scarfed down a few more burgers at the barbecue, because I was already starting to feel the hunger. I heard a stomach growl, but I couldn't tell if it was me or Mack.

"A lousy roommate makes life lousy in the Army," Sgt. Cookson once told me. "So if you have a lousy roommate, shape him up or make his life miserable until he quits." Things could go sour in a jiffy if Mack didn't learn to spit-shine properly, or if he was the type to leave his beard in the sink after shaving, or if he was in the habit of leaving his gunky tube of toothpaste lying out with the cap off. Or maybe he has BO. That's the real killer—sharing a room with some guy who smells like gym socks, or bad breath, or pee.

I turned my head to Mack, who stood on the opposite side of the doorway, and tried to make out his face in the dark. The rest of our flight stumbled over each other, cursing in whispers and trying to position themselves accordingly. Mack's lips moved silently but I couldn't make out his expression.

When I heard the clickers approaching, my head shot forward in the appropriate eyes-front, don't-look-around position.

Clickers are steel plates nailed to the soles of parade boots to make marching snappy; they make it sound a lot keener than it normally would. A few select fourth-year cadets thought it would be intimidating to put clickers on their Oxfords. Generally, as I found out later, only jackasses with control issues did this, but still they were right. It was intimidating.

The clicking got louder until it was directly on top of me; in my periphery I caught the red glow of a cigarette being raised to someone's lips. The glow got brighter as he inhaled.

"What the fuck do you think you're looking around for, Recruit?"

I caught a stream of smoke full in the face as he exhaled: Marlboro Lights over stale coffee breath. He was close. Really close. I figured he was bluffing, had to be. Nobody could see in this darkness.

"Looking for your Mommy, Recruit?" he whispered.

"I wasn't looking around—"

"Don't fucking lie to me you piece of shit. How do you address me?"

"I'm not lying, sir!"

"I haven't bloody well received my commission yet, Recruit. And I doubt that you're in a position to promote me."

"Excuse me, but I can't see your name tag, Mister."

"Mister! Mister fucking what, asshole?"

"I don't know," I said.

The cadet brought his cigarette up again and inhaled, the ash inches from my nose. The red glow illuminated a craggy, pockmarked face. From his expression this man looked more like an ex-con than an officer in training. I decided to keep my mouth shut. It occurred to me only then that I might not have a clear picture of what exactly I'd gotten myself into.

"The name, Recruit, is Mr. Stocker." There was a pause. I wanted to tell him he had a fitting name.

"Well?" he blew more smoke in my face. I was sure smoking in the building was against regulations.

"Yes Mr. Stocker!" I said.

"I mean everybody!" Mr. Stocker turned and addressed himself to the rest of the flight: "Does everybody understand?"

"Yes Mr. Stocker!" we screamed.

"That's right recruits. Your mommies and daddies are all gone now, so you've got nobody to cry to for a long, long time." He nodded and smoked for a bit, then ground his butt out on the wall beside my head.

"Now: get in the push-up position!"

There was a stunned moment of silence, and then we hit the floor. I knocked heads with one of the girls across the hall, though I didn't know she was a girl until she started whimpering. A girl whimpering in the dark with the smell of sweat and fear is not a nice thing. I reached out and touched her hand, just to let her know she wasn't alone. I heard Mack whimper then.

"Fuck off," somebody said.

It's like that. When it's a guy whimpering, you want to find his face and give it a smack.

We shuffled around, knocking into each other, trying to find enough leg space. The hallway was a painful mess of heads, elbows, knees and feet. And I'd had plans to polish my parade boots and iron my CFs for the morning inspection. I'd hoped to prepare before recruit term started, but apparently it already had. Right away, they'd taken away the privilege of personal time.

When we were all down on the floor, the lights came on.

"Look up! Look up you bags of shit!" Mr. Stocker sneered, his upper lip curled like a lemon rind. Pressed against the cold floor, I could appreciate that sneer. I could appreciate his position, and its relation to mine. What bothered me, and what I could not ignore, was the strong urge I had to please him.

We did push-ups until half the flight was moaning. I couldn't stop my arms from shaking, but I was still able to move up and down. When I looked up, there were only about five of us still holding the Proper Push-up Position, in a sea of Jell-O flesh and blotchy faces. Mr. Stocker clicked down the hall towards me. He had a mug in his hand, and I could smell coffee. Coffee! The very idea at a time like this seemed preposterous.

"What's your name, Recruit?" He kicked me lightly in the stomach.

"Kempt, Mr. Stocker!"

"And yours?" he toe-tapped another guy in the ribs.

"Gaze, Mr. Stocker!"

"And you?"

"Mann, Mr. Stocker!"

"You."

"Weiland, Mr. Stocker!"

"You!"

"Wommersley, Mr. Stocker!"

"Well," Mr. Stocker said. "All you keeners are blading your buds. November Flight, looks like these five young bucks want to keep doing push-ups. They think they're special. So we will continue, and while you're all sweating down there, perhaps the five of you can ponder the importance of working together."

Soon we were grunting and shaking, coughing, farting, snotting and sobbing all over the cold linoleum. Seeing the girls across the hall was starting to get under my skin. I'm not insulted when it's me getting cock, but to see a woman face-down and sputtering and being publicly humiliated and toe-tapped in the gut—all for training purposes—is horribly insulting for everyone involved.

"You people are tremendously out of shape," Stocker said. "I think it's high time you got some exercise. You all look a little too fat for my liking. Don't you think we could use some exercise, Recruit Weiland?"

"Yes Mr. Stocker!"

"Well, November Flight, it seems that Recruit Weiland wants to go for a run. That means all you saucy fatties are going for a run! You have now got—and I'm timing you—five minutes to be formed up here in PT gear. Five minutes is bags of time, recruits! Bags of time! Dis-missed!"

I scrambled for the door and collided with Mack, who was trying to squeeze through at the same time. He was all limbs.

"Go!" I said. He looked ready to shit himself. I followed him in and flicked on the light.

"Oh my goodness!" Mack said. All our kit was upside down. Every uniform we had was strewn on the floor. The beds, which we had made with care that morning, were completely stripped. A pillowcase hung from the curtain rod. My toiletries had been dumped with Mack's into the sink. We scrambled, looking through the mounds of clothing feverishly for our CF-issue grey polyester PT shorts. I remembered them well—they chafe the crotch even when you're not moving. I yanked off my shoes and found a PT shirt under a pair of my CF trousers. It was stenciled PRENDERGAST across the chest.

"Mack. Mack! Here's your shirt," I said. I tossed it at him but he dropped it. I made a mental note: can't catch a shirt—not a good sign. His eyes were googly with panic and his mouth was loose and flappy. He struggled into a pair of shorts. I found a pair myself and hopped into them, but the damn things bloomed out like diaper pants. Our five minutes was almost up.

I retrieved another t-shirt from beneath Mack's scarlet dress coat. It was too tight and barely reached my shorts, but I could already hear other recruits slamming to attention in the hall. I threw on a pair of grey wool socks. Sweat poured off of me as I laced up my runners. I looked up at Mack.

"You ready?" I said. I didn't want to be the last one out. Then I noticed his feet. The clown had put his drill boots on again.

"Are you mad? Where the Christ are your runners, man?" I said.

"I forgot to put on laces," he said. No laces, so he just figured drill boots would be acceptable. On a run.

"We're screwed," I said. "Every time you make a mistake, you screw me. And every time I make a mistake, I screw you. You get it?" I said. Mack nodded. I noticed there were beads of sweat covering his face, his eyes had a hard time staying still. I could smell his breath across the room, and his lips twitched, and his reddish-blond eyebrows moved up and down. He had sallow skin, and a weak chin. For a moment I wanted to tap it.

I turned off the light before we went back into the hall. I paused, waiting for Mack, so that we'd come to attention together. Josh Weiland from next door was already outside, looking tanned and fit. I envied his perfect fitting PT gear. His roommate was still inside their room.

"So you're ready, Recruit Weiland."

"Yes, Mr. Stocker!"

"Ready to go for a jog?"

"Yes, Mr. Stocker!"

"Where's your roommate?"

"He's ... looking for his shoe, Mr. Stocker."

"Well if you're ready, Recruit, why aren't you helping him?"

"Yes, Mr. Stocker!" Weiland tore back into his room to help Wommersley.

"Weiland get the fuck out here!"

He popped his head out of the room: "Yes, Mr. Stocker?"

"Out HERE, at attention, you fuck-wit."

"Yes Mr. Stocker." He slammed to attention.

"You must ask to go help your bud, now that you're at attention."

"Permission to help Recruit Wommersley get ready, Mr. Stocker."

"Are you fucking daft, Recruit?"

"Pardon, Mr. Stocker?"

"Have you forgotten how to report already?"

"No Mr. Stocker!"

"Well?"

"Oh. Recruit Weiland, J., Five Squadron, November Flight, One Section reporting!"

"You're in Three Section; One Section is my Section. You're not in my Section."

"Recruit Weiland, J., Five Squadron, November Flight, Three Section reporting!"

"Yes?"

"Permission to help Recruit Wommersley find his shoe, Mr. Stocker!"

"It's mighty white of you to think of him. Sure, go ahead."

Josh tore into the bedroom and smacked straight into Wommersley who was on his way out. It sounded painful. Josh went sprawling on his ass and Wommersley landed on top of him. I thought my gut would split. It's funny when you're not the one getting cock. Stocker screamed at them until they were up on their feet in the position of attention.

"Okay N Flight that took way too long," Stocker said. "I assume all of you have seen that we helped you reorganize your rooms since you left them gashed before the barbecue. You must learn how to panic! You have to learn how to get things done efficiently—to do this you must help each other meet the timings required of you. And you," he said, approaching me, "did you change your fucking name, Kempt?"

"Uh ... no, Mr. Stocker."

"Then why the fuck does your t-shirt say Prendergast? You people are pathetic. You've got four minutes—no, three-and-a-half minutes to be back out here with your uniforms on. Dismissed!"

We came out in our uniforms and then had to go back and change into PT gear. Over the next three hours Mr. Stocker shouted himself hoarse. We couldn't seem to get it right. We must've changed forty times, and never did end up going for that run. After the first hour everyone's uniform was dark with sweat. Finally, Mr. Stocker seemed bored with the drill.

"Three minutes, N Flight," he said. "Not too bad for the first night."

It sounds odd to say it, but I was proud of our timing. I thought we'd be spared until morning at least. I fantasized about the urinals: fragrant piss pucks, cold metal taps, tile, grout, porcelain and condensation, piss piss flush. I had to pee bad. None of us had had the chance to relieve ourselves since before the barbecue, and I'd swear my teeth were floating.

"It is now 21:00," said Mr. Stocker. "You have half an hour to be formed up for your next timing. Since we have your watches, I will keep time for you. At 21:30 you will be outside your doors in full CF dress: that's tunic and tie, long-sleeved shirt and parade boots. Your rooms will be ready for inspection. Any questions? DIS-MISSED!"

I felt betrayed; what about our timing? We'd changed in less than three minutes! That had to count for something. Then I remembered that nothing really counts in military training and that it wasn't going to stop until rook term was over.

The ensuing half an hour was a blur of impossible activity. First thing I told Mack to watch the door. I unzipped and was almost pissing before I could even aim at the sink. Probably still the best piss I've ever had—the kind where you get shivers, a cold knife singing right up your spine.

"What are you *doing*?" Mack said.

"What the hell does it look like? You think we'll get another chance for this?"

He just gaped, staring at my penis with his mouth open. I considered turning my heavy stream in his direction, just to snap him out of it.

"Just watch the door, will you?" I said.

Mack turned around. He never stopped moving; his orange head bobbed up and down inconsolably, his freckled arms flailing around his sides in exasperation. He looked like a big panicky bird, trying to flap his way out of our situation. "This is crazy. This place is crazy," he said. He kept saying it. "This is crazy."

I finished my piss, shook off and zipped up. Mack fumbled with the clothes on the floor, looking for a place to start. I glanced across the hall and caught one of the girls perched awkwardly above the sink with her pants around her ankles, her thick, dark thighs squashed flat on the countertop. She saw me looking and flipped the bird. I liked her immediately.

"Your turn, Mack," I said.

"Forget it," he said, bobbing. "I'm not going to pee in a *sink*. That's disgusting."

"Suit yourself." I didn't have time to argue. We only had about twenty-seven minutes, and I had to find a logical place to start. I knew I couldn't count on Mack. The bunks had to be remade, but nothing could be accomplished until all the clothes were off the floor.

At first I started working *with* Mack, picking up our uniforms one piece at a time, but he kept bumping into me, muttering, "This is crazy."

I grabbed both sets of parade boots and my shoeshine kit and slammed them on his desk. "You can spit-polish, right?"

"Yes," he nodded.

"You do these, I'll work on the room."

I hung the uniforms like we had in the reserves: one set facing the other to distinguish whose was whose. I checked that all the buttons were done up and that there were no loose strings hanging. As I did this, I counted. I counted slowly, aloud. I was at four minutes by the time the clothes were off the floor and the PT gear was folded and put away in drawers. I had to count because they'd taken our watches. They'd confiscated almost everything that wasn't military issue.

I was thorough. I even folded Mack's gitch, knowing the Cadet Section Commanders (CSCs) would be sticky about everything. Even our gash drawer, for personal items, which was supposedly off limits during inspection, was empty and dust-free. It's my experience that when they give you something like the freedom of a gash drawer, it's usually a test—an attempt to fake you out and make you lazy.

I tackled our various personal items: books, papers, toiletries, not much. These went neatly into desk drawers, beneath the sink, and behind the mirror of the medicine cabinet. When I rinsed out the sink I was at nine minutes, give or take. I checked on Prendergast. He was still on the first boot.

"Mack! Shift it! You've got about twelve minutes to finish the other three."

I grabbed the sheets and made the beds. We'd each been issued one pillow, two white DND sheets, and two grey wool fire blankets. I had to pull the beds out and move them around to get behind them, and do proper hospital corners. I paused for a second.

"Shit!" I said. I'd stopped counting without thinking about it. Now I had no idea how much time was left. And not knowing was worse than not having enough. Mack was on the third boot.

"The fourth, the fourth!" I said.

"Huh?" he said. He looked as if he'd just woken up from a nap.

"Do the last one! We don't have much time!"

Mack, startled by the notion that we didn't have much time, jumped up, knocking the tin of polish to the floor. The clatter of the tin scared him even more, and he jumped back, dropping the boot in his hand. The boot landed upside down on its gleaming toe.

"Cripes!" Mack said, and judging by the way he said it, "Cripes" was a big thing for him. He must have really meant it. I picked the boot up and checked inside, thankful to see *his* name in black Magic Marker and not mine.

"Sorry about your luck," I said, "but we have to get dressed." It was bad luck for Mack, and I remembered the Colonel's motto: never trust people with bad luck.

We dressed in our CF uniforms. When I was done, I found Mack staring dumbfounded at both ends of his tie.

"Here, gimme that—" I made a quick double Windsor for him and threw it back.

"Thanks." He actually smiled. Just then he looked like a little kid. I didn't have the heart to tell Mack he was doomed.

"De-froust your beret," I told him.

"What is froust?" he said.

"The lint, man! Take the lint off your beret!" Doomed. I de-frousted my own beret—my old one from the reserves—and put it on. The new one I'd been issued was somewhere in a duffel bag, where it would stay. This one was sunbleached and formed perfectly to my head from a summer of heavy wear.

Then I brushed my teeth.

"What are you *doing*?" Mack said.

"I advise you to do the same."

"I'll do it before bed. We don't have time, Herbert!"

"We've got to *make* time, man. Do you believe that they'll tuck us in, make sure we brush our teeth? 'Don't stay up too late recruits! Do you have clean jammies on?'"

"They're not going to let us brush our teeth?"

"Think about it—if they're not giving us a chance to piss, they're sure as hell not worried about our dental hygiene." I gulped down greedy mouthfuls of water. "And make sure you drink every chance you get. We're going to sweat a lot and you don't want to dehydrate."

Mack stood there for a moment, and then, slowly, undid his fly. He did it sadly, as if by pissing in this here sink he was letting down his mom back in North Bay and everything she stood for. Holding onto the towel rack he broke the seal and let out a low moan.

"Feels good, eh?" I said.

"Ooohhh," he said. I thought he might cry. It had been over thirteen hours since we'd last had the chance to piss.

"That's called sweet release, Mack," I said. I tried to calculate exactly how many cadets had pissed in this very sink over the years.

I heard a thump-thump of someone coming to attention outside. I'd hoped we would be first out this time, but I wasn't going to make the mistake of going into the hall without Mack, who took some time pissing and then floundered for his beret. He put it on ass-backwards, and resembled a GI version of the Pillsbury Doughboy. I tried to help him stretch it, flatten it, form it—do *something* with it, but to no avail. I poked him in the stomach and giggled.

"Tee-hee!" I said. It was lost on him. He had discarded his sense of humour. Mack was doomed.

"From now on," I said, "we come to attention *together*, we leave this room *together*, we do everything *together*."

"Okay," he said. He nodded.

In the hall I checked out our surroundings out of the corner of my eye. That's what the CSCs would call *deeking*. I spotted two large speakers attached to the ceiling above my head; I stole a glance to the other end of the hall, and noted that there were two more.

"Don't look around Recruit!"

I shot my eyes front. Two seniors were standing off to my right. I hadn't heard them approach: neither of them was wearing clickers.

"You don't learn very quickly, do you, Recruit Kempt?" one of them said. "Mr. Stocker told us that you had an attitude. That you liked to deek around."

"All right November Flight," said the other one. "Time's up! Everybody out in the hall!"

The CSC of one section was Mr. Kincaid, a tall, lanky, and clean-cut cadet who, despite his booming baritone voice, rarely got excited or upset. And two section had Mr. Hackman, who was shorter and given to making sarcastic jabs rather than yelling. It was obvious to me, seeing these two, that Mr. Stocker was the one to watch out for.

As Mr. Kincaid paced up and down the hall eyeballing us, Mr. Hackman strolled about casually, checking dress and deportment and making snide remarks.

"Recruit French!" he said.

"Yes, Mr. Hackman?"

"You've got an IP, Recruit."

"Pardon, Mr. Hackman?"

"An Irish pennant—you see this—this thread coming out of your epaulette? Here, put it in your mouth. There: uncomfortable, isn't it, Recruit French? Having a string in your mouth. But that's what an Irish pennant is, and now you won't forget. And you, Recruit: how do we stand properly at the position of attention?"

"Sir?"

"I'm not an officer yet, Recruit."

"Sorry, Mr. Hackman."

"Oh, not at all, not at all. Now, do you have an answer to my question?"

"Mr. Hackman?"

"How do we stand properly at the position of attention? No—never mind, you obviously haven't the faintest. I'll tell you: not like you're standing! That's the correct answer—oh dear, you look like a wind-up toy, Recruit. First you should close your mouth. Relax your arms. Close your fists. Chin up! There. Well… almost. Mr. Kincaid, what does this facial expression make you think?"

"Looks like she might have to shit, Mr. Hackman."

"Work on that, Recruit. I want to see a vast improvement. And don't have a bowel movement in your uniform."

She looked like she'd take him seriously—that she'd spend time *practising* standing at attention. Tears rolled down her cheeks.

"You keep crying, Recruit," Mr. Hackman said, "and maybe, just maybe, all this will be nothing more than a bad dream."

Mr. Kincaid gave a speech.

"For the next six weeks," he said. "You people belong to us. Reveille is at zero-six-hundred-hours. Don't worry about alarm clocks—we'll wake you up ourselves. Lights-out is at twenty-three-hundred-hours, and from that time until Reveille you will be racking in your pits. If anyone is caught out of bed during this time, the entire flight will receive the necessary punishment.

"Over the next six weeks you will have various squadron duties to attend to. Your Recruit Adjutant, Ms. Pfaff, will explain these duties in further detail tomorrow.

"The only time you are not required to be in uniform is when you are racking in your pits. You are required to wear headdress everywhere other than in your rooms, the academic buildings, and, obviously, the mess.

"You will march everywhere, swinging your arms shoulder high. When inside, you are required to perform square drill— no wheeling around the corners in the halls. You must make a proper left or right turn on the march, if you desire to change direction.

"Upon meeting any barmen—those cadets appointed with three bars or over in squadron and wing HQ—you must acknowledge them appropriately. You are expected to know their names by tomorrow morning. Outside of your rooms you are forbidden to speak to each other without specific permission.

"When marching in a group, you will be in a formation. Always. If it happens that you are going somewhere by yourself—which I don't foresee for some time—you must double the parade square when crossing it. To do this you come to a halt, check left and right, then double-time it to the other side. There you will halt, check right and left, then continue at the standard quick-march pace. Failing to do this will get you remedial drill.

"If you're wondering about leave passes—don't. Nobody will be stepping off this campus until Thanksgiving. Now go change into shower gear for shower parade."

Two minutes and thirty seconds later, Mr. Hackman ran us around the halls in our towels and flip-flops for shower parade, where we had to scream "November Flight" over and over in unison. The showers were freezing, and we had thirty seconds to clean up. Soap wasn't allowed. I stood to the side of the nozzle and drank.

When we got back to our rooms, we found them gashed again. They had thrown every uniform, every piece of military kit we had—right down to our bootlaces—all over the floor.

"Oh my God," Mack said. "Again? This is crazy. This is too crazy." He looked at me and I saw he was crying.

"I pretend it's always going to be this way, then I'm not surprised when it happens," I said.

"Ten seconds till Lights Out!" Mr. Stocker screamed from the hallway. His voice made me jump and want to hide: I am Pavlov's dog already. I hit the lights and was in the top bunk before Mack could take his glasses off.

Breakfast

My Flight, November Flight, was part of Five Squadron, or Brock Squadron, named after the British soldier Isaac Brock. He died fighting for Upper Canada in 1812. How do I know this? I had squadron pride coming out of my ass after our college history lectures with Ms. Pfaff, the Recruit Adjutant.

Major-General Brock was first in command at Quebec, but was eventually appointed as Lieutenant-Governor. Ms. Pfaff maintained that Brock was a real go-getter, and had it not been for him we would have lost Upper Canada to the Yanks.

According to legend, Brock defeated Hull at Detroit "without firing a single shot." That's a battle I would have paid cash to see. He fought with a motley crew—some Reg Force soldiers, some militia, some settlers armed with forks and pickaxes, and all the Indians he could coerce. He had some big brass balls, if you're to believe our version of the story: dressed in brilliant red, he led the charge against American forces at Niagara for about ten seconds until he took a bullet in the chest from a sniper. He died, but not before Upper Canada was saved. As a monument, there's a 185-foot monument over his grave in Queenston Heights. I've seen the pictures: it looks like a giant erect phallus.

To pay tribute, our squadron traditions include wearing "crazy" pants at wing functions, sporting the colour purple, and painting lobsters on our faces. Why lobsters? Because of the B-52's song "Rock Lobster." Rock rhymes with Brock. What a tradition!

But we, the ladies and gentlemen cadets of N Flight, were not much concerned with squadron traditions as we passed through rook term together. We were getting to know each other in the kind of compressed situation that tends to linger. I got the impression that it was the kind of thing that I had to go through to understand—like war, or abuse, or child labour. All the theory in the world can't make me understand it, but once I lived it I was connected to everyone else who has lived it. I might pass some recruit in the hall—someone I've never met, never even had a chance to look in his eye, let alone shake his hand or learn his name—but I will feel kinship. We panic together, march side by side, and chew silently across from each other in the mess hall. These guys and girls are going through the same hoops, so odds are they feel the same things I do. That reason alone is enough. I'll fight for him. I'll fight for her. I don't have to know their names. Even Mack, who brings me to a boil at times with all his flubbering and blubbering—even Mack I'd stick up for if it came down to it. No question.

Mack was in a bad way though. Inside the system he became a victim. All I can say to that is better him than me. We were in Mr. Hackman's section, which wasn't a bad section to be in as long as your dress and deportment were at a high standard. Mack's wasn't. He understood nothing about training, and thought these people were just being mean. These people included me at times, as I'm afraid I didn't really help Mack out all that much. On several occasions it could even be said that I bladed him.

As it turns out, Mack lasted until midway through second term, which was longer than I initially gave him. I think his breaking point was when Josh Weiland, next door to us, came to collect me for dinner one night when we were finally allowed to eat. Instead of me he found Mack, the geeky little tosser, coming aboard himself furiously while sitting at *my* desk. Which started me thinking that Mack was a bit of a poofta. Josh had an entertaining description of Mack jumping up immediately and yanking on those retarded CF-issue grey sweatpants.

"I'm just doing Chemistry, ah… um, some laundry… uh, Herbert's not here." Josh did a good impression.

"Mack's boner was caught up in his waistband, for crying out loud," Josh said.

It didn't take long after that. Josh had all the other first-years on the lookout for Prendergast; whenever Mack would march by the Academic buildings there'd be a group of first-years hanging out the windows:

"Hey! It's Mack the Whack!"

"Yo, Fast Hands, how's your vision these days?"

"Hey Whack! You get off yet today?"

It didn't matter that every guy was jerking off whenever he could. We just needed a lamb for the collective slaughter and Mack was it. Mack was the ransom we had to pay for holding ourselves hostage. In a way I knew it was wrong, but it was acceptable because it was necessary. We needed him, and if it hadn't have been him it would have been somebody else.

After the incident Josh and his bunkmate Bilbo Wommersley would say good night by banging against our paper-thin wall, groaning and shouting in mock ecstasy. That cracked me up. From the top bunk I laughed out loud, even knowing that Mack Prendergast was silently going sour inside. He was retreating within himself, becoming an island. As a result I was getting closer to my comrades, and it felt good not to be the one who was isolated.

Not long after Mack finally fell asleep in his tear-stained pillow that first night, we were woken at 05:00 to the deafening noise of April Wine's "Oowatanite." The music was so loud that Mack and I had to scream at each other while making our beds. Then came The Sex Pistols' "Anarchy in the UK," accompanied by the furious shouts of all three CSCs as they paraded the hallway in clickers, banging the butts of their rifles against our doors.

I kept telling myself that they didn't matter, that it was just a game, that eventually this would all be over. I knew the CSCs couldn't get to me if I didn't care. By the fourth day I would awake with a start, in a cold sweat, listening to the speakers hiss and crackle just moments before the big show.

The music was a painful, distasteful medley that lasted for roughly seven-and-a-half minutes, and in that time we had to shave, polish, make our beds, get dressed and dust our rooms.

And that first morning, after they had gashed our rooms so badly, we also had to pick up all our kit off the floor; nobody was well turned-out for inspection, but that didn't matter since we had to rush to breakfast before picking up our last and most important piece of gear: our C7 rifles.

The C7 is Canada's version of the M-16, with magazines manufactured by Mattel. At RMC, the C7 is nothing more than a prop for parade and a pain in the arse.

We clomped over to the mess in Yeo Hall in three ranks, under the auspices of Mr. Stocker: "Shoulder-high, recruits! Kempt! Don't look around! Left-wheel! Swing it around Weiland. Harrowsmith! Recruit Harrowsmith! Inside man steps short, outside man steps long! Or woman, in this bloody case."

Sue Harrowsmith was short and kind of squat in stature, and she would eventually offer herself to almost every male cadet in N Flight. Maybe in the whole wing. She started out rook term with a roommate, but I never learned her name as she was one of the two who quit on the second day. Rumour from Basic Officer Training was that Harrowsmith was always ready and always willing—the kind of girl that's handy to have in an army. She used to say that what we were learning at RMC applied realistically to the manager's position she'd held at Tim Hortons.

"Tim Hortons!" Josh said one day. "Figures. She's like the fritters—chunky and glazed." Sue was a person that I was too embarrassed to connect with, but probably could have. She had a rough go of it, I think. I heard later on that eventually she was shamed into failing out in second year after some creep bronco-fucked her. A bronco fuck is a popular pastime among the infantry types or those trying to get into the Ritz—RMC's underground male-only club. Another rite of membership was the red badge of courage—eating a girl out when she was on the rag. The method of bronco fucking, as explained to me, is to screw a girl doggie-style, and right before you blow your wad you slap her in the ass and say something like, "You're the ugliest fuckin' bitch I've ever seen in my life." Then you hang on. There was a close-to-undisclosed statistic floating around that over half the women of any year at RMC were at some point raped by either their fellow cadets or their senior officers.

I wasn't exactly new to the idea of crass and illegal behaviour, but nothing had prepared me for this aspect of soldiering—this reckless abandon of the norms of society. I wondered if the Colonel had been in the Ritz Club—something I could never ask him.

As we marched over to get our rifles that day, I stared at Harrowsmith bear-marching and wondered how she ever made it through Basic. I just wanted to scream at some people: "Why did you sign up for this?"

It wasn't until we were inside the mess and had joined the long line of sweaty, petrified recruits, that I remembered how famished I was. The smell of the rich food seemed extravagant, and I sneaked a peek at the holy spread on a large centre table: dozens of cold cereals, and massive bowls of raisins, brown sugar and fresh fruit. Surrounding this display were three refrigerated trolleys with sneeze-guards. One housed a juice bar—tomato, apple, orange, grapefruit, pineapple—and another contained yogurt, sliced tomatoes, lettuce, cheese, cretons. I was about to check the third when I felt Stocker's humid coffee-breath in my ear:

"You fuckin' steady-up now Recruit Kempt. You cunts just get the hot plate and that is fuckin' *it*."

I shot my eyes forward and stared ahead, just a cunt anxious for the hot plate. Not one of us had eaten since the barbecue, which seemed to have happened years ago. I was already thinking about seconds.

We moved along in file, and we were close to the steam line when somebody dropped a cup. It was one of those plastic drinking glasses that makes a brutal racket, and it bounced across the floor, loud. I could make out scores of cadets in uniform in my periphery, and none were talking. They were watching us.

The bouncing cup drew a few startled looks from the recruit line-up, and the seniors were ready with a barrage of curses. The mess hall went from silence to instant mayhem. Every senior stood at the same moment—some on chairs, some on tables, some right in front of our faces, so close that we could feel their breath and spittle, and they lobbed verbal artillery at us:

"Don't look around, recruits!"

"Eyes-front, dogs!"

"Get your hands by your sides you pieces of shit!"

"Put your fucking faces straight you pieces of shit!"

"Don't look around! Don't look around!"

Tango Flight of Seven Squadron, or Wolfe Squadron, was just ahead of us in the steam line, and in small, deeking glimpses I noted that they seemed to be as agitated and hungry as we were. They looked terrified. Once again I found it comforting, during all this yelling and screaming, to know that the torment and the panic were somewhat standardized. In the large picture of the system we were in, what I was going through was not unique or special, and for that I was grateful.

Eventually we made it to the plate stacks; the civilian cooks were a refreshing reprieve from RMC cadets.

"Hey there buddy, you look a little knackered," said a fat man behind the steam line. He wore a starched apron and held up his spatula, "What'll you be havin'?" I was surprised to remember that people spoke like that.

I looked at everything and couldn't decide. I seemed to be incapable of choosing even one item. There were trays of thick-sliced, fatty bacon, pale, greasy sausages, inserts filled with pancakes, French toast, hot syrup, lumpy oatmeal and hard-boiled eggs.

"How about hotcakes and sausage?" the man said. I nodded, and took pancakes and sausages, listening to Stocker berate Mack at the back of our line for taking a piece of fruit. The fat man leaned across the steam line.

"You ride it out easy, hear?" he said. He had this voice like Leonard Cohen—all whiskey and cigarettes. "These bastards have been getting pumped for your arrival for weeks. Don't sweat it—the novelty will wear off in a few days."

"Sure," I said. "Thanks."

"What's yer name kid?"

"Verbal," I said.

"Well, Verbal, I'm Frank. Enjoy your breakfast." Frank winked.

At that moment I wanted to take my plate and go to the back of the kitchen with Frank, sit beside him on a couple of old milk crates and shoot the shit.

"Thanks," I said. Then I heard the clickers.

"You got your fucking food Kempt, now shift it!" Stocker was right beside me, in my ear, on top of me, and the panic was right back in my belly. "And you sir," Stocker said to Frank, "would you kindly refrain from talking to my recruits. I believe your job is to slop the beans. Move it Kempt! Forget the fucking eggs, it's too late now."

We marched in single file over to the recruit section of the mess, and sat at the N Flight table. This section was off limits to other cadets. For the unwashed only. I vowed no mistakes, no looking around. I would just stare at my plate until everything was gone.

"Steady-up!" screamed Stocker, just as I was cutting into a sausage. "Are you heathens just going to shove your filthy snouts into the trough, or is someone going to say grace?"

"I'll say grace, Mr. Stocker," said Noel Gaze. He looked inches away from eating his own arm.

"Oh dear. Didn't we teach you slugs how to report to a senior cadet?"

"Excuse me Mr. Stocker! Recruit Weiland, J., Five Squadron, November Flight, Three Section reporting!"

"Yes, Recruit Weiland."

"Permission to say grace, Mr. Stocker!"

"Go ahead, Recruit," he said.

"Rub-a-dub-dub, thanks for the grub, yay God!" Josh shouted. Bilbo Wommersley broke into his big farmer-boy grin. I thought for sure Stocker would put the boots to them for insolence, or mischief, or conduct unbecoming a recruit, but he just said, "Okay recruits. Dig in."

Billy and Josh had the fighter pilots' sense of adventure, danger and humour. They'd never flown anything bigger than gliders, but one could tell that's where they were headed. Both were the type who wanted to fly before they could even crawl, and they were undoubtedly destined for the cockpits of multimillion dollar jets.

During rook term, though, the distinction between Army, Navy and Air Force was faint. We were all just meager recruits eager for the hot plate and a bit of rest. I tucked in, anxious to get some energy in me. I focused on the pancakes first—

"Steady-up!" Stocker said.

We put our forks down again and sat at attention. My eyes beheld Caruthers and Smith sitting directly across from me.

Dave Smith had been roomed with Thomas "I went to Appleby" Caruthers. Smith was a zipperhead; all he talked about was tanks. I think he'd taken in too much TV at an early age, and his parents had too much money. Smith was doomed to live in fantasyland for the rest of his life. His hobbies, other than war movies, included building model tanks and collecting large amounts of expensive gear that he would never use. For instance, although we were not allowed to have personal items in our rooms, there was storage off our hallway— where half the boxes in there were marked *SMITH: CIVVY KIT*. He had state-of-the-art diving gear—we're talking brand-new tanks, expensive regulators, wetsuits that would make the Navy Seals blush. All the bells and whistles, but the guy couldn't name one occasion when he'd actually used the stuff. But Smith and his shit came in handy whenever N Flight planned a graunch. Somebody would say, "If only we had some fishing line," and Smith would shoot back, "You need fifty-pound test or eighty-pound test?"

But his fancy-pants kit wasn't enough to save him from harm and humiliation during zipperhead training: despite his encyclopedic knowledge of tanks, word was he just couldn't keep up physically or emotionally. The instructors tore him apart and fed him to the wolves. He ended up failing out of phase training and spending his summers in the admin platoon at Gagetown, gluing and painting models of tanks. All this I didn't know until much later, but if someone had told it to me then, that first morning of rook term as I was staring across the breakfast table at him and Caruthers, I don't think I would have been at all surprised. It was all there in his eyes.

Caruthers was lanky and awkward, and an insufferable mouth-breather. His lifelong passion was the infantry, though he didn't have the first clue how to deal with other people. When times were tough, he languished in his Appleby days, often repeating his favourite saying, "What one man can do, another can do." Might have been a good saying from somebody else, but Caruthers always came off so candy-ass when he said it.

Caruthers was intelligent in the sense that he made top three in his Engineering class. But he was also senseless in a way that his leadership abilities came from passages of history textbooks and his favourite films. He was the type of officer who would be fragged someday by one of his own troops.

As I stared at Caruthers, starving for a flapjack and waiting for permission to eat, I found his mouth-breathing and dead eyes made my stomach turn. I tried to look over his forehead in an attempt to blot out the rest of his face, but I kept going back to that mouth, hanging open, dry flecks of skin on his lips, bad breath. I wanted to jump across the table and punch his lights out.

The intensity of what I felt was alarming. Later, I felt guilt for the thoughts that had stirred up in the mess hall, and at times I made an extra effort to give a nod or a smile to Caruthers, if only to let it go.

"Do you people," sneered Stocker, "normally eat your meals without something to drink?"

Chrissakes.

"Excuse me, Mr. Stocker! Recruit Kempt, V., Five Squadron, November Flight, Three Section reporting!" I said. I saw the pattern developing, and figured there was no point in wasting time.

"Go ahead, Recruit," Stocker said.

"Permission to get a drink Mr. Stocker!"

"Well, November Flight, looks like Recruit Kempt can only think of himself. Sure you can get a drink, Kempt. Everybody else steady-up until he gets back. Go."

"Mr. Stocker, I meant for the whole—"

"Too late now. Should've thought of that earlier. You'd better hurry up before breakfast gets cold."

I grabbed the biggest cup I could find, and was jostled and yelled at a few times while looking for something to drink. Finally I spotted two large stainless steel milk dispensers, and drew a glass of cold, bubbly chocolate milk. I hurried back to the N Flight table, dodging fire from unfriendly senior cadets.

"Chocolate milk, Recruit. Fancy. You must be special."

"Excuse me Mr. Stocker! Recruit Kempt, V., Five Squadron, November Flight, Three Section reporting!" I said.

"Yes?" he said.

"Permission for the rest of N Flight to get a drink!" I said.

"Not enough time. Should have thought of that earlier, Recruit Kempt."

"Permission to share my chocolate milk with November Flight, Mr. Stocker?"

"If you want to speak to me, Recruit, you must fucking report!"

I stammered, and my mind went blank. I didn't care even about breakfast anymore—I just wanted to lie down—even for fifteen minutes, and have a silent rest in bed. I couldn't remember how to report, and I was tired all of a sudden.

"Excuse me, Mr. Stocker," Billy piped in. "Recruit Wommersley, B., Five Squadron, November Flight, Three Section reporting!"

"No Wommersley. Too many people from Three Section reporting this morning."

"Excuse me Mr. Stocker! Recruit Terranova, T., Five Squadron, November Flight, One Section reporting!"

"What is it Recruit Terranova?"

"Permission for Recruit Kempt to sit down and share his drink while the rest of November Flight eats."

Stocker mulled this over, then nodded his head. I was hungry again. I sat down quickly, passing the cup to Gaze, and then cut eagerly into my pancake for a big bite.

"Recruit Kempt!"

I couldn't speak, having shoved a huge syrupy wad in my mouth.

"Recruit Kempt! Steady-up!"

My arms shot to my sides and I sat up, chewing the doughy mass as inconspicuously as possible.

"Recruit Kempt, Recruit Terranova asked permission for the rest of November Flight to eat. Not for you."

I swallowed hard and stared ahead, waiting. The rest of N Flight ate, and ate with abandon. It was hard to watch, and just as I was about to report for permission to eat, Stocker was on his feet yelling that we had twenty seconds to be formed up outside. Breakfast was officially over.

Left, Right, November Flight

The roster for Two Section, Mr. Kincaid's Section, read: SUMMERS, MACDONALD, LEBREQUE, FARR, PASTERNAK, LACROIX, LABONTÉ, SOSA. Sosa punched out on day three when he found out he'd got a job as a lifty in Whistler. His father had teed off with the Commandant a few times, so they processed his release immediately. He walked through our hall one last time wearing cargo pants and an Independent t-shirt as the rest of us were marking time in our raincoats. He picked up his snowboard from storage and waved to us as we chanted: "Left, right, November Flight; Left, right, November Flight…"

"See ya homies—don't work too hard," he said.

I never heard from Sosa again, though I did see a picture of him in *Thrasher* a year or so later. Turns out he was in Japan skating with the likes of Tony Hawk.

Skippy MacDonald, a salt-o'-the-earth Cape Bretoner, roomed with François Lacroix, a separatist from Trois-Rivières.

"Here's a teaser," Skippy liked to say. "Why the fuck would you join the Canadian Army if you're a separatist?" Lacroix kept to himself mostly, and was badly out of shape. He had flabby flesh and smoked unfiltered French cigarettes.

"The Quebec politics of paranoia have him and his generation by the balls," Skippy liked to say. Eventually Lacroix stopped talking to us altogether, and we referred to him as the Spy. The deal with RMC was that anyone could leave of his own volition at any time during the first year. Lacroix was a VW (Voluntary Withdrawal) by Christmas exams.

Agnes Lebreque started with a roommate who cleared out on the first night. Agnes cried over it for days, I imagine because she didn't want to be alone. I would have traded places with her in a New York minute. Agnes was different, though. She had arms like matchsticks, legs like two pieces of spaghetti with knots tied in them for knees. Agnes also had a rare skin condition and a full head of grey hair. She was only twenty years old but could have passed for a grandma. How she got through the preliminary physical fitness test is beyond me—I guess they must have had a rough time filling the gender quota the year we signed up.

Jean-Claude Labonté and Paulo Pasternak shared a room. They both grinned like thieves, especially when the chips were down. When the CSCs were severely pissed off and giving us cock, there were always explosions of laughter from their room as Labonté tried to dress Pasternak in time for inspection. Either one of those guys would have made a good roommate. Mack and I never laughed like that. Pasternak had this doughy, lazy expression when he grinned, his mouth framed by baby fat and a veneer of innocence. Pasternak had a fertile mind, I think, always receptive to new ideas. He wanted to make films. I asked him once why he was studying Engineering at a military academy.

"I thought it would be interesting," he said. He was never downcast or angry, a rare type who never felt bad for himself— he just didn't like seeing others down.

Labonté would laugh at anything. The guy could make even Agnes or the Spy feel like some kind of wiseass comedian. I think that people who know *how to* laugh deserve more credit, being so valuable in tight situations. What was most peculiar about Labonté was his nerves. All I had to do was knock on his door and I'd hear him scream and hit the floor. This had something to do with his father being a never-convicted Montreal drug lord; as a child, Labonté was witness to routine domestic intrusions by la Sûreté. They would come armed with handguns and search warrants. By four years of age Labonté despised cops.

And then there was Daisy Summers: her name summed her

up pretty well, I think. I'm sure we all rubbed a few out thinking about Ms. Daisy from time to time. She was truly a knockout in the all-American, California-girl sense of the word. Natural blonde-on-blonde hair, wide blue eyes and Hollywood tits. The CSCs handled her with kid gloves and she was the only cadet in N Flight who started out with her own room. She ended up quitting halfway through rook term, due in no small part to the fact Kincaid had been tapping her since day three. How professional.

One Section had the worst go of it. Mr. Stocker must have sat up for weeks dreaming up ways to be cruel. And since he took a perverse interest in my welfare, Hackman offered me up as a sacrificial lamb whenever Stocker wanted to have some fun.

There were two girls in One Section: Tina Terranova and Becky French. Tina, the girl I caught pissing, had beautiful Italian features—wonderful face with smooth, dark skin. Her body was bulky, but it was a smooth, strong, solid fat. She was hard-headed, too, and didn't get riled easily. Becky, however, was about as useful as tits on a bull. She whimpered during every panic drill, and moved slowly and stupidly. Tina took to scolding her, which was kind, as it was the only thing that kept her from falling apart completely. When I had laundry duty during our second week, French piled her panties, stained with vaginal discharge, on top of the heap. She didn't have the sense to conceal them, much less the sense to wash herself. I couldn't help dry-retching in front of her. I know the CSCs didn't give us time to shower, but she had a sink in her room like everyone else.

It's like I said before: we knew each other, and much more than we ever would have wanted to, given the choice. The two people Stocker enjoyed playing with most in his section were Noel Gaze and Scott Mann. They were Army types, pretty hard soldiers both of them. Stocker had them out every morning at 05:30 doing remedial drill, and running circles on the inner field every night after dinner. He gave up eventually when he couldn't break either of them. They never let the panic seep into their eyes, they never complained. His mistake was that he took them on together, and he always punished them together, like he was trying to break them at the same time. They just got stronger.

Eventually Stocker gave up, disinterested with his own section, and concentrated most of his time on me. It would be nice to say that I held fast like Gaze and Mann. I'd like to say so, but the time eventually came when I'd do anything to please him, to make him happy, to have him give me any kind word or a nod. I couldn't help myself.

The Old Eighteen

Marching back from drill, C7s tucked neatly under our right arms, we walked right by the Cadet Wing Commander, Mr. Hutch, and the Cadet Wing Training Officer, Mr. Palourd—the highest ranking cadets on campus. They were the two people we absolutely *had* to acknowledge.

"Who did you miss, recruits?" screamed Ms. Pfaff. Nobody knew; nobody had been paying attention. For our sins we got an hour's worth of wall-sits.

To fully grasp the meaning of a wall-sit, put your back against a wall or a door—as long as it is a stable vertical surface it doesn't matter which. Bend your knees and move your feet out until your thighs are parallel to the floor. Your arms should be fully outstretched, parallel to your thighs, and a wet mop will simulate a rifle nicely. Stay in this position until your entire body shakes, and don't release yourself. Do the collapse. Have somebody scream at you while you lie panting and huffing on the floor. Repeat.

After the wall-sits, we changed into our PT gear. Unfortunately we were too slow in doing this, so we changed back into our uniforms. When we couldn't manage to do this fast enough, we did more wall-sits before changing back into PT gear. This we did slower than the first time, so we pumped off one hundred push-ups before changing back into uniform. We managed the uniforms alright then, so we were allowed to change back into our PT gear. Then we went for a run.

I felt the sensations on my body as if somebody else owned it. Burning, itching, chafing—it was very impersonal. Only my hunger seemed my own. We ran in formation around Point

Frederick where (I would learn later) a fourth-year cadet had blown the back of his skull all over the flagpole the previous year. Evidently he'd *really* wanted out of the Army. Some time after recruit term, after I had met and befriended Cecil Witherspoon, Cecil told me that his flight had found the corpse—jogged right by it one misty Saturday morning. The body had been removed by the time breakfast was over. It never made the local news, not even a mention in the *Kingston Whig-Standard.* DND was thorough with its laundry, and didn't like outsiders seeing the dirt. I think, in a very serious way, that cleaning up the dirt had become part of Dad's job.

We didn't find any dead bodies on our run, but we constantly had to go back for French, Lebreque and Smith when we attempted Heartbreak Hill at Fort Henry. Kincaid was leading the run, and when the three stragglers made themselves known by collapsing pathetically on the steep incline, he sent four of us back to get them, to "pick up the trash."

Smith, too proud to admit he was out of shape, feigned injury and had to walk back on his own to the Medical Inspection Room (MIR). Gaze and Mann grabbed Becky French, who was crying and blowing snot bubbles, and dragged her up the slope. Josh and I took hold of Agnes and hoisted her by the armpits. I couldn't believe how light she was—she couldn't have weighed more than ninety pounds. After we took a few steps she started shaking her damp head and flailing those matchstick arms around.

"Easy Lebreque!" Josh said. "We'll carry you up okay? Don't fucking make this harder for us."

She moaned and sobbed until we were halfway up, then she started convulsing and shrieking, and managed to kick both of us. We dropped her and she hit the ground like a rag doll, crumpling on the dirt trail.

"What's the problem?" I said.

"I ... I ... I peeeed," she said, rolling over. Her grey issue shorts were like charcoal, darkened with urine. Even as she said it a stream of bright yellow washed over her skinny, blue-veined thighs. She wept.

Kincaid jogged down to see what was taking us.

"Kempt! Weiland! What the fuck is... oh. We got a pisser here, do we?" He thought for a moment. Agnes rocked back and forth, eyes wide open.

"Quit your fucking moaning, Recruit!" Kincaid said. "I'm trying to think... Ah, fuck it. Kempt, Weiland: haul her to the top. Everybody's waiting."

We picked her up again and charged up the hill, trying, in vain, not to let her piss-soaked parts come into contact with us. Everybody at the top was jogging in place on heavy feet, thighs completely burnt out from the wall-sits earlier. Caruthers and Mack puked up bile, and French was coughing snot. We threw Agnes in the back of the line, grateful to be rid of her. It was hard enough to take this on my own without having to cart someone else through it. Although that, I suppose, was the point: this was the summation of our valuable training. It was the whole point of the College; hell, it was the whole point of the military. Still, I wanted nothing to do with someone else's urine.

Eventually everybody made it back to Fort Champlain—sweaty, grass-stained and out of breath. We changed in and out of shower gear a few times before shower parade. Again there was no hot water, no soap. I had enough time under the nozzle to rinse my underarms and drink a few greedy mouthfuls of icy water.

After our shower we had another college history lesson. Ms. Pfaff explained that there would be a test on the parade square near the end of rook term, where questions would be put to us by Mr. Hutch.

"You must study hard, recruits! The college history quiz gets big points for the Commandant's Cup."

The Commandant's Cup was a piece of silver designed to bring cadets together with the glue of camaraderie—the sticky paste of squadron pride. There were competitions such as the Wing Harrier Race, a foot race involving the whole student body; the Wing Regatta, where races were held in kayaks, canoes and whalers; the Director of Cadets' Inspection, which gave points to the best turned-out squadrons; the Cadet Wing Sports Day, an intramural mock-up Olympics; the Recruit College History Test, a systematic formula to increase college pride and instill a sense of hero worshipping; and the Recruit Obstacle Course, the final and most heavily weighted event towards the coveted cup and a year's worth of bragging rights.

As we stood in the hallway reciting various trivia about RMC, it dawned on me that I'd spent so much time standing in that spot, staring straight ahead, that I knew every crack and fissure in the doorway across from me. I knew every feature of Becky French's flat, pasty face: the three nose hairs protruding from the right nostril, the soulless vacuity of her eyes, and the way her forge cap was too big for her pumpkin. It tilted to the left and hung too far back, exposing a shiny crown and often a stray lock of her mousy hair. If I made the mistake of catching her eye, she would wheeze through her nose and smile like the village idiot. Like now.

"Recruit French, do you find something funny?" Ms. Pfaff said.

"Nope Ms. Paff."

"It's Pfaff, Recruit. Tell me when the college first opened."

"Um, eighteen-seventy... six?"

"Right. Don't sound so sure of yourself. Who were the first cadets, French?"

"I ... I don't know Ms. Fuff."

"You should. Anybody else?"

We were standing "at ease," but if you wanted to speak you had to come to attention, slamming your foot down to get noticed and sticking your right arm out, parallel to the ground, fist clenched. We were big on right angles.

"Recruit Caruthers, T.R.J, Five Squadron—"

"Don't bother reporting Caruthers, we haven't got all day."

"The Old Eighteen, Miss Pfaff!" Caruthers said.

"Very good, Recruit Caruthers. Recruit Prendergast, when was the Royal Military College of Canada Degrees Act passed?"

"Um... 1878?"

"1878 what?"

144

"1878 Ms. Pfaff!"

"Wrong. 1878 is when Her Majesty Queen Victoria granted the college the right to use the prefix 'Royal.'"

"Ms. Pfaff!" Pasternak slammed to attention, grinning.

"Yes, Recruit. Well? Go ahead!"

"1959, Ms. Pfaff."

"Correct. Now: what is the role of RMC?"

"Ms. Pfaff!"

"Somebody other than Recruit Caruthers."

"Ms. Pfaff!"

"Yes, Recruit MacDonald."

"The role of the Royal Military College of Canada is to educate and train officer cadets and commissioned officers for careers of effective service within the Canadian Forces."

"Keener," Ms. Pfaff said. "You all have fifteen minutes before your next timing. You will, upon dismissal, be seated at your desks studying your recruit handbooks. Questions?"

"Ms. Pfaff!"

"What is it, Recruit Labonté?"

"Are we getting to 'ave lunch?"

"Maybe, Recruit. Any more SFQs? Yes, Recruit Harrowsmith."

"What is an SFQ, Ms. Pfaff?"

"It's a Stupid Fucking Question, Recruit. Dis-missed!"

Weak-limbed and light-headed, I attempted to retain which graduating class had donated Watt's Walk, but the ability to concentrate eluded me. I envisioned loaves of fresh-baked bread from my mother's oven—or her cinnamon rolls, gooey delicious. I moved on to a healthy portion of butternut squash soup and before I knew it I was smacking my lips on the Colonel's famous barbecue ribs and some grilled baguette. Still hungry, I helped myself to a pound of sizzling Lone Star fajitas—the chicken and mesquite grilled shrimp combo—and washed it all back with a cool Corona; insatiable now, I started working on a caramel latte and two servings of deep-fried ice cream. By the time I found myself at Haveli's with an order of Murg Makahni and a glass of shiraz, my head had hit the desk.

"Recruits! Get out here!"

I bolted upright, and a thick string of drool flapped upwards, splashing me on the forehead. I grabbed my beret and nodded to Mack, who was rubbing sleep from his eyes. We marched out screaming the required "Lights out!" and came to attention in tandem.

Mack was growing on me, a little bit. We didn't laugh like old mates, but we were working together. We had to—there wasn't a choice in the matter. Looking back, I bet Mack hated looking at my sweaty face as much as I hated looking at his.

It had been a long morning, but it was finally lunchtime. Hackman was in the hall and I had a shiver of gratitude that it wasn't Stocker taking us to the mess hall.

"When I dismiss you, recruits, form up in three ranks outside," Hackman said.

"Mr. Hackman!" Stocker shouted, coming into our hall from outside.

"Oh, fuck," I whispered.

"Well hello, Mr. Stocker," Hackman said. "I was just about to herd the pigs to the trough."

"Well we have a problem, Mr. Hackman. It seems that not everyone here knows who the Old Eighteen are."

"Is that so."

"Yes. Ms. Pfaff just brought it to my attention now."

"We can't have that, Mr. Stocker."

"No we can't, Mr. Hackman."

"I guess they're going to have to learn."

"They most certainly are, Mr. Hackman, they most certainly are."

"Who should go first?"

They were bad actors. The CSCs probably figured that if this scenario had the appearance of immediacy it would seem more terrifying. And I just knew in my bones who they'd pick. I *knew*.

"Well, Recruit Kempt looks like a studious individual. I'm sure he'd do the flight proud," Stocker said, face-to-face with me now.

He whispered, "Stand at ease Kempt and fuckin' stand easy." I did as told, unwilling to focus on his face.

"Up you go," he pointed his finger to the ceiling. That was the first time I noticed the chin-up bar. Fuck. I knew from summer training that I had maybe fifteen chin-ups in me, but I only had seven, perhaps eight names.

I hoisted myself up cleanly and paused, hoping to make up in deportment what I lacked in information.

"Excuse me Mr. Stocker! Recruit Kempt, V., Five Squadron, November Flight, Three Section reporting!"

"Yes."

"Permission to begin Mr. Stocker!"

"Begin."

"Wurtele." One.

"Freer." Two.

"Wise." Three. I considered feigning a slip and cracking my skull open on the floor. They'd have to let me off then. They couldn't expect me to know all eighteen names if I was bleeding from my skull.

"Davis." Four. I could manage the fall cleanly if French would only shift to her left.

"Reed." Five. I looked down the length of the hall, hoping Gaze or Mann or even Caruthers would pick up on my subliminal plea for help.

"Denison." Six.

"Irving." Seven. I wondered what they'd dream up as punishment. The chin-ups didn't sting yet, but that hardly mattered since I only had one more name. Coming down after Irving I hesitated slightly, almost imperceptibly, not wanting to give up this last, weensy shred of knowledge. On my way up I lost it, and had a panic attack. *What was the name? C'mon, it was a double name—there were two of the same. Wise? No. God I'm hungry. Wurtele? No it wasn't a W.*

I couldn't think, and with my chin hovering over the bar I hesitated again.

"Davis!" someone shouted.

Who said that? I went down and came up again.

"DesBrisay!" yelled Mack. Oh, good old Mack.

I went down. I came up.

"RIVERS!" This time it was not only Mack, but Caruthers and Harrowsmith and MacDonald, as well. By the time I finished, mumbling and lip-synching the last ten names, everybody in N Flight who knew the Old Eighteen were shouting them out for me.

"Excuse me Mr. Stocker! Recruit Kempt, V., Five Squadron, November Flight, Three Section reporting!"

"Yes."

"Permission to dismount Mr. Stocker!"

"Yes. Next—Gaze!"

"Mr. Stocker?"

"Get the fuck up there, Gaze!"

"Yes Mr. Stocker!" It wasn't the Old Eighteen he was after. He just wanted to dish out some more cock.

Not everyone in the flight could do eighteen chin-ups, so Hackman designated Josh and me to spot those who were having trouble. Mann was up after Gaze, and Stocker let everybody stand easy and mill around the chin-up bar to shout out the names of the first gentleman cadets to ever have to put up with this shit. It was a sacred moment, being given a privilege for the first time we'd been together. We could smile at each other, look around, shout out encouragement: "C'mon Harrowsmith! You can do it! Dig deep Lacroix!" It was exhilarating, and for a moment I forgot about my hunger, proud to be a part of this RMC tradition. I was sure we were doing a tremendous job—obviously we'd made some rapid progress in the way of teamwork.

The last person at the chin-up bar was Lebreque—little granny piss-thighs. And here I was with Josh, lifting Agnes up for the second time today. We didn't care, though; the emotion was contagious. As we hoisted her up to the bar we didn't even bother letting her try one single chin-up on her own. We were exuberant. N Flight was screaming out the names now in proud unison.

We got swept away with the excitement, and feverishly thrust Agnes up harder and harder until her head was bouncing through the chipboard roofing. Stocker and Hackman and the rest of the flight laughed as we threw her up higher, and she moaned. It seemed as if we could toss her skinny body right through the roof.

Recruit Poopshooter

We didn't make it to the mess until the steam tables were shut down. Somehow I got caught as the first in line—the leading sheep in a long line of bleating. Mr. Kincaid, our shepherd, directed me to halt at the self-serve table in the centre of the mess, where we were told to load up on dry bread and fruit.

We marched back to Champlain quietly, baking under the midday sun, which was strong for September. With a bit of food in my belly, I was exhausted. No one yelled at us. So, without panic and adrenalin, and with the warm buzz of the afternoon, I almost dozed off. To shake the cobwebs, I looked around at the college grounds for the first time.

From where we were on the peninsula, by Point Frederick, I could see downtown Kingston across the water. The ferry to Wolfe Island was going by and blasted its horn. I had been hearing that horn regularly for days and couldn't figure out what it was, and now here I knew. Mr. Kincaid marched us on past our dorms, and around the point to the pier. Beyond that was the boathouse, and then Navy Bay, which separated the string of immaculately kept playing fields from Fort Henry Hill. The stone buildings of RMC were old to me, as old as anything I knew, and strong. They reeked of the military, but our military from a more grandiose and proud period. Mackenzie Building and the Stone Frigate Dormitory were ancient, by Canadian standards. I knew from my recruit handbook that the building which housed the mess was Yeo Hall, and that the Military Wing HQ and the Registrar's office were situated in Mackenzie. The much feared and dreaded drill instructors were housed in the Old Hospital beside it. The Stone Frigate, home of One

Squadron, or Hudson Sqn, was also known as "The Boat" and was the oldest building on campus. Having the most call for tradition, Hudson Sqn was located away from the other dorms at the opposite side of the parade square. One half of the cadets at The Boat looked out onto Lake Ontario and Fort Henry. The other half faced the parade square: the echoing marches of early morning Flag Parade and the caterwaul of amateur bagpipes.

The most precious gem of landscaping on campus was the inner field. Here was a carefully groomed rugby pitch, with the flagpole, the parade square and the imposing view of Mackenzie Building and its clock tower at one end. At the other end was the stone wall of Fort Frederick, and looming behind it, the Martello Tower. One side of the field held a view of the water through some saintly old maples, and the other was flanked by Fort Haldimand—four stories of dorm-room windows where cadets could watch the action when there was no room in the bleachers. They'd lean out and cheer from above, stacks of young men and women, grateful for a free afternoon, and the liberty to jump and shout and take in some rugby.

After marching us all the way around to Watt's Walk, Kincaid suddenly double-timed us back to the barracks. Soon after we were grunting on the floor in N Flight halls, arms locked in the push-up position. Becky French had left her rifle insecure.

"All right you fuckin' pansies," drawled Stocker, "it looks like they didn't teach you weapon security at Basic Officer Training. Well I'm more than happy to teach you myself. Down! Hold it! Up! Steady! Hold it! I said hold it Lebreque... ah, Christ. Down!"

"Okay, I want everybody to squirm and snivel and whine on the floor like Lebreque. You have to learn to work together, recruits. That's it... Gaze! Why aren't you sniveling? That's better. Good!

"Now, Lebreque, you stand up. No... come here. Everybody else continue squirming! Okay, Recruit Lebreque, take a look. See? That's how pathetic you look... Prendergast! I didn't say to stop moaning! That's better. Isn't this frustrating to look at,

Recruit? Look at them! Why would you want to frustrate me like this… Oh, that's clever: what the *fuck* are you crying about? I wonder, Recruit—are those tears shed for yourself, or for your pathetic comrades? No, don't answer. I'll tell you something— and this goes for all of you—if you think this is tough, we haven't even begun! This is *nothing!*

"Take a look around, Lebreque. Take a good look. No. Better yet, stand easy and walk around. No! *Stroll* around. Stroll! That's it! Get a good look at their faces. See them squirm—for you, Lebreque. This is all *your* doing. You gonna piss your pants? And look here! What do we have here? It seems Recruit Kempt is enjoying this—he's trying to bugger his roommate! Hey Prendergast, are you just going to let him give it to you up the ass like that? Jesus Lebreque—quit your fucking sobbing!"

While twisting and moaning and snivelling, Mack and I had manoeuvred into a compromising position. I tried to squirm away, dusting the floor with my beret as I moved.

"No no no," Stocker admonished. "You two stay like that! We've got to know who's queer, right, so the lads can watch their wee-wees in the shower. This is too much! Okay, switch it up now. Prendergast, get in behind Kempt and give him some good loving. Everybody else, on your feet! Stand easy, relax: this is a learning experience."

I attempted a smile in order to play along with the charade, but my show at good sportsmanship backfired. And now Mack, who was more afraid of Stocker than he was of having his dignity compromised, wriggled behind me on his side, pantomiming anal sex.

"Look at Kempt's face!" Stocker said. "I think the sick little fucker is really enjoying himself!"

"Excuse me Mr. Stocker—" I said.

"Not yet Kempt. This is educational. I think we will now refer to these two as Recruit Ass-Bandit and Recruit Butt-Pirate. What do you think, November?"

I heard relieved laughter, and understood. Everyone was just thankful to be released from the floor. I couldn't blame them.

Like I said, it's funny when you're not the one getting cock. I tried to report again, but Stocker ignored me.

"We'll keep this our little secret. Fags are allowed in the Army now anyway. You two can happily pummel each other up the poopshoot if you so desire—I can say that, I *can* say that—that's not harassment. I'm only speculating that they can if they *want* to, which certainly seems to be the case."

More laughter.

"Excuse me Mr. Stocker! Recruit Kempt, V., Five Squadron—" I hit Mack in the leg so he'd stop humping me, "November Flight, Three Section reporting!"

"Yes."

"Permission for Recruit Prendergast and myself to join the rest of the flight!"

"He's still smiling!" Stocker said. "I'll bet you two haven't been lonely in that little den of sin you occupy. Tell me: do you pound each other on the top bunk or the bottom? You like it when he pumps you full of cream, Recruit? From now on, room inspections will include your bedsheets! We can't be leaving nasty cum stains on our hospital corners, can we?"

I was hungry, I was tired, and I needed to piss. He was making me nervous. His craggy face, his nicotine teeth, his harsh, raspy, sardonic voice—I hated and feared him, but despite myself I wanted him to respect me. I couldn't figure out what I had done wrong.

For the next few weeks I was known as Recruit Cockchugger, Ballsucker, Fudgepacker, Dicklicker, Assmuncher. You name it. I tried to brush it off, or get used to it, but never really did.

Stocker finally let me and Mack up off the floor, and turned on the whole flight again. We panicked into our rooms to unlock our rifles and brought them out for another session of wall-sits. We brought our rifles back into our rooms and locked them up again. Back out in the hall. Push-ups. Get the rifle. Wall-sits. Lock them up.

To be properly secured, the C7 had to be broken down into two pieces: the butt end with the trigger mechanism was locked in our barrack boxes, and the muzzle portion was fastened to a chain by the door with a padlock. Every time we left our rooms now, we had to scream "Lights out! Weapon secure!"

We practised this a dozen times until Stocker thought we understood. Then we went for another run. And then we did something else, and got in trouble for it, so we did more wall-sits and went for a run.

After a hazy afternoon of panic drills, I found myself standing in formation outside Yeo Hall. It occurred to me that it was dinner time, and I recalled distantly that I should be famished. I knew I was hungry, and when I remembered how much I nearly doubled over from the sudden pain.

On the menu was Hawaiian steak and spaghetti, with a choice of mashed potatoes or french fries. The vegetables were peas.

"Everyone will get Hawaiian steak and mashed," Stocker said at the steam line. "This is truly an RMC cultural experience."

Hawaiian steak turned out to be a thick slab of steamed, pressed ham, topped with a pale pineapple ring and a maraschino cherry. To me it looked wonderful. Being in the mess had brought back the intense awareness of my stomach— my guts were moving and making noises. I got lost in the smells, and felt the pangs come over me in waves. I lost my head and dug in.

"Recruit Kempt! Holy fucking audacity! What the fuck is it you're doing?"

I looked up at the table, my knife and fork poised to find the path of least resistance through the ham, and realized everyone was steadied up. I sat at attention.

"Excuse me Mr. Stocker. My mistake."

"You're fucking right it's your mistake! Now why, Recruit Kempt, would you have the audacity to charge ahead when everyone else is steadied up and we haven't said grace? Hmm? Nobody has asked permission to begin."

"I don't know, Mr. Stocker, I ..."

"You don't know?"

"I forgot ..."

154

"No. You didn't *forget*, Recruit. I'll tell you why: you are self-centred. You are not a team player. You have no excuse. Say it."

"I have no excuse."

"What?"

"No excuse Mr. Stocker!"

"Well?" he said.

"Excuse me, Mr. Stocker, Recruit Kempt, V., Five Squadron, November Flight, Three Section reporting!"

"This should be interesting. What?"

"Permission to begin eating, Mr. Stocker?"

"Sure. Go ahead, Recruit—stuff your face."

We bent towards our plates.

"Steady-up!" Stocker said. I looked at him. This was no joke anymore. I needed to fucking eat. I was so hungry I was inches away from jumping across the table and choking him. I wanted to sit under the table with just my piece of ham and chew it in peace.

"Recruit Kempt asked only for himself, as he is wont to do, so only Recruit Kempt may begin," said Stocker. "Tell you what: N Flight now has six minutes to eat, but nobody will start until Kempt is finished. Kempt, you will eat using square drill: eyes front, no looking down at your plate, and your fork must come straight up from your plate until it is directly in front of your face. From there your fork will travel a path parallel to the table until it reaches your mouth. When you have taken a bite, your fork will travel the same path back to the plate to retrieve another morsel of food. You will report to me when you are finished, so the rest of your buds can eat. Remember you're on a clock. You may begin."

While everyone else sat at attention, I ate according to square drill. I managed to tear off a piece of ham and a bit of pineapple, but as I got it up to mouth level, the pineapple fell off and hit the table with a wet slap. I got to the ham between my teeth without a problem, but had some difficulty pulling it off the fork. With some effort I managed, and, with my hand following the prescribed path to my plate, I choked the meat down in dry swallows. It must have come from a hundred-year-old pig. Anxious to avoid the Hawaiian steak, I stabbed at my plate until I found the peas. I brought them up to face level without a hitch, but as they came closer to my mouth they started bailing out individually. Peas in my lap, peas on the table, and the rest down my shirt before I got the empty fork between my lips. I went back along the ninety-degree path and poked around for the mashed potato. This presented little difficulty and I proudly managed a mouthful.

By now I had wasted at least a minute, and started feeling guilty about the rest of the flight, even though Wommersley was about to burst into laughter across from me. I knew it must have looked hilarious, but I felt like I would weep, because at that moment I realized that this was it. This bit of mashed potato was the last food I'd have until breakfast. I would have done anything—wall-sits, push-ups, Heartbreak Hill, *anything*—if only I could eat a whole plate of food in peace.

"I just want to be an infantry officer for fucksake I don't need this bullshit fork-and-knife school," I mumbled. I brought the fork back to my plate and stabbed the ham with all my strength. Winking at Billy when I'd brought the whole slab up to mouth level, I launched it at my face. At the last instant I deeked my head and the Hawaiian steak sailed over my shoulder, into the crowd of recruits from Four Sqn.

"I'm finished, Mr. Stocker," I said.

"What the fuck?" somebody screamed behind me. Billy lost it—he couldn't believe his eyes—and bent over, howling. But hearing the tone of voice from behind me and looking at the expression on Stocker's face sucked all the vinegar from me. I steadied up, sitting neatly at attention.

"Excuse me Mr. Stocker! Recruit—"

"Shut yer fuckin' hole, Kempt."

An angry CSC from Four Sqn approached the table: "Mr. Stocker," he seethed, wiping his cheek. "I just got pelted with a hunka ham. Would your recruits know anything about this?"

"Recruit Kempt, sit-at-ease and relax. Look this way. This

is Mr. Rooney," Stocker said, indicating the beefcake of a boy beside him. "Explain to Mr. Rooney why you hit him with your dinner."

"My sincere apologies, Mr. Rooney, sincerely. I was eating square drill and then I don't know wha—"

"Explain," Stocker said, "why you hit Mr. Rooney with Hawaiian steak, Recruit Kempt. Give him your excuse."

"I ... I have no excuse, Mr. Rooney."

"Sorry little girl," Rooney said. "I couldn't hear you. What was that?" He cupped his sausage-like fingers around his ear.

"I have no excuse Mr. Rooney!"

"Okay then, Recruit. Mr. Stocker, perhaps you might refrain from punishing this young recruit. He obviously meant no harm. I would prefer to personally teach him some manners, though, if he can spare the time."

Stocker whistled. "He can spare it." Rooney grunted and walked off.

"You're in for a treat, Kempt. Steady-up!" I did. "Now that Kempt has finished, November, the rest of you may eat."

And that's when it started in earnest. For the next month I took one minute to eat my meals using square drill, and then steadied up to watch the rest of N Flight clean their plates. After three days, I experienced dizzy spells and grey-outs. I dreamt of food every night. I could barely get through the push-ups and wall-sits without passing out.

On day four of this new diet, I passed out during shower parade. Later that night I wrote a memo to Captain Underwood, Five Squadron Commander, illustrating my concern that N Flight wasn't getting enough nourishment. Stocker ripped the memo up in my face while I marked time.

"Recruit Bumfucker, you've screwed yourself now, along with everyone else."

We did wall-sits and push-ups for three hours, and the allotted time for meals was cut down by one precious minute.

Up to Here

Thinking about Ruth during recruit term at RMC was like thinking about a story I had once read, and liked, but couldn't quite remember. It was like Ruth had happened to someone else. During the first few days, I thought of her from time to time, but as the hunger took over, she was an image with no substance or plot—like a half-remembered dream. The constant array of panic drills, combined with drill classes on the parade square and runs up and down Fort Henry Hill, had made me almost forget her completely when the letter came from Ottawa. It was a one-pager. As happy as I was to receive something from outside the college, it would have been better not to hear from her.

For mail-call, everybody in the flight was required to do as many push-ups for a letter as the postage indicated. If we couldn't do all the push-ups at one time, it had to be worked off slowly before the mail was handed over to the recipient.

"It seems," said Stocker, holding the letter beneath my nose, "that Recruit Kempt has mail from his boyfriend in Ottawa. Are you jealous, Prendergast?"

"Prendergast subscribes to free love, Mr. Stocker," I said.

"We have an arrangement, Mr. Stocker," Prendergast said. Stocker ignored us for once and ordered everyone into the push-up position. We pumped them off slowly, stopping every few minutes for Lebreque, Harrowsmith, French and Lacroix. Eventually I got my letter.

When I looked at it I got dizzy and had to lean against the wall. Her handwriting on the envelope made me feel queasy, and I had the impression that there was an emergency somewhere and I was missing it.

I didn't open it for several days. Finally I read it in my bunk at night by the dim lights of Fort Frederick parking lot.

Dear Verbal,

I hope this gets to you before Friday. As I write, I think that you must be just starting your first year. How are your classes? Or have you started school yet? I know you're probably very busy, but I was really hoping I'd have a letter or a phone call by now. The last one I got from your officer training was ages ago! I miss you lots, but I'm proud of you.

You've missed some killer parties, but we'll make up for it. I have great news: I got tickets to the Tragically Hip next Friday—they are playing at Fort Henry, which is, according to Chantal, right beside your school. So I'm hoping you'll have the night off and come with—I bought an extra ticket just in case. Please try! Otherwise my flight for Paris leaves Sunday, and I won't see you until Christmas!

I miss you tons, and think about you every night. Every night before I go to sleep I say good night to you.

Love always,

Ruth

P.S. The concert starts at 7:30. Chantal and I will be in Kingston at 4 to meet up with some friends of hers at a bar called the Toucan. We will be there until 7 from which time I'll wait at the gates with your ticket. Please try. Sneak out if you have to! XOXO

Deeking

By the end of the second week of rook term I'd lost over twenty-five pounds.

After day six of my square-drill fast, my memory of specific events is sketchy. I remember doing wall-sits that Friday night at 18:00 thinking: *Ruth is at the Toucan now.* Later, I'm convinced to break my will entirely, Mr. Kincaid took us for a run around Fort Henry while the Hip played inside. Delusional, hungry, exhausted, I swore that night I could smell Ruth's perfume.

I could have written her, but there seemed to be no point: she'd be in Paris by Sunday night.

"Recruits! Out in the hall! Now!" said Hackman. "Come on you lazy recruits, don't waste my precious time."

"Lights out! Weapon secure!" Mack and I slammed to attention simultaneously. We were moving well together, finally.

"Mail-call," Hackman said. "Recruit Prendergast, you've got an IP on your beret. Recruit Kempt owes me twenty for not checking you over properly. Recruit French, get that froust off your lapel. Okay recruits, I've got a thick one here: everybody down and give me eighty-two so that Recruit Summers can get her mail."

It took a while but we did them, then I pumped off an extra twenty for the Irish pennant. The letter for Summers was the only letter Hackman had, but Stocker came down the hall towards me holding a parcel. There was a whistle around his neck.

"Recruits stand-at-ease! Okay, stand easy. Looks like Recruit Backdoorman wants everybody here to do 563 push-ups. Who's Paula, Recruit? Is that your Mommy?"

"Yes Mr. Stocker."

"Well Kempt, I'm willing to bet my snake belt that there's kye in this package. What do you think—did Mommy send you some munchies?"

"Probably," I said.

"Probably what, fuck-face?"

"Probably yes, Mr. Stocker!" I said.

"Tell you what I'm going to do: rather than have November Flight work this off over the next three hours, we're going to have a little fun. Stand at ease and stand easy. Everybody look," he said, holding the parcel over his head. "When it hits the floor, you've all got four minutes to consume anything inside. Go!"

Stocker launched the box in the air and it crashed to the ground in the middle of the hallway. It was torn apart in under ten seconds. I saw a Tupperware full of cookies, two bags of peanut M&Ms, one lemon poppy seed pound cake, and some chocolate. As the savages ripped into my mail, I noticed a painting of a horse beneath Caruthers' feet. Seeing Ailish's art there, being torn beneath his gash boots, reminded me suddenly of her face, how peaceful it was when she painted—her impeccable concentration, her tongue covering her top lip. It was a mistake that her gentle offering had to come into contact with this place. My life here was something that would frighten her, something she would never understand. From Ailish's eyes, this made no sense.

A well of self-pity rose up within me. I knew it was pathetic but still I wanted it to come. I willed it to come. Besides my hunger, I hadn't felt anything concrete for days and suddenly this spectacle reminded me that I was still alive, that there was life outside of this place. I missed it desperately, and my thoughts turned to Ruth, how I had been within one hundred metres of her only three days before and now she was on the other side of the Atlantic. I had no way of getting a hold of her until she wrote me with her address.

I didn't move for the parcel but stood there, fists clenched, my face soaked with fat, soggy tears. I wanted everybody to stop stuffing their faces and look at me so they could witness how alive I was, how devastating their actions were.

Stocker blew the whistle once, twice, three times, and finally everyone cleared out and stood at attention beside their doorways, mouths full of sweets. Wrappers scattered on the floor, the painting shredded, crumbs and stray M&Ms littering the torn carcass of the cardboard box.

I would no doubt have continued blubbering from my guts, but the whistle did something to me. Something warned me that it would be worse, way worse, to let anyone see me like that. The self-pity dried up and left me with a moment of understanding. I saw clearly that I would no longer play by their rules. I walked to the refuse and collected the painting, then returned to my doorway and assumed the position of attention.

That night after shower parade, for which the dress was now CF raincoats and flip-flops since too many towels had fallen off during our hallway runabouts, I lay in bed plotting. Nobody had seen me crying, or if anybody had, hadn't mentioned it. After lights-out I heard Mack toss on his bunk.

"That was shitty what he did with your package, Verbal," Mack whispered. "He really has it out for you."

"Yeah, sure," I said. "I saw your cheeks bursting with pound cake, asshole."

Mack didn't say anything after that. I waited in the darkness until I could hear his breathing steady-out. When I was sure he was sleeping, I knew he'd be out cold until the panic music started in the morning. I slipped out of the top bunk and opened the window, wondering why I hadn't had the balls to try this before.

November Flight hallway was in the basement of Fort Champlain, so the windows opened out to ground level. My window happened to face Point Frederick parking lot where traffic was sparse at this time, which I judged to be about midnight.

Emerging from the window headfirst, I caught a rush of terror mixed with perverse power. It seemed too easy. I halted when

I heard voices from an open window above me, but moved on after reassuring myself that I was invisible in the darkness. Creeping along the stone wall, I gained confidence with the thrill of breaking rules. I had put a civilian t-shirt on before climbing into bed, so that if somebody saw me they would take me for a third-year import from Royal Roads in Victoria or CMR in St. Jean. I walked casually beneath the lit archway that joined Fort Champlain and Fort Haldimand, and then down through a creaky doorway into the basement of Haldimand where the Four Sqn lounge was located.

The squadron lounges were strictly off limits to recruits. Each squadron had one—a large room with DND couches and comfy chairs gathered around a TV at one end, and a kitchen table, a fridge and toaster oven at the other. Every night at 22:00 the mess put out kye, a crate containing loaves of bread, jams, jellies, peanut butter, milk, chocolate milk, orange juice, and, the odd time, sandwiches.

Entering the darkness of the lounge, I saw that the TV was on. Some cadets were watching *Platoon*. One of them turned to look at me, but as I was clear across the room it would have been impossible in the darkness to make anything out. I saw the silhouette of his head turn back to catch the part where Barnes shoots Elias. I made for the fridge.

There was bread. Four slices! I grabbed what was there and a handful of jam packs. Since I had no pockets on my jogging pants, I could only take one milk. I walked out briskly, fighting the urge to run.

"Hey!" somebody shouted. I froze.

"I never noticed that part," the voice said. "Did you see that? Rewind it and watch Barnes' hand."

I caught my breath and walked outside, thinking my heartbeat would give my position away, it was so goddamn loud. I considered going back to N Flight Halls with the loot, but decided against it, not wanting any compromising evidence in the room. Instead I raced back to the shadows and followed them beyond the wall surrounding the Martello Tower. I picked a spot by the old cannon at the tip of the peninsula and dug greedily into the jam, dipping huge wads of dry bread into each packet. It beat anything I'd ever eaten.

When I was done I threw the garbage into the barrel of the cannon and sat down in the grass. I looked across the water at all of Kingston. Lake Ontario shimmered quietly, throwing back the glow of downtown harbour. There must have been a full moon out. I breathed deep and my stomach growled. I lay in the grass, digesting, and fell asleep. When I woke up I panicked, and crawled back into bed.

Creeping around at night, with greater and greater stealth, eventually seemed normal, just like it eventually seemed second nature to piss in my sink, to perpetually stink, and to be thankful for long draughts of icy water in the shower.

Word spread that French, Lebreque and Harrowsmith had all contracted yeast infections, but it didn't matter. We could no longer even smell ourselves.

I ate my "meals" using square drill, but this only amused me now. The nights were mine. This newfound freedom was exhilarating; the food I managed to scrounge was sometimes only a few crusts of bread off the lounge floor, but by the old cannon everything was delicious, sugared with forbidden freedom. I expanded my horizons from Four Sqn lounge to the Two and Three Sqn lounges in Fort LaSalle.

Sometimes, feeling cocky, I sauntered back to the Point, my arms laden with bread, peanut butter and the odd box of milk. Or a SunPac orange juice: those tiny, dense aluminum cans, usually rusted at the seam, with foil pull-tabs to open them. They normally went down like battery acid, and were probably just as unhealthy, but even a SunPac tastes sweet at midnight.

I learned to zone out on our runs; I could keep up without any difficulty and was thus rarely yelled at during PT. I put up numbly with the endless string of panic drills. Once, when little Sue Harrowsmith left her weapon insecure, even after saying

"Weapon Secure," Mr. Kincaid had us change into half of our military wardrobe. We wore everything at the same time; we put on drill boots with our CF work dress and then our raincoats. Over our raincoats we had to wear our college-issue wool turtlenecks and, finally, our winter gabardines. On our heads were the ludicrous college-issue astrakhans, high-riding furry hats with big red flaps, designed for winter wear. Reporting in the hall laden with this kit, we marked time for an hour while he blared Billy Idol's "Hot in the City." Marching in place is harder than it sounds (especially when someone's yelling at you to get your knees "waist-high") and Agnes and Sue passed out within half an hour. Suddenly the drill seemed very funny; I really appreciated what he was making us do, and with two cadets passed out from the heat of it, I couldn't stop laughing. We were a comic picture, all right—especially Becky French's expression, the astrakhan bobbing on her head, sweat streaming down her face.

"Left, right, November Flight!" we screamed. "Left, right, November Flight!"

It was genius, how foolish we looked! We'd been marking time and sweating, listening to "Hot in the City" for over forty minutes when the music switched to ABBA. I burst out laughing. Kincaid didn't even hear me, the music was so loud. I had to look around then, and I saw that Mack marched earnestly in place beside me, red-huffed and breathing heavily. He was soaked with sweat, but still stared straight ahead. Everybody else looked the same, exactly the same, staring straight ahead, marching, going nowhere. It was lovely. How had we all allowed this to happen to ourselves?

Notes from Underground

Military-issue jogging pants, while ugly, are nonetheless extremely comfortable. Most recruits, no matter what their true size, ended up with triple-XL. They were like fat-man pants on little kids, and Josh, Billy and I started hiking them up and running around the halls when the CSCs weren't looking. We cinched the waists up around our necks so we had these ill-fitting heads attached to these huge, deformed pairs of legs. We also took to running down the polished linoleum hallway and then skidding past every door on our asses, waving in at each room. The three of us were tighter after we'd sneaked out together. I brought them some food and in return, they did me one better. They showed me the time capsule.

That particular evening, we agreed to meet at the cannon after the clock tower struck 01:00. Deciding to surprise the boys, I sneaked out just after midnight and stole over to Four Sqn lounge to grab the fixings for a jelly sandwich. The lounge was empty so I took my time, checking an empty pizza box on one of the coffee tables. Then I browsed the freezer.

After opening the door, I must have stood there for a full minute looking in. It was treasure: an unopened pack of Player's Light King-Size Regular. I pulled them out and shut the freezer door quietly. I wanted to run outside with them, but I controlled myself and opened the fridge door to get some bread. Instead, I found a dozen fresh donuts from Tim Hortons. I snatched up the box after peeking inside. I closed the fridge door and the light went out. I stood there, a pack of tailor-mades in one hand and a box of donuts in the other, letting my eyes adjust to the darkness. I wanted to run, but I walked toward the door softly.

"Recruit, halt!"

It was a trap. Somebody had been sitting there the whole time, watching me in the darkness, lying in wait. I could see the charge report now. It would be an expulsion for theft. Theft! It would make the *Kingston Whig-Standard*. The Colonel would never speak to me again. Dismissal With Disgrace—it would make the *Globe and Mail*, perhaps. Adrenalin pumped through my veins as I scanned my options, which were nil. I was euchred.

In a cold sweat I decided to wait for my captor to speak again. When he didn't, I turned around slowly. Running was useless.

I could barely make out a figure in the corner, sitting as still as he was.

"You're the skinny recruit from Brock," he said. I could only make out the dim outline of his shoulders and head.

"Yes sir," I said.

"Don't let that bastard Stocker get the best of you—you hear? That piece of shit should never have been given the authority."

"Yes sir."

"Enjoy the donuts. It's shit food but it'll fill the hole and give you some energy. Don't make yourself sick on the smokes."

"Yes sir." I turned to leave.

"Recruit."

"Yes sir?"

"This too shall pass. If you make it through, don't forget what this feels like. There will be others like you, count on it. Be there for them. Understand?"

"Yes, sir," I said.

I walked out into the night. I never found out who that guy was.

Billy and Josh were already at the cannon when I arrived with the big haul. They were speechless. I didn't tell them about the guy in the lounge. That part was for me alone. Instead, I made like I'd ripped it off right under the noses of some cadets from Four Sqn. We tore into the donuts—four apiece: I had a bear claw, a chocolate dip, a sour-cream glazed and an apple fritter.

Stuffed, we lay back on the grassy hill and smoked. After some time, the ferry to Wolfe Island passed by.

"So that's what that noise is!" Billy said.

"You know what makes me sick," said Josh, exhaling, "is that while we humour ourselves by deeking out of our rooms and skidding in the hall, Queen's frosh are at this very moment out on the piss and getting laid, or on their way there."

"Yeah," I said. I hadn't thought of that. My happiness at a box of donuts and a pack of weeds seemed childish.

"This school is a far fucking cry from what I thought it would be," said Billy.

"Thain why doncher header back to the faaarm, Biiilly-boyee?" Josh said.

"Fuck that, man. I'm gonna get that piece of paper, and I'm gonna get me a jet."

"Yeah."

They both stared at the sky, where their thoughts were. Watching them watch the sky, waiting, I knew that after rook term we would wait for second year, and then we would wait for graduation. Every class at RMC kept a strict calendar counting down the days to grad. But after graduation, for most of us, that yearning would never leave. There would always be something in the way, always another concrete and visible milestone to be reached, a hurdle that had to be jumped.

I saw it then—us, the family. I saw my father in retrospect through all of our moves, and how he had to keep punching his ticket. The next training course, the next promotion, the next posting, the next tour.

The yearning was there for us now, the three of us felt it as we stared out over the lake, crawling inside ourselves. Finding the impetus, weighing it.

When the clock tower struck two, we rose without a word, shook the grass off and scurried back to our hallway.

"We've got something to show you," said Billy. Josh nodded.

The three of us crawled through the window, and Josh pulled out his gash drawer.

"Billy, pass Verb your maglite."

I took the flashlight and Josh motioned to the open drawer space.

"It's in the back. Pull it out."

With my face close to the cold floor, staring in with the beam of light, I understood this was no ordinary gash drawer. It had a huge space behind it where part of the wall had been knocked out. There was a large, old ammo box sitting there, behind which I could make out the gash drawer of the next room. My room.

"Jesus Christ. Anyone else know about this?" I asked.

"Just you. We'll keep it that way."

"This is unreal," I said. "How long do you think these rooms have been attached?"

"You haven't seen anything yet, Kempt. You need to check out that box."

I pulled out the old metal crate with some effort and opened it as quietly as possible. I could hardly believe the stuff that was in there: letters, worries, advice spanning a hundred years or maybe more. There were a couple pairs of old, faded silk panties from a raid on Queen's, and there was a 7.62 casing with a note, identifying it as the suicidal round from the flagpole incident. There was the watch of the kid who drowned during the obstacle course a few decades before we got there. I listened to it tick.

"I wound it," said Billy.

I dug my hand in and pulled out postcards and journal entries and lists of desires dreamed up by dozens of sweaty, scared recruits. I got choked up all of a sudden and couldn't speak.

"Crawl through, Verb. We'll put the box back and you can slide it through your side," Josh said.

"Borrow my maglite," Billy said. "Just leave it in the time capsule when you're done."

I nodded and crawled into the hole, pushing my gash drawer out as quietly as possible. Mack was snoring. I climbed out on our side and he didn't even stir. Then I waited a minute in the dark, listening to his breathing, while Billy put the ammo box back in.

"G'night Verb," he whispered. "Happy reading." He slid his drawer back into place. I took up the box and opened it. I reached into the bottom and pulled out a form.

Royal Military College of Canada

To: Dr. R.W. Bradbury   *KINGSTON,* AUGUST 18, 1930

SIR or MADAM:

(1) _____ THOMAS LEITH BRADBURY _____
     having been nominated a Gentleman Cadet of the Royal
     Military College of Canada, I have the honour to
     forward forms of Declaration. You are requested to
     obtain the signature of the Cadet to Declaration No.1,
     to attach your own signature to Declaration No.2, and
     to return both to me as soon as practicable. It is also
     requested that intimation may be given of the religious
     denomination to which the cadet belongs.

(2) The fees and allowances payable on behalf of a Cadet
     while at the College, are:
     First Year
     Annual Fee $100
     Outfit Allowance 250
     Expense Allowance 200

         Total $550

(3) Each Cadet is required to pay an annual subscription
     of $20 to the College Recreation Club. This sum covers
     all subscriptions for sports and recreation, including
     the June Ball. A separate cheque for this amount,
     made payable to "The Recreation Club, Royal Military
     College," must be brought by the Cadet, on joining,
     and handed to the Staff Adjutant. The Commandant wishes
     parents to supply Cadets with not less than $5 nor
     more than $10 per month, for pocket money. This sum is
     considered sufficient to cover incidental expenses of the
     Cadet.

(4) Each Cadet should, on joining, bring with him the
     following articles, marked conspicuously with his name
     and initials:

1 pair, black leather slippers.	12 handkerchiefs.
3 pairs, pyjamas.	4 hand and 2 bath towels.
1 dressing gown.	1 brown Holland clothes bag.
3 woollen undershirts.	1 pair, heavy boots.
3 pairs, drawers.	1 each, hair brush and comb.
6 pairs, woollen socks.	1 toothbrush.
4 flannel shirts (without collars).	1 clothes brush.
	1 blue or black bathing suit.
1 nail brush.	1 sponge and bag.
1 trunk.	Bible and prayer book.
1 valise or suitcase.	Hall & Knight's Trigonometry.
Hall & Knight's Algebra.	

No civilian clothing or private furniture (curtains, rugs, easy chairs, eiderdown, etc.) is permitted to be kept in a cadet's room.

(5) During the first two years of the course, cadets are required to submit applications for permission to visit in Kingston; such applications to be accompanied by a written invitation. This regulation is intended to prevent them from forming undesirable associations. The Commandant would, therefore, be pleased to be informed of the names of friends in Kingston, to whose homes cadets may be invited. Kindly advise the Commandant as to whether or not you wish your son to be allowed to smoke.

There were more papers like these. Hundreds more. Letters, advice, bitching, moaning, anecdotes. What did it mean? Christ on a cracker—what did I care? It made me feel better. I knew that much.

THIS IS TO CERTIFY that Gentleman Cadet HEELIS, having completed the full course of instruction and term of Service prescribed by Regulations is entitled, from marks recorded in the Books of the College to receive a Diploma of Graduation and to have entered thereon Pass or Distinguished for the subjects herein specified.

Mathematics and Mechanics
Geometrical Drawing and Descriptive Geometry
Military Engineering
Artillery
Tactics and Topography
Military History
Imperial Military Geography
Military Organization, Administration and Law

```
Civil Engineering and Surveying
Physics
Chemistry
English
French
Drills and Exercises
```

I went through some of the paraphernalia: old name tags, grad pics, clippings from the *RMC Review*, the *Arch*, the *Kingston Whig-Standard*. There were black-and-white photos of the obstacle course, spanning years and years. All of them looked the same. It was as if everyone who came here stopped with time: muddy crewcuts, oily rags, weary happiness and relief.

Excerpt from RMC Review, *December 1933. By Cadet Bradshaw: Little Misery was "THE" obstacle. A sloping bank, a greasy wall, a ten-foot drop into muddy, oily water, over a greasy pole, under a submerged log, out by a greasy incline, all made it the most difficult obstacle of a difficult course. A minute of squelching brought us to the next obstacle, the suspended barrels. The "Greasy M" was our next encounter. Finally came the "Rat Trap." My memory recalls vividly the groans, the ejaculations of various temperatures, the thumping, kicking, heaving and panting that seemed to come from the very boards of the platform. Gradually unlovely head succeeded unlovely head as they emerged from the top of the barrels set at the end of the trap. Wet, sooty, slimy, tired bodies dropped to the ground. A sprint of twenty yards to the finish line brought a happy feeling and a smile to all of us. The race was over; we had all finished; the Fourth Class and the College were one.*

There was a conservative Playboy centrefold from the fifties, maybe, and another, riskier, centrefold from what looked like the seventies. I put the maglite in my mouth and beat off quietly looking at them. When I was done I continued reading:

September 23, 1940. I have been ready and smartly turned out every morning and still I'm collecting slips. We go through at least fifteen minutes of confusion every morning before the call of "Dress," and every senior has his complaints—shoes not shined well enough; a missed polished button; a sword sling not blancoed, always something. Then of course each senior has to be whisked clear of lint (which of course settles on our blues) and as well we must answer to the flat calls of "Recruit Here"—or the parade calls—and everything at the fast double. Notwithstanding the swim in the lake at 6:00 am, I am always hot, sweating and worried. There are always three inspections before the battalion forms up. Three opportunities to collect slips for mistakes in drill or dress. It seems I'm committed to every defaulter's parade at 6:15 am and 4:00 pm. It is most unusual I survive getting caught for some infraction: "Your hair is too long," "You didn't shine your shoes," "You slept in your uniform," or "This rifle is filthy, why isn't it clean?" To which the answer must be "No excuse." To which the inspecting NCO says "Put a slip in my room." I don't know if I'll ever get used to this.

No excuse. Boy, could I ever have a chat with that guy. I'd like to sit down over a pint with any of these guys. It was as if they had been reading my mail—all of them.

OCTOBER, 1928

At last it is Sunday again, when we can sleep until nearly seven. This morning I have an awful lot of stuff to clean for Church Parade, for in addition to my own Senior, CQMS McCorkadale's equipment, I have half of Sgt. McClure's, since his recruit, Vass—lucky man—has four days' ex-recruiting for some minor exploit. McClure, being a gentleman, has given the other half of his uniform to Irvine for cleaning. At that I have to polish or blanco three great coats, two scarlet tunics, two white belts, three brown belts, two sets of accoutrements, and one pair of overshoes. It is necessary to get all this ready before breakfast, in addition to making up my room. After breakfast, we make up our Senior's room, interrupted by calls to whisk the guard commander, CSM or Under Officer on duty. If we don't look nippy over our senior's needs, we won't have time to get ourselves ready for Church Parade ...

All the way down to St. George's Church we have the sergeants yelling at us: to swing our arms properly, to swing them higher to the front or rear, or to watch our covering. If you happen to be tall and are immediately in front of a bevy of them at the rear, you are a "sitting duck," as Vass calls it. Vass—lucky man—is not tall.

In church you are so tired, and everything is so peaceful that you doze off every few minutes, and you have to be prodded in the back by a classmate. If one of the hymns happens to be one of the eight college ones such as "Fight the Good Fight with All Thy Might," or "All Hail the Power of Jesus' Name," the cadets sing at the top of our voices, high in the balcony reserved for us, and the commandant looks up with a disapproving frown. Otherwise no cadets sing at all, and the congregation sounds piteously weak by contrast...

Back in "B" Company I head for my room, but I hardly enter the flat before the seniors are bellowing for me, at the top of their voices. Never was there such a bloody mess as I—I'm a damned disgrace to the College—I did everything wrong on Church Parade, I was checked up, and I still made no attempt to march properly—I didn't give a damn, that was the trouble—and that was the attitude of my whole damned class. Now I was to get moving up and down the flat, 180 to the minute. "Faster, faster, get moving damn you!" yell the seniors. "Don't bend your arms at the elbow. Stand up and make something of yourself!" And off I go again...

Dinner on Sundays at the College is the best meal of the week, but with all the "shit" flying, the recruits do not get much chance to enjoy it. Meals take place amid three varieties of surroundings; the seniors may have been on an exercise, or on ride or other appetizer, and be interested in their food, and not in us. Or they may have come from a series of restful classes and be in jovial mood, making us tell jokes throughout the meal. Or they may arrive in a bad temper from their own frustrations (more frequent in winter I notice) and we do nothing right—whence we are under fire from the beginning of the meal to the end...

After several parades we now have time to get over to Fort Frederick for an hour. The Fort is the recruits' haven; here behind thick stone walls, we huddle around the fireplace, and forget our troubles for a while. How we bellyache! How the hardships, grievances and scrapes, melt away for the time being...

Skeletor

The postcards started arriving. N Flight pumped off 115 for this little gem from Spain:

Hey Verbal! As you can guess I'm in Spain. Went to a bullfight the other day with a couple girls I'll be living with in Paris. Don't have an address yet but when I do you'll be the first one to get it. Trapped right now in a bus station in Pamplona because it's siesta. 14C/rainy. These lazy bastards, or bastardos, will sleep any time they can. Been wonderful so far—wish you could see it with me. I <u>love</u> sangria! You haven't tasted <u>real</u> sangria till you've been to Spain! My biggest issue with the Spanish is that they don't speak English! I'll write as soon as I'm back in Paris. Lots of love, Ruth.

Her words were a drag. It wasn't as if I expected her to understand what I was going through, what *we* had to go through just so I could read that tripe. She had no way of knowing that all two hundred recruits did push-ups for each flight member's mail, that the other thousand cadets had done it before we arrived— and that all the ex-cadets, our *ex-buds*, had been assuming the push-up position for mail-call since the Old Eighteen started the whole thing off. Still, it seemed a gyp. A few days later we got another hefty workout for a postcard from France. The picture was of a broken and sad little bust, covered with graffiti, the face unrecognizable:

Hi Verbal! Got back earlier than expected. Haven't settled in at my pension yet but I'll write when I do. Thought you'd like this: it's Jim Morrison's tombstone. Isn't it the saddest? Didn't actually see it, but I liked the postcard. Haven't seen the cathedral you asked me to take pictures of, but when I do I'll send you a roll. I guess you couldn't make it to the Hip before I left. I was pretty let down, but I guess you must be busy. Got to run. Switzerland next week! Love Ruth.

I wished she had to do as many push-ups as we did before she sent the damn things. At least then she might try making them worth the postage. I started thinking of Ruth as callous and unromantic for stuffing her face with cheese and chocolate and wine. My imagination was unhealthy: I saw her putting on fresh layers of youthful, hedonistic fat, constantly smoking hash, complaining when her raclette was served cold, when her Alsatian wine was not cool enough, when she had to spend another long day heli-skiing somewhere in the Alps. One day, three postcards arrived at once.

"Well well well, Recruit Kempt! Seems we have a few today," Hackman said. "Let's see here… one from Paris, one from… Zermatt, and—hey—this one's from London. These," he snickered, waving them above his head, "are going to cost you dearly, N Flight."

"Excuse me Mr. Hackman! Recruit Kempt, V., Five Squadron, November Flight, Three Section reporting!"

"What?"

"You can throw them out, Mr. Hackman," I said.

"What was that, Recruit?"

"Pardon, Mr. Hackman—I would prefer if you just threw them out."

He shrugged and smiled at me as he ripped them up.

I wanted Ruth to have to piss in a sink, to feel the grey wool fire blanket and look at me, shocked: "You have to sleep with *that?*" I wanted her to be touched by the sight of my face, to see the hollow sockets my eyes had become. And while I shamelessly wanted all of this, I knew that I could never expect anybody to understand except the people in this hall (and the ex-buds in the time capsule). That was the sad thing, since I didn't even like most of them.

Mr. Gaston, our Cadet Flight Leader, started taking us out for PT at least three times a week and lectured us on the importance of teamwork. Ms. Pfaff was to be seen more regularly—always pushing to instill a sense of squadron pride. She made us huddle together one day and make up a November Flight hymn, an original war cry for the fast approaching obstacle course. It made me want to barf:

> *Hoo! Haa! November Flight!*
> *We'll sock it to ya with all our might!*
> *Brock rocks! We never stop!*
> *We're in your face until we drop!*

"We should all memorize it, November!" squealed Harrowsmith, rubbing against my arm.

"It's lame," Mann said, staring openly at her tits. I looked at her tits, too.

"C'mon!" Becky French wheezed through yellow teeth. "Let's sing it again guys! With lots of squadron pride!"

We sang it again with lots of squadron pride.

"Shouldn't it be, 'We're in your face until *you* drop'?" I said.

"Yeah," said Gaze, "why are WE going to drop? It doesn't make sense."

"What do you mean?" French said. She looked at him like he'd just asked her to understand fourth-year quantum mechanics.

"No. We'll keep it how it is," Josh said. His face was tired. "It's fitting."

We were all tired. If we weren't out getting pumped for the obstacle course, we spent hours on the stinky hot asphalt of the parade square, with the Drill Sergeant Major barking out commands we could now follow instinctively. Of course, the Drill Sergeant Major always had new movements to add to our drill portfolio. These were broken down into squads for the ease of instruction so that even the dumbest tit could eventually get it right. The minutes stretched into hours on the sunbaked asphalt, and the drill staff were eventually forced to give us water breaks once people started thundering in, fainting with bayonets fixed to their rifles.

We learned the format for the ex-cadet parade and practised it until it was no more difficult than breathing, or walking. As far as parades go, this was an important one as it would signify, when it took place for real, our official acceptance as cadets of the Royal Military College. If we weren't practising for this parade, we were learning the drill movements for the Recruit College History Test.

Eventually I received my first duty as the Squadron Runner. SR duty was always filled by a recruit, or first-year, and entailed marching throughout squadron halls to check the dozen or so boxes for outgoing mail. This had to be done three times a day, which ensured one of the most efficient inter-campus mail systems to be found anywhere.

Checking the boxes required square drill, and marching into foreign territory. Seniors lurked around corners and between doorways. Some of them would even follow me, ready to shout "Recruit halt!" at any moment.

As SR, whenever I came to a mailbox I had to halt, execute a snappy left or right turn, stand-at-ease, stand easy, and then thoroughly scour the box. It was important to ensure there was nothing at the bottom, because oftentimes seniors enjoyed fooling the SRs with a tiny little scrap of paper, just so that they could dish out cock later. One fourth-year wrote a memorandum on a tissue then blew his nose into it, and gave me hell for not delivering it on time. I thought somebody had just left a snot-rag in his outbox, and left it there.

"You must pay attention to detail, Recruit," the fourth-year said.

Once the mail was collected I had to come to attention, execute another left or right turn, and then quick march it to the next mailbox. It would have been an easy duty if they hadn't spent so much time making it difficult.

In a broad way, Gertie stayed beneath the neat folds of my mixed-up melon; she lurked in the dark corners, frowning, arms crossed. When her letter came I felt a sick tremor of betrayal, and all of it came back: Buttercup, the Colonel, the August 17 Chicken Killing. It seemed like someone else's life—some kid I used to know. My anger towards her blind knowledge of where I was and what I was doing was astoundingly bitter. Did she even know that Gramps was dead, I wondered. She's the one who took off, so I didn't see what right it gave her to assume anything about anything.

Looking at it another way, I have to admit it was pretty remarkable that she knew how to find me. What was more worrisome to me was the thought that, however remarkable it was, it was not at all surprising:

Herbie: If you are reading this (and I know you are), WHY? I'm watching NRA numbnuts on TV asserting that guns don't kill people: people kill people. If the guns weren't there, would it happen as much? What would you say to this I wonder. Do me a favour and buy the 10,000 Maniacs album In My Tribe. You, Herbie, with the quarter-inch cut of your hair and your army-issue green.

Every day you make choices Herbie, and these choices are based on one of two things: FEAR or LOVE.

You've been afraid of him your whole life. When is it going to stop? You've feared him so much you've fallen in love with the Army-boy ideal. You have tried to quell your fear with enslavement. Freedom scares you Verbie—freedom to you would be slow torture. By your own will.

And I'm positive you are reading this. You freakshow, I love you. I'm sure this piece of paper will find its way into your hands, and you will read it, be glad to hear from me, but deny everything you already know. Then you will dream up some flashy form of revelation—something to do with the Kernel (whom I love as

*well—more than you could ever know). But you are wrong on
both counts, Herbie. You are wrong to live through Dad. And you
are wrong to live through me. Don't live like a second-hand soul,
brother. All you owe yourself is yourself: Herbert Kempt. And that
is the same thing you owe the rest of the world.*

Why? How COULD you, Herbie?

Had I forgotten something? I took her letter to bed like Linus'
blanket, and pressed my thumb to my forehead to think. She
was absolutely right. The whole time I'd been in this body I'd
been a carbon copy of this then that, an emblem of gutless self-
sacrifice. Still, I was a soldier. Maybe that's all a soldier was—stale,
completely unoriginal. Not everybody can be original. But just
because I couldn't be unique—like the Gerties and the Ruths of
this world all doing the same thing trying to be original through
their travels—didn't mean I was so different. Just because it
wasn't unique was no reason to quit the Army.

Gertie, wherever she was, knew I was here. So what. She was
ignoring the real reasons how, or why she knew what she knew.

I'd make it. I'd hold the reins, eat snakes. I'd become the
Colonel if that's what it took.

It was late. I got up out of bed and snuck across the inner field
and onto the parade square. In the middle of the parade square
I squatted, staring up at the clock tower as it struck three. The
commissionaire walked fifty feet away from me, but he didn't
see me. I was still as the night, a professional hidden in this wide
open space. I emptied my bowels, leaving a long steamy coil of
shit for the whole college. If they wanted me they'd have to take
all of me.

In the morning I sat up in bed, wiping sleep-snot from my eyes
and anticipating the music; the crackling hiss of the speakers
powering on was enough to alert me in the morning. This time
the static didn't send the normal wash of panic through me.

"Morning Mack," I said, hopping off the bunk. The music

started right after I plugged the iron in. I stepped up to the sink casually to piss, humming along to April Wine.

Mack, standard-issue recruit terror in his eyes, stared at me in disbelief. Something had changed. Now we both knew it. I put my face right in front of his.

"What the fuck are you staring at, jackass?" I said. Mack turned around and made his bed. I took the Kiwi cloth off the toes of my spit-shone gash boots, and got dressed while dry-shaving. I made my bed next, whistling while I ironed the corners. The music was cut short, but I couldn't have cared less. There was no reason to panic. The CSCs were yelling and screaming about a surprise inspection by CFL Gaston. Word spread quickly that someone had shit on the parade square and practice was going to be held up while the college looked for the shitter. I knew I was safe then—it was clear they had no idea.

All three CSCs were on deck to ensure everything went smoothly, anxious to show off how much they'd accomplished with us in our several intense weeks together. Out in the hall, Mr. Gaston stared at me in disbelief.

"Holy Hanna, Recruit." Mr. Gaston was a well-meaning cadet, but was nonetheless an absentee leader, and obviously a tad surprised at my weight loss. "Recruit Kempt," he said. "Have you been eating properly?"

"I eat everything I'm given, Mr. Gaston!" I said.

"Mr. Hackman: see that Recruit Kempt eats a large breakfast."

"Yes, Mr. Gaston," Hackman said.

Stocker glared hard. I could feel his look on me as he approached, clicking away on those infernal clickers. I wanted to laugh at him and his stupid clickers. He could shove his clickers up his arse.

"I was just noticing his gaunt features yesterday, Mr. Gaston, when I gave November a big feed of kye," Stocker said. "I think he kind of looks like Skeletor. Perhaps that should be your new name, eh Kempt? Recruit Skeletor. What do you think?"

"I was kind of getting used to Recruit Bumfucker," I said, "but of course you can call me anything you please, Mr. Stocker." I looked directly at Stocker and saw him wince.

"What's this?" Gaston said. I pretended the question had been directed at me.

"Oh it's been sort of a running joke between myself and Mr. Stocker, Mr. Gaston. He came up with the idea that I'm a faggot, and he has the greatest names for cocksuckers. Just yesterday I was Recruit Pillowbiter."

"It's a good thing you have a sense of humour, Recruit," Gaston said, his voice sober. "Otherwise, something like that could be viewed as harassment."

"Surely not, Mr. Gaston. This is all in good fun."

He continued inspecting my uniform and boots. He brushed a piece of lint off my epaulette.

"Good turnout, Recruit," he said before moving on. "Mr. Stocker: I'll have a word with you outside please."

Half an hour later, for the first time at RMC, I had a full, honest-to-goodness meal in the mess. It was a breakfast of lumberjack proportions: waffles, scrambled eggs, pancakes, bacon, sausages, ham. And maple syrup! Rivers of it! Nothing beats the taste of maple syrup when it collides with ham.

Hackman didn't steady-up the flight once, and I, finally, didn't have to eat using square drill.

I ran my hand along my pants pocket, feeling the outline of Gertie's letter, and couldn't help smirking, my mouth full of kye. To hell with her and all that she thought she knew.

That night I broke into the squadron storage area and stole a ball of string and a can of lighter fluid from Smith's civvy kit. I squirted the whole thing into the Point Frederick cannon—all over the garbage I'd thrown in the barrel from every midnight snack. On top of the lighter fluid and the garbage I put Gertie's letter. I made a fuse out of the string. Then I let 'er go—whoosh!

By the time I got to the bottom of the hill I was sprinting, and I looked back when I heard a small pop. Flames shot about six feet out of the cannon. I ran through the parking lot, by the guardhouse and down Precision Drive. I ran to the Arch. I had the feeling that I was on the verge of understanding something important. I took a shit directly beneath the Arch, and when I was done I jumped off the wall into Lake Ontario and swam back towards the point. I undressed in the water, letting my jogging pants and t-shirt sink to the bottom. I watched the fire die out and then I snuck back into bed, naked and wet. I shivered under the fire blankets.

NCT

When the time came to perform, having practised and performed the drill movements for the Recruit College History Test a thousand times, we executed them perfectly, like zombies. The ordeal took forever, as we had to march to the dais individually and report to the Cadet Wing Commander, who would then ask us questions about RMC's past. I rolled my eyes up, trying to tell the time on the clock tower without moving my head, and thought that the most dreaded sound in my military training so far was the thud of the second hand, a reminder of inactivity and delay.

What is work? Was I working now, standing in the sun? Work has to be performed between such and such an hour for so many days per week and for so many weeks per year. These fragmented tickings necessitate that the day be processed uniformly, separate from the natural rhythms of human experience.

Whoever was cleaning up my feces beneath the Arch was working, and was surely aware of the present moment.

On the parade square, I recognized my own movements to be those of an automaton. I could see the heat rising from the newly blackened asphalt, felt the trickles of sweat breaking free from my neck, my pits, my shoulders, and pooling at the small of my back. I was acutely aware of it during drill practice—the timing, that is.

If the DSM barked: "Move to the left in threes... Left turn!" My right foot lifted immediately as I pivoted on my left without thinking. On completion of a ninety-degree turn, I slammed my heel into the ground. Usually, the staccato of all other heels would indicate that the timing had been missed. The wool of my pants would start to seem an inch thick, and the pins in my feet from endless marching, turning, halting and slamming would eventually be replaced by flames. The crotch sweat would come: I'd prepare for the itch that couldn't be scratched. Ultimately I'd give thanks for not fainting, having seen more bodies crash onto the square, bayonets fixed to their rifles. Although, thundering in was definitely better than taking a knee when you felt woozy. If any soldier took a knee, shame would follow him indefinitely. It was usually the skinnier guys and the bigger girls who went down first, and they served as an early warning for the rest of us.

I snapped to attention when I saw Harrowsmith returning from her test. My turn. I stepped one pace forward and halted. Executing a perfect left turn, I marched out through the rank and file of November Flight and up to the dais.

"Excuse me Mr. Hutch—"

"Don't bother reporting, Recruit Kempt. I can see your name tag clearly."

"Yes, Mr. Hutch."

"Tell me in what building the library is housed?"

"Currie Building, Mr. Hutch."

"You don't have to keep repeating my name, I've had the same one my whole life. Just answer the questions, Recruit."

"Yes, Mr. Hutch."

"Who is the Currie Building named after?"

"General Arthur Currie."

"What was his role in World War II?"

"He led the Canadian Corps and was instrumental in the final hundred days. He occupied Mons as the armistice took effect."

"Very good, Recruit. Are you a History major?"

"Negative, Mr. Hutch."

"Where'd you get the time to study?"

"In the heads after Lights Out."

"Well then," he said, "let's see if we can stump you. Six Squadron: who is it named after?"

"Joseph Brant."

"Tell me about him."

"He was a Mohawk Chief as well as a soldier. He was conversant in Latin and Greek and at least three Native dialects. He was a Protestant."

"Okay. Can you tell me, Kempt, who attached himself to Brock's troops after Sir Isaac's final battle?"

"It was Tecumseh, the infamous scalping Yank-hater."

Mr. Hutch paused for a moment.

"This one's easy, so you better not fuck it up: who led the Canadians in our victory at Vimy, if you can call it that?

"General Julian Byng."

"When?"

"Easter Monday, April 9, 1917. And you can call it a victory."

"Casualties?"

"Ten thousand by noon, I believe. Low by the standards of that time."

"That's not low by any fucking standard, Recruit. That's ten thousand dead soldiers. What's your classification?"

"Infantry, Mr. Hutch."

"Well I'll be. Ducimus. Have you read Berton's *Vimy?*"

"No, Mr. Hutch."

"Every self-respecting Canadian should."

"Yes, Mr. Hutch."

"I'm impressed, Kempt. Good turnout. Mr. Stocker told me to grill you, but I can't see why."

"He has a crush on me, Mr. Hutch," I said. Hutch laughed.

"I want you to sing the college cheer for me, Kempt."

"Sing, Mr. Hutch?"

"That's what I said."

"Beer, Esses, Emma ..." I squeaked.

"Have some balls, Kempt. Bite it out! I want you to sing it so that your whole flight can hear you. Don't look around. Sing it or you fail."

"BEER ESSES EMMA, TDV! WHO CAN STOP OL' RMC? SHRAPNEL, CORDITE, NCT! R! M! C!"

"You have a lovely voice, Recruit," Hutch said. "Now what does Beer Esses Emma stand for?"

"BSM, or Battery Sergeant-Major."

"And TDV?"

"That's easy, Mr. Hutch: Truth, Duty, Valour."

"Okay. This is your last question, Kempt: what does NCT stand for?"

I had no idea.

"I have no idea, Mr. Hutch."

"You did a good job, Kempt. Well done."

I was about to dismiss myself when Hutch said:

"No Cunt Tonight, Recruit. Bet you'll never forget that."

Book 3

Those of you with nothing to fall back on,
you will find, *are* home.

–David Mamet

The Bridge

From the first day of courses I knew I was doomed to fail physics. It was my very first class in M-7, and I took my seat just as it started, at 08:00 sharp. There was a special introduction from the Dean of Engineering, who wore an expensive dark suit with a yellow polka-dotted tie. He had thin lips and a sparse mustache, and though he said he was an ex-cadet himself, I could hardly believe it.

"You are the Elite," the Dean said. "Capital E." He frowned, then jabbed his finger at everyone in the room. "You are Engineering students, about to embark upon the most important course of study to society at the best school in the country. Lights, please."

The lights clicked off and a short film played—a montage of old footage of bridges and buildings collapsing. While the film played the Dean turned his back to us and wrote out an equation that spanned the width of the three chalkboards. When the film was done the lights snapped on.

"That last shot of the suspension bridge—swaying and crumbling and extinguishing the lives of dozens of innocents— that is what happens when you take this," the Dean tapped his stick of chalk on a minus sign midway through his grand equation, "and do *this!*" With a powerful stroke he changed the minus sign into a plus, pressing the chalk so hard against the blackboard that the entire stick crumbled to dust. He rubbed his hands together. "It is your duty to study hard," he said, before walking out of the lecture hall. It was a grand beginning, and I knew then that I wanted nothing to do with Engineering. Of all possible ways to spend my time, building bridges was perhaps least among them.

After that day, classes ran from 08:30 until 16:30, Monday to Friday, with an hour break for lunch. We still had to be formed up for inspection and marched over to Yeo Hall for breakfast, but after that we were free to march in gaggles of twos and threes over to the Massey Building—the closest safe haven from the edge of the parade square, and where most of the first-year Engineering classes were held.

I got to know M-7 well. It had the appearance of being, at one time, a comfortable lecture hall. Years of cadet attendance had worn the fabric of the swivel-down theatre seats until it was threadbare. The once-white paint had yellowed to a tired cream colour, and the wall behind the last row of seats had been systematically stained in patches from the hair oil of the thousands of cadets who had fallen asleep over the years with their heads back and mouths open.

There was a clock in M-7 but it didn't work, and the hall was so overheated that, even when we took our wool tunics off and loosened our ties, it was hard to stay awake. Everybody slept. All I had to do was walk into M-7 and my lids would feel heavy. I'd no sooner sit down than I'd feel my feel my head falling forward and drool seeping from the corner of my mouth. It got so bad that I wondered if the administration was pumping some sort of nerve agent, as a test, through the ventilation.

Winter was the best time for napping, not only because of the added comfort of long johns under our wool pants, but for the cushy splendour of our winter headdress. In October or November we traded our blue wedge cap with chinstrap in for the black astrakhan with the red flap, which was like wearing a fluffy, portable pillow. If you couldn't tell a first-year cadet by his shoulder flashes, then you could certainly spot him from the drool encrusted on his astrakhan.

Anyway, I didn't mind sleeping in physics class because I knew I was doomed after that first day. After the Dean left the hall, the instructor, Dr. Racy, explained the course objectives. He got Wommersley up and had him stand by the door.

"When I say so," Dr. Racy said, "I want you to fling the door open. The rest of you observe closely and objectively. I want you to pay attention to my every movement." He started bobbing up and down, doing these deep knee bends, and twirling around in a circle while simultaneously clucking his head back and forth.

"Open now!" he screamed. Billy threw open the door with a grand gesture and after a moment, Dr. Racy drew himself up sharply and puffed a few times as he caught his breath. He cleared his throat and spoke in a low, almost menacing, tone.

"By the end of this course you will need to know enough about physics to tell me everything about not only the velocity and acceleration of my nose as it is bobbing up and down, spinning in a circle and moving back and forth—but you will also have to calculate that *with respect to* the motion of the doorknob as the door is flung open."

He went on with his lesson I presume, but at that moment—like a narcoleptic on cue—I promptly embraced unconsciousness.

Dry the Rain

I went for another swim after taking a shit on the Commandant's lawn. At 03:00, shortly after I had crawled back into my bunk, they came. At first I thought they had come just for me. They were nameless and faceless; all three of them wore masks. They were jacked up on that nefarious combination of caffeine, nicotine, adrenalin, power and low self-esteem. They were dangerous.

November Flight scrambled out of bed. We reported for duty in our gitch and drill boots. They had come for all of us.

"Dognight," one of the three yelped in a terse voice, "is a *tradition* at RMC." He wore a rubber Nixon mask. The second boy was a Stormtrooper, and the third wore a mask of *The Scream*.

Later I would find out that these, the directors of our Dognight, were a select group of third-years on whom were bestowed the privilege of roughing up the fresh meat the night before the obstacle course.

I was freezing in my gitch, and tired. The Stormtrooper barked at us to mark time. We rarely marked time without music, and it felt sinister. It felt like anything could happen, that everything was about to happen.

"We have a treat for you, recruits," said the Scream. "We ordered take-out." He brought out a Little Caesar's pizza box: inside was one piece of Hawaiian pizza.

"One piece for the flight," said Nixon, shoving the box at French. "You take a bite, Recruit, chew for ten seconds, then spit half of it out."

Everybody had to follow this drill, and after the first ten recruits there were no fresh bites left to take. The box was passed around until there was only a lump of chewed pizza (dough, pineapple and ham) the size of a teaspoon—it had gone around four times by then. When I was chewing, I swear I could taste Mack's bad breath.

"Suit up!" said the Stormtrooper. "PT gear, rain gear, toques. Move!"

They took us for a midnight jog around Fort Henry. Fortunately it was raining, because with the raingear and toques, it would have been too hot otherwise. I can't remember how many times we had to go up and down Heartbreak Hill in the dark, but I eventually collapsed, which pissed me off because I'd never before collapsed on a run. Not one person was standing by the time they threw the logs on us.

"A straight line, recruits!" barked the Scream. "It won't hurt so much if everybody does their part! Gotta muck in for the team, November!"

Thomas "I went to Appleby" Caruthers, ended up right beside me. I swear it felt like I was in labour, trying to do a sit-up at the same time as everybody else, with this bloody log on top of us. If we were out of sync, it meant somebody down the line was getting crushed.

"Up! Hold it! Down! Up! C'mon you bags of shit—work together!"

I felt the wind get knocked out of me, and heard Mack sobbing. Caruthers leaned over and barfed on me, but I didn't even care at that point. We were all covered in mud anyway.

"Excuse me Mister ... um, Recruit Weiland, J., Five Squadron—"

"Shut-the-fuck-up, *you!*" screamed Nixon. All the girls were crying, now, and half of the boys. Caruthers whimpered. I heard two more people puke somewhere down the line.

"Sickness! Sickness won't help you, November Flight!" The Scream and the Stormtrooper told us to push the logs off, and when we did, Nixon made us pick up the vomit with our hands and smear it on each other's toques. After that, they graunched us. All of us. They smeared us with ketchup, margarine, peanut butter, mustard, mayo, honey, shaving cream, toothpaste, oatmeal. The smell alone was enough to make me puke, but I held it in until they made us do a few more wind sprints up the hill. Almost everybody was retching by then, anyway. After picking up our barf we had to pass it around to each other. Then we were lined up against the stone wall of Fort Henry and pelted with eggs.

"Regulators, saddle-up!" the Scream yelled. They double-timed us back to the N Flight halls to introduce the game of Hot Iron/Cold Iron. I had never heard of this game before, which is probably why I came away from it with a nasty burn on my cheek. Well, it wasn't a real burn; after recruit term I learned that it was a psychological burn. Whatever. The fact is I had to walk around for the next three days with the imprint of a clothes iron on my cheek. It bloody well *felt* like a real burn.

What they did was walk around us with a steaming iron, saying "Hot iron, hot iron." Nixon came dangerously close a few times, and I started believing that he was actually trying to burn me. Eventually the Scream came up behind me and pushed the iron right in my face. I screamed, and started blubbering like a fool. My face was burning up, even though the iron that touched my face was not the hot iron, but one that had been chilling on ice.

"Fucking pansy recruit," said the Scream. I didn't even try to collect myself. It wasn't until later I saw I'd wet my pants. So tired. The PT and all the late nights seemed to catch up to me right at that moment. It didn't seem to matter much that I was crying, anyway. I held my cheek and made out like it was the pain that was bothering me, not that they were scaring me.

They pushed us all into the bathroom where we stood under the freezing showers fully clothed. When we were all shivering and blue-lipped, they had us shut the showers off. We all lay face-down and they turned the lights off. The floor tiles stank. My face was on fire. People were moaning and shivering up against each other. I think I might have been moaning, too.

I felt a warm trickle hit my raincoat, my neck, my toque, my face.

"They're fucking pissing on us, man," Billy whispered to Josh.

I was hoping he would laugh. But he didn't. He didn't make a fucking sound.

~

Don't You Believe a Word

When construction was finished, the obstacle course was impressive. On the big day, it rained all morning and we were soaked right through before the starter pistol was fired. We huddled together as November Flight, one unit of fire blankets and squadron jerseys, shivering. We tried to muster up enough squadron pride to make our cheer sound convincing. *We're in your face until we drop!* We sported maroon headbands to match our jerseys, CF-issue Rambo runners, black poly-cotton blend slacks and green web belts. Everything would be thrown in the trash when we were done.

The second-year cadets, in charge of organizing and building the obstacle course, were obviously fond of firehoses. There were firehoses everywhere, maybe two or three of them per obstacle, on average. It's a rough estimate, because it's hard to count them when they're being sprayed in your face; the spray was powerful enough to knock a grown man down.

Everywhere there was shouting and cheering. People screamed at us, but we couldn't hear what they shouted. They screamed anyway, and pointed their fingers this way and that, indicating in what direction we should run next. I thought they must be idiots for not understanding how bone-tired we were.

And my family was there. This was the Big Event, after all. I caught a glimpse of Ailish at our second obstacle, riding piggyback on Dad, shouting my name. I thought of how she was looking at me, or looking up to me, as a big brother, and I tried to act accordingly. I shouted encouragement at my buds, knowing even as I did it that they couldn't hear a bloody word and that it wouldn't have mattered if they could.

I climbed a greased plastic sheet at Fort Frederick in order to stand in front of a firehose so that the rest of the flight could pyramid themselves to the top. A few obstacles later I caught Ailish's pretty little face again by the moat of the Stone Frigate— she was holding Mom's hand and shouting something. I couldn't even pretend to shout encouragement by that point. My parents should have known better than to bring her down to Kingston to see me like this. We were swimming through the moat, which stank even though they had filled it with water and soap, and I tried to shout something to Ailish.

"Keep your mouth closed, Kempt!" Ms. Pfaff screamed. Later I found out why: the murky water of this stagnant obstacle had served as a receptacle for shit, piss and puke to drunken senior cadets for weeks. We were swimming through a sewer, and all these people, even our parents—especially our parents, were laughing and clapping and spectating. This gave new meaning to "unlovely head after unlovely head" rising to the surface.

There were no long swimming obstacles over five feet deep, and there hasn't been since a recruit drowned after being forced to swim around the Point, even though he was so petrified of water that he had only ever bathed by sitting on the edge of the tub and sponging himself. Rumour had it he was reported missing after the obstacle course, and the military had phoned his family to inform them he was AWOL. They apologized and sent their condolences the next day when they found his bloated body floating in Lake Ontario, and were nice enough to hang his picture on the memorial staircase in Mackenzie. I looked at it once, even though that staircase was off limits to cadets who hadn't yet graduated. The inscription read: "Drowned while attempting the obstacle course." I've heard it said that drowning is a peaceful way to go, but who would be the authority on that?

We pushed on relentlessly for hours. It was a feeling beyond exhaustion, and I stopped caring about what anyone thought— I didn't care that I was dragging my ass. I wanted to give up. I wanted to stop running, stop moving and crawl into the earth with a fire blanket for warmth. I wanted to weep, or have someone punch my lights out. The last obstacles are a blur: my body could barely move, like when you're being chased in a dream and you can't run away, or you just can, but not nearly fast enough.

It dragged on, hour after hour, until finally, soggy and stupid, we shuffled to the bell at the flagpole to signal that November Flight had finished.

From what I'd read in the time capsule, I should have felt exultant. These people surrounding us were all laughing and clapping for us, telling us how great the obstacle course had been. Stocker even came up and congratulated me personally. He clapped me on the back like an old pal.

"I met your father—why didn't you tell me he was Colonel Kempt? That guy's a legend." He was all smiles, telling me what a tremendous job I'd done during rook term. He gave me a smoke, even. All the seniors beamed at us, and welcomed us to the fold, like they had cared about us all along.

We were whisked away for a few snapshots before our long-promised showers. Somebody handed me a Polaroid of N Flight in our moment of glory. We were some messy cats. I looked around at our ragged crew as we did an airborne shuffle back to November Flight halls: every single one of us was caked in clay and oil and water and blood. An army of stinkers. I held the Polaroid gingerly so as not to muck it up too much with my shrivelled, greasy fingers. I had it in mind to contribute the Polaroid to the time capsule. It looked like all the rest—even I would be hard pressed to tell the difference between this picture and a grainy black-and-white one taken over fifty years ago. And I thought about how, after the first obstacle, when we were already soaked with mud and grease and rain and sweat and mud, not one gentleman or lady cadet of N Flight was distinguishable from another.

Maybe this was really how it was done—to have us become one being—a being with the solitary purpose of growth through survival. The Great Unwashed absolving ourselves of the past weeks in inches—eking closer with each obstacle as a higher form of penance. If this was what was happening, the whole focus seemed misguided.

When we got back to the barracks, I took a few minutes to sort through the time capsule, looking for another obstacle course picture, and I came across a journal entry. When I came to the signature, something took me—from outside and in—like my heart was plucked from my chest cavity, forced upwards through my throat and placed in my mouth, where it lay pounding. The journal entry was signed *Recruit David V. Kempt*:

I go to bed pondering RMC life and what it's all about. On the very first afternoon that we hit the College a bare six months back (but seemingly eons ago) when we gaily dismissed our taxis on the square and entered the portals of the Administration Building unsuspecting into a cataclysm of commands shouted by a group of awesome gold-braided gods, it was made clear why we had come to the College:

"Why did you come to RMC, Kempt?"

"Permission to say, to go into the Infantry."

"No you didn't. Why did you come to RMC?"

"Because my father wanted me to."

"Hell no. You came to RMC to be made a man of. Do you get that, Kempt?"

"Yes."

"Bite it out!"

"YES!"

"Well then, we shall devote the entire year to doing this."

To be made a man of! As I savour the memory of the pleasant afternoon and evening just over, and my temporary freedom from the shackles of recruiting, I recall this promise.

To be made a man of? To be made a man of! Perhaps that was the uncomfortable sensation I was feeling.

Ms. Pfaff took the girls to the third floor for their hot showers. The boys of November were outside in the hall, stripping bare. I heard them hooting and hollering, and they jumped up and down like a bunch of victory-crazed Zulus before swarming the heads. Mack poked his face in the door.

"Hot showers, Kempt!" he said. "Let's go, man! We made it! November Flight rocks!"

"Rock on, Mack." I shut the door in his face and shoved everything back into the time capsule. I couldn't understand how my old man had held the same ammo box in the night here decades ago—maybe had even had the same bunk as me. I had nowhere to put that information in my head, so I stripped down and hit the showers.

The taps were all running and the bathrooms were hot and steamy. I stood with the others, surprised by my body's gratitude, basking in that warmth after scouring the mud and sweat from every follicle and pore. Stocker and Kincaid brought in cold beers which we drank while we showered. Somebody wondered what the girls were doing. They should have, I think, been showering with us. After working together the way we had, we had earned that much.

Even then, in the steamy showers with a cold beer in my hand, the proper sense of elation, of accomplishment, escaped me. I tried to catch a wave of feel-good-times as everybody shouted out "We're first-years!" and ya-hooed, but I missed it. I felt queasy and light-headed.

"Congratulations November Flight. You're first-years!" said Mr. Kincaid. I thought I'd go deaf with the hoorays and the ya-hoos. I could even hear the girls screaming down the hall with Ms. Pfaff. We stood naked, and accepted more beers and laughed about what a tough ride rook term had been but we'd made it through together, etc. I wanted to go lie down, but Stocker handed me another beer.

"You'll make a good soldier, Kempt," he said.

My knees gave out, and I slipped and smashed my forehead onto the wet tile. I was out for a minute or so, and I came to with

Stocker helping me up and the boys standing around, staring. They told me I'd gone into convulsions for a few seconds. It was embarrassing, standing there dripping with my cock hanging out. It wasn't embarrassing before I passed out, but suddenly I felt skinny and weak.

It's clear now that that's when it started. It started then, after finally being released from the abject authority of this guy who was smiling at me and holding out a beer.

It was at that moment that I began to think that everybody was lying.

On the Teat

It wasn't very difficult getting laid at RMC; you just couldn't be too choosy. As Cecil Witherspoon liked to say, "There's massive amounts of fucking going on in this place."

What happened at Thanksgiving was just a fluke, and it meant nothing, really. I didn't see the point in writing Ruth in France just to tell her I'd fooled around the first weekend I was allowed out of the college. I was tempted to, though, when I thought of all those postcards she'd sent.

Tina Terranova, the husky Italian girl, offered me a ride to Ottawa. Tina struck me as the type who found herself powerless to have anything more than quick, loveless flings, and even though these flings weren't satisfying, she kept having more. She had plenty of experience, soft, soft lips, and deep brown eyes. After her, I would never look at big women the same. The right type will make me weak. And yet Tina wasn't as tough as she made out. There were enough hints to tell me that she was unhappy with herself, unhappy with her body. She probably thought being loose made her more desirable. That's the thing—she needed to be desired. I found her situation as convenient as she did mine.

No sooner had we pulled onto the 401 than Tina laid down the rules.

"Don't mention the College and don't mention the Army," she said. "Off-duty is off-duty."

"Okay," I said. I couldn't think of anything to say. She had effectively ruled out anything we had in common, other than sex. It was a quiet drive, but it didn't bother me after some time. We listened to a crummy mixed tape she had—bad recordings of Indigo Girls, Sarah McLachlan and Ani DiFranco. If I had a nickel for every girl that subsisted musically on one of those three acts, I could put myself through a normal school.

So while we rolled down the highway, I was thinking more and more about how sweet it would feel to have a little action with her, and the more I thought about it the more I couldn't stop thinking about it. Pretty soon I was at the point where something had to happen or I thought I might die. She wore this short suede miniskirt, and I kept glancing over at her legs. When we were ten minutes out of Basseville my arousal peaked, and the need seemed imminent. I had this outrageous hard-on, like a pulsing beacon to the crotch of my pants. Without thinking too much about it, like we'd already discussed it, I reached over and put my hand between her thighs. Her response was short and to the point, like any good soldier.

"We'll stop and have sex," she said.

"Full marks there for initiative and decisiveness," I said. "Critical Requirement No.7 of Being an Officer is above the line."

"Not talking about the Army means not talking about the Army. I just need you to fuck me, Kempt."

"There's an abandoned farmhouse two clicks from my place," I said. I'd been thinking about going there since we passed Brockville.

"Nobody lives there?" She cupped her hand over my crotch.

"No. I don't think so," I said weakly. There was that familiar ache. Neither of us could wait, and neither of us could even pretend to fight it. It was all about logistics now.

"You drive us there," she said, pulling to the shoulder. She slid over to the passenger's side as I got out and walked around. By the time I had the car in gear, she had my fly open and was giving me a hummer. With this buzzing noise in my head, I drove. I drove like I was driving a goddamn tractor, barely keeping it on the road, but finally I pulled up the old dirt driveway and parked out of view from the highway. When I parked, she didn't even try to kiss me; she leaned over my seat and hit the recline. I shot back and she went back to work with her mouth. She was a genius. She was in complete control.

She paused every so often and then halted completely, afraid that I'd come before we could have sex. She turned around and lifted her skirt around her waist, and I pulled this big, black silk thong off of her, down the length of her tanned, fleshy legs. I had the sense that I was on a mission, that I had a definite objective.

We moved into this complicated position, and I went at her with my tongue and two hands and all my limited knowledge until she screamed, and bucked her hips up high. Her ass and thighs were suspended for a moment, her flesh heaved and quivered over my face.

We clambered awkwardly into the back seat and I ripped her shirt off and she undid her bra. I asked her if she had a condom.

"No," she moaned, pulling my hips towards her, "but it's all right, I'm on the pill."

I kissed her then, for the first time, and tasted her clean lips. She shoved her tongue inside my mouth, moaning, then pulled it out and gave my face and cheeks these quick, little licks.

"I'm clean."

"Okay. Me too," I said. I didn't care if I wasn't. I didn't care if she wasn't. She obviously didn't care, either—we were too far gone to care. Halfway to the finish line is a bad time to look for your shoes. I moved, found her, and then I fell apart.

"Fuck me deep and quick," she said.

My God did that woman have a womb! Soft and warm and squishy. Her womb was, as the Kama Sutra would say, of the cow-elephant persuasion. I'd like to say we made love eight ways from Sunday, but things just fell apart.

"What's up?" she said.

"It's been a while, I don't know," I said. "It just left me."

"C'mon Kempt. I'm counting on you."

I lay on top of her, sweaty with shame, thinking suddenly about the Girlfriend, who hadn't seemed like much of a problem before. Now Ruth was lying between us. I wanted to get off Tina and go home and shower and never speak to her again. I wanted to call Ruth. Then Ruth drifted away, and I felt empty, and light. It was warm in the car and the windows were fogged up. I listened to Tina's breathing, and her heart. I turned my head and found her full, pink nipple and pulled it softly with my lips. I closed my eyes and sucked.

"Oh Jesus," Tina said, rising. "I'm not here to nurse you, Kempt." She opened the passenger door and pushed me out, then hopped out herself, pulling her skirt down with one hand while reaching for her shirt with the other.

I pulled up my pants and walked up a hill to a patch of soft grass in a clearing by the old boarded-up farmhouse and watched her drive away. The sun was warm but there was an October chill in the air and I could smell the leaves that had already turned and fallen. I had this sick, worried feeling in my stomach, fearful that Ruth would find out, fearful that Tina would tell everyone I was a lousy lay. A flaccid soldier.

I went home and spent Thanksgiving shit-faced with my old man.

Conduct Prejudice
to Good Order

I took the CFB Kingston bus back to the College. Tina arrived back in November Flight halls about the same time—I saw her come in with her bags. I could hear her keys jingling, and feel her trying to get my attention. I ignored it.

My old man had given me a stainless steel flask when I was home and it was filled with Cragganmore eleven-year-old scotch. I nursed that while Mack talked about his mom and how they'd had a wonderful weekend together. His mom had given him new glasses and a *cowboy hat*, for crying out loud. His parents were split and his dad was pretty much out of the picture. Mack sure loved his old lady.

"It was a great weekend," Mack said. "Mom's not even like my mom—she's like my best friend!"

"I believe you," I said.

"It was a wonderful weekend," Mack said for the twentieth time. I wanted to ask him if he'd had sex with his mom. There were little beads of sweat on his upper lip and his eyes looked huge behind those new glasses. I was an imposter in that room, especially since recruit term was over. I went to the mess and ate dinner alone, then I took a walk around the point and finished off the scotch from the flask. I wanted to go some place and act natural, or not act at all—where I wouldn't have to think about what impressions people were getting from me, and what the consequences of those impressions would be.

I slept and woke up for PT and went to classes after breakfast. In class I thought about lunch and after lunch I thought about dinner until rugby practice, and after dinner I'd take a walk around the point. I did this every day for weeks. I couldn't seem to focus on schoolwork and was often sleepy. Solving calculus problems seemed pedantic and unnecessary. My academic advisor sent me several warnings about my increasing absences from my Engineering classes. I wrote Ruth only once, to tell her things were fine, that I missed her, etc. She was in the Netherlands getting high. I gathered that much from a postcard she sent.

I usually ate on my own at the mess, now that we didn't have to form up and go in a group. The other cadets seemed to go in larger groups, or in twos and threes. It's not that I didn't want to eat with the others—it's just that I found myself alone most of the time.

My simple routine made it bearable, and nobody paid me any mind until I flunked half my midterms. To whip me into shape they shipped me stateside with Seven Squadron for Remembrance Day Parade. While half the cadet wing got sent to the Hill in Ottawa for parade, the other half stayed in Kingston for a ceremony by the Arch and a piss-up at the Legion. Not me, though. I was on a coach bound for Arlington National Cemetery.

Seven Squadron was Wolfe Squadron, after Major-General James Wolfe. Back in the day, on the Plains of Abraham that is, they had the true thin red line, only two men deep. Armed with Brown Bessies, they pulled off what Sir John Fortescue called "the most perfect volley ever fired on a battlefield." Wolfe ordered his men to hold their fire until the enemy was within forty paces. The recruit handbook states that Wolfe quoted Thomas Gray's "Elegy Written in a Country Churchyard" as he lay dying: "The paths of glory lead but to the grave." Sometimes I thought I'd like to go back in time to see old Wolfe sprawled out on the battlefield and give him a few words before he passed on. I'd hold his head and whisper in his ear: "Hello, *bonjour*. Goodbye, *au revoir!*"

My going down to Virginia had nothing to do with Wolfe Squadron, though. They'd been chosen to represent RMC because their drill was so keen. When their muster came up short, my Squadron Commander kindly offered my services. I guess he figured that rubbing shoulders on parade with a squadron full of keeners could only help my slack and idle body.

The Americans put us up in a hotel on base. Army stuff everywhere I turned—heaps and heaps of it. They must have more kit on that base than we have in all of Canada. The mess was as big as a warehouse, and the food was worthy of a decent hotel.

The service itself took place close to President Kennedy's grave. While I stood there at attention beside JFK's bones, a white-robed padre belted out a prayer in a sober voice. A first-year I knew from Seven Squadron played "The Last Post." I looked up at the Cross of Sacrifice. It was something else, boy. Imposing! It stood seven metres high and was five metres long, with a bronze sword imposed on the face. It must have weighed three tons, easy. I had a mild panic attack just looking up at it. The brainchild of King's government, it was erected in 1927 to honour Americans who died wearing Canadian colours. These guys came to Canada, enlisted with and fought for Canada, and died for Canada before their own country had anything to do with the Great War. One had to wonder what the hell had motivated them. But I wasn't thinking about those guys. I was thinking about Gramps lying on a beach, looking across at the remains of his fragged leg.

Military college life kept happening, but I paid as little attention to it as possible. Despite my squad com's efforts to make something out of me, by Christmas I'd flunked four exams. My squad com was a nice man, and probably a good soldier. I could tell that every time I spoke with him, he struggled with an urge to shake me and scream "Wake up!" He didn't have much of a poker face. I wasn't fitting into the program, and both of us were baffled as to why.

The night before our holiday-leave passes kicked in, I went out on the town with the rest of N Flight. It was best to stick together outside college grounds, because we were dead giveaways in our number-four dress blues. There was always a pile of Queen's students revving for battle, so we moved in packs. It was rare to see an RMC cadet on his own.

The large crew of us got shit-faced at Dollar Bill's, then we split up and I drank with Wommersely, Weiland, Gaze and Mann at Cocamo's. It was hard to talk to those guys with the dance music pumping, and they talked a bunch about planes and motorcycles, which I know nothing about. I maxed out my brand-new credit card to be a big shot and pay for all their drinks, and then took off on my own. I walked up Princess Street to AJ's Hangar, looking for a fight the whole way. I wanted to get beat up badly. At AJ's I paid $20 cover to see Sloan play. They were already into their last set but I would have paid double.

I got a few looks, on account of my uniform, haircut and posture, but I didn't give two pisses about that.

"What are you doing here all by your lonesome, soldier?" the bartender said.

"Just because I'm in the goddamn Army doesn't mean I can't enjoy a goddamn rock show," I said. He shrugged and bought me a drink. I was pretty buzzed at that point, but at that nice level where I could still hear and enjoy the music without being self-conscious. The drawback of being buzzed like that was that it never lasts, and I end up completely sideways.

After the show, I stood in place for about five minutes, amazed at what I'd just heard. I was thinking about buying a guitar, maybe taking some lessons, when I noticed that I'd been semi-surrounded by a group of girls. They looked like Queen's frosh, and all of them were stunningly hot.

One of them, a girl with green eyes and chestnut hair, smiled and something took me. There were no further thoughts of how I could be a rock star—only of how I could get next to this girl and stay there for as long as possible.

She introduced herself and pulled me over to a table with the others, and they ordered fancy drinks. It turns out they had all been through high school together in Perth, and had all come to Queen's to live in the same house and continue their studying and partying together. They asked about the Army, and the college, and my uniform and whatnot.

At first I couldn't believe my good fortune, but then I saw that they weren't really attentive listeners, and their eyes kept roaming the dance floor and the bar. My uniform, being different, was just another beacon to their table. I was there to draw attention and curiosity.

I didn't mind, though; it seemed like a fair trade to me. I even managed to speak to the green-eyed girl some. She studied psychology but was thinking of switching into world religions. She was an only child and wanted to work with orphans. This girl was an open dreamer, her life was out of a storybook. Every time she said something, she'd smile, and every time she smiled it didn't matter a damn to me what she'd said—I agreed with her. Part of me wanted me to snap out of it, but I couldn't leave her side.

The girls got me hammered on sugary drinks and then took turns dancing with me, and eventually I think they all left with other guys—the guys they had presumably come to the bar to get.

I walked back to the college, weaving down Princess Street and across the causeway. I thought about going for a swim, but I could barely stand up so I stumbled into bed. Mack had gone home early for the holidays so I had the room to myself.

I lay down with my uniform half-unbuttoned, and the spins started. I turned the light on, but the spins were still there every time I closed my eyes, so I stripped down to my gitch and forced myself to puke in the sink.

I crawled out the window, more out of habit than anything else, and went for a swim off the point. When I came back in I brushed my teeth for about half an hour while taking a hot shower, and then put on some clean sweats. I almost felt like I could have another drink when I finally lay down in bed. I recalled the green-eyed girl at the bar, and while I was trying to memorize her face it became clear that those girls were using my uniform no more than I was. They had just used it for a couple of hours. I had been using it day in and day out for months.

Then I remembered that Tina Terranova was across the hall, probably sleeping. Like mine, her roommate had already departed on leave. I hadn't said five words to Tina since Thanksgiving weekend, but now I kept playing it over and over in my mind. I wanted to make it up to her; more specifically I wanted to redeem myself.

Eventually I got up and went across the hall and opened her door. The light from the hallway fell across her bed and she rubbed her eyes. "What the hell are you doing Kempt?"

I didn't know exactly what I was doing. I said nothing, but crawled over the foot of her bed and put my head between her legs. I reached up and felt her tits. She had a dark silk camisole on, and matching silk boxer shorts. She was warm and heavy from sleep, and there was sweat at the small of her back.

"Come up here," she said.

I moved up and I kissed her and must have passed out. I came to later and went back to lay down in my bunk. The spins had gone, and I slept long and hard.

The next morning, late, I took the military bus from CFB Kingston to Ottawa International. I sat in the back to try and sleep off some of the hangover. I should have paid the thirty bones for the public bus—it would have been worth it to avoid wearing uniform, but I'd spent so much money on drinking, and I wanted to get Ailish something nice for Christmas. I had already bought Mom oven mitts, like I got her every year. I'd bought Dad a bottle of Jamaican overproof rum.

Thankfully, the bus was nearly empty. There were two or three Air Force officers from Trenton, and several cadets I didn't know. That was one good thing about base transport. On the public bus there was always some guy—often an unwashed ex-con—that would wink conspiratorially and suggest that if he didn't get to smoke a cigarette soon, he would have to open a can of whoop-ass.

In this respect the CF bus wasn't so bad. There were just a

handful of Air Force staff weenies going home for the holidays. Christmas in the air.

I thought of Ruth, and then right away remembered Tina and last night. What kind of guy was I, I thought. Where had I learned to treat women like that, I wanted to know. Where had I ever learned to treat myself like that. I felt a tremendous guilt, yet in thinking about it I had a hard-on at the same time. Then I got angry with Ruth.

The problem with Ruth was I couldn't picture her without seeing some buff ski instructor named Hans carrying her up the Alps to the log cabin he built with his bare hands. And I was sure that Ruth and Hans only ever make it halfway through their cheese and chutney plate before he gives it to her on the bearskin rug by the glowing hearth.

I needed more sleep. I couldn't seem to get a sense of what was real; I don't even know if there *are* bears in the Alps.

Eventually I slept soundly, and when I woke up I had drool all over my cheek and arm and we were already pulling into the airport. Two captains looked over their shoulders at me and whispered. I guess they figured flaking out and drooling on your uniform is un-officer-like behaviour. It is, as they say, Conduct Prejudice to Good Order. I wanted to ask them, "So how are those desks you're flying?" Instead I sat up, feigned shock, and pretended like I'd lost my bearings. I straightened out my tunic, and they went back to discussing the sorry state of the Sea King helicopters.

Super 8

Dad picked me up. In the car I couldn't wait, and pulled out the rum. I wanted to show him it right away.

"Whoa—the strong stuff," Dad said. "I guess we'll have to have a 'welcome home' eggnog."

"Yesiree," I said. I can't stand eggnog.

"Good to have you home, Herb. Welcome home."

Welcome home indeed. I was greeted at the door with the smell of shortbread and the light sounds of Bing Crosby. A little ball of flour tackled my ankles.

"HEY! Could this be … is it … Oh my goodness! It is! Ailish! Did you shrink since Thanksgiving?"

"She refuses to grow," said Mom, hugging me. "How are you, dear?"

"Ailish! Watch his uniform!" Dad said.

"It's okay, Dad. Dry cleaning's free."

"She has to be more careful," he said. He went to the cabinet and poured drinks.

"You look sharp Herb," Mom said. "That blue suits you."

"Thanks."

Ailish stared at her hands guiltily, rubbed them together.

"Care for a bevvy?" Dad said. I saw he had poured two doubles.

"Sure." I lifted Ailish up and sat her at the table. "You better help Mommy finish," I whispered, "and make me a super big one."

"Put your bags in the laundry room and come see the tree." Mom said. She sounded a bit like she was giving drill instructions.

The living room was busy. One corner had the ever-growing Dickens Village, and another the nativity scene. I counted four wreaths and at least five miniature sleighs filled with candy. Eight tiny reindeer everywhere. Mom must have cleaned White Rose out of candles. She kept getting new decorations each year but refused to throw anything out.

The tree was packed with shiny balls and Christmas lights, half of them those annoying blinky ones.

I noted that Gertie's favourite ornament was hung at the bottom of the tree, but I didn't have the heart to ask who'd hung it. Dad came in, handed me an eggnog. It looked pretty watery.

"What is this—a triple?"

"Merry Christmas, Herb. Good to have you back."

"It's good to be here." I said. I wanted a shower.

Ruth's flight got in two days before Christmas. Dad let me use the Datsun to pick her up, but he handed me the keys like he was doing me a big favour, even though he wasn't using it anyway.

I got nervous as hell on the airport parkway. It'd been five months since I'd last seen her, but it seemed like a lot longer. I thought it might be possible that she wouldn't like me anymore— she didn't even know me anymore. I kept picturing the last time we talked, and I knew that I wouldn't say the same things now.

And who was to say Ruth wouldn't have changed? Her and that goddamn Hans, specimen of the master race. In the parking lot I had a hell of a time composing myself; after I put money in the meter, I sat in the truck and told myself over and over that *There is no Hans.*

I went inside to buy a pack of smokes. I wasn't smoking full-time yet, but I would be eventually. I went outside for a hot one and fed the meter. When I went back in her plane had touched down and she was clearing Customs.

Ruth stepped through those automatic doors that whoosh open. We made eye contact and somehow I moved across the space between us. We were face-to-face, smiling, but I felt tired and she looked tired.

"Hey," she said.

"Hey, girl," I said. It was awkward, and I wasn't sure if I should hug her or kiss her or what. I took her bags. "It's good to see you."

"You too," she said.

"How was your flight?"

"Fine," she said. "It was good."

"Good, good. Okay. I'm parked outside."

"Okay. Thanks for coming to get me." She looked at me funny.

"Sure," I said. We walked out together. After I started the truck I couldn't stand it anymore, it was like there was this thick wall of ice between us. So I grabbed her and kissed her.

"Wow," Ruth said.

I kissed her again, and it turned into a pretty heavy make-out session right there in short-term parking, with the engine idling.

"I had a bad case of nerves there for a sec," I said.

"I know," she said. "I couldn't sleep on the plane."

"It's weird. Why's it feel so weird?"

"I don't know. I think I've put on weight."

Girls. You could be talking about anything at all and then, from way out of left field, they'll bring up their weight. Of course, now that she'd mentioned it, she looked like she had put on a couple of pounds.

"Don't be ridiculous," I said.

"You don't think so?"

"I really missed you."

"Me too."

"Do you know that the French would say *You missed me* when they really mean *I missed you*," I said. Ruth laughed.

"I was living in France, Herbie!"

"Oh yeah." I had nothing to say for a minute, so we kissed again. Then I put my hand up her shirt, and slipped under her bra. Her nipple hardened.

"Hmm. When do your folks expect you in?"

"It doesn't really matter."

"Are you hungry?"

"Not really."

"I'll get some snacks," I said.

We stopped off at the closest Loblaws to pick up strawberries, kiwi, brie and a baguette. Ruth waited in the truck.

"I'm having a bit of culture shock," she said. How does someone have culture shock in their own country, I wanted to know.

After Loblaws I drove to the LC and got a bottle of Wolf Blass, spent a fortune on the grey label. I felt like a lunatic, racing all over the west end. I wished I'd *planned* something for her homecoming—instead I'd spent the last three days in front of the TV.

When I got back in the truck, we didn't even speak. Without even asking her I drove right to a Super 8 Motel. I had to run my debit card into overdraft for the room, which meant that Ailish wouldn't get a present this year.

In Room 101 we drew the blinds, hit the lights, and were undressing each other under the covers before you could say *Welcome home.* When my hands got hold of her underwear I had to turn the bedside light on.

"Don't," she said. "I don't want the lights on. I'm all fat now."

I could tell her a hundred times that she was a rake and I'm sure she still wouldn't believe me. But what underwear! Only, this wasn't underwear: it was a divinely braided string of silk, a white silk g-string, so delicate that I felt it would disintegrate between my callused fingers if I rubbed it.

"Do you like it?" Ruth said.

"God, they must have some great panty shops in France."

"*Panties!*" she roared.

Then something crossed my mind: "How many times have you worn these?"

"Just today. I bought them for you, not for me."

"Oh is that so," I said. "How's Hans?"

"What!? Could you please turn off the light? I'm all fat."

Oh sure she'd gained a few. Chocolate and cheese. I could tell from the extra tension on her bra strap. And her thighs were slightly more ample than they'd been before. She was sexier than ever.

"You are amazing. Really. A total babe. I mean it."

"Shut up," she said.

I went downtown, swam away on her honeystream. I found a Zen-like consciousness within the art of cunnilingus. With a nifty Venus Butterfly, I dug up deep groans. Eventually I couldn't take it slow anymore, and hammered home my resolve. We peaked together, I came inside her, and said foolish things. During orgasm I think I said I wanted to die for her.

After some time we ate the brie and the fruit.We had sex again and then napped peacefully, drying out. Every so often I would wake up and reach out for her, pull her in close to me. After some time we slept deeply, only to awake in the darkness, half-consciously groping. We rediscovered the familiar warmth of each other, although this time it was much slower. I wanted to stay like that forever, my mouth pressed into her neck. I had never known sex to be so all-consuming, and felt at times as if she and I were standing back, capable of watching ourselves move and taste and touch.

When it was all over, I was a little down. It was depressing to think that that was it—there in the Super 8—that was as good as it was ever going to get for us. But somehow I knew it was.

Navy Bay

After my night at the motel, I spent a night out with Icky and Won-ton. The next morning I slept in, and woke up on the couch at 17:00, surprised to find myself at home. What day is it? What time is it? What happened last night? What did I say? How did I get home? The usual questions. I dug up fragments from my tortured head, pieced them together gingerly.

Things had been uncomfortable between me and the boys until we all got on the sauce. I half remembered crying to Won-ton, or maybe Icky, about the Army and/or Gertie, but it was hazy. I recalled punching a hole in drywall somewhere. That's all I could remember.

Mom came down the stairs all gussied up.

"Are you ready, Verbal?"

"Are we going dancing?"

Dad came downstairs in a suit. "I'll warm up the minivan."

"Mass is at 5:30, mister," Mom said. "Didn't I tell you we were going to the 5:30?"

Ailish skipped into the room in a frilly dress. I was still in the same goddamn clothes I'd worn the night before.

"I think I'll pass. I've got a big head on me today."

"Very funny."

"I don't, um, go to Mass anymore, Mom," I said. She gave me a look.

"It's Christmas, Verbal. I don't care what you do when you're not at home, but you can stand to go to Mass once a year." We stood facing each other, a showdown.

"That'd be hypocrisy, Mom. Then I'd be one of those just-in-case Christians you make fun of."

"You're my son. It's different," she said. I shrugged. Suddenly I was eager to get back to the College.

I had to pick up Cecil Witherspoon, who was flying in from Winnipeg, at the airport in my new van. A Christmas present to end all Christmas presents, the van was already my new and real home. Mom and Dad had spent my RESPs on the van since the government was picking up the tab for my education. Hard to believe, but they spent my entire college fund on a custom VW bus.

It had been Ailish's idea. She'd found the plans for Gertie's dream vehicle when painting in her room, and Dad got the same guy that worked on Buttercup to put a new engine in a vintage, immaculate body. He'd followed Gertie's plans to the letter: purple metal flake paint job, deep purple shag rug, sink, toilet, stove, icebox. The table in the back converted to a bed. It had a CD player and, get this, an 8-track stereo. Mom had commissioned Icky to find 8-tracks—you should see the selection: Sabbath, John Denver, Neil Young, The Beatles, Cream, Zeppelin, Zappa. How he managed to find a copy of Beastie Boys' *Paul's Boutique* is beyond me—that must have cost a fortune itself.

Cecil's flight got in right on time, and we drove back to RMC, feeling pretty swanky in my new ride. We smoked butts and shot the breeze.

"Santa was good to you," Cecil said, looking through the 8-tracks.

"God," I said, "if Gertie could only see this thing, she'd die. She'd probably come home right away."

"I would," Cecil said. "Fuckrights. This van is the business."

Cecil Witherspoon was by far the most unlikely RMC cadet ever. He was in Eight Squadron, or Mackenzie Squadron, and was the most bitter human being you'd ever care to meet. He hated the military, he hated Engineering. He loathed his squadron, and the thought of RMC made him want to puke. It was a wonder he could get up in the morning. It was always hard for me to put my finger on what motivated Cecil, but whatever it was, it was something powerful.

Cecil never said anything lightly, and I suppose that's why I respected him so much. That and because he was so bitter. And his sense of humour was magnificent, although it was also quite bitter. I never felt too bad after listening to one of his tirades. When I first spoke to him we were marching across the parade square, on our way to class. He was a smaller guy, just over five-foot, and was marching in front of me just as casually as one can march. Almost *strolling*.

"Hey little man," I said. "Nice ass." He whipped his head around.

"Thanks, buckshot," he said. "You want to pump it full of cream?"

"Steady-up," I said.

Cecil also had great taste in music, which set him apart from ninety-eight percent of the cadet wing immediately. He was born and raised in the Prairies, and while this would depress most people, Cecil would get weepy with longing just by talking about wheat, for crying out loud. What he saw in the Prairies escapes me, but when somebody loves something that much, you have to respect him for it.

We blasted *Paranoid* on the way back to Kingston. I was feeling great until I took the Old Fort Henry exit off the 401 and snaked down Highway 15.

It hit me suddenly. Coming down the hill was enough to make me queasy, and when I entered the gates, I started shaking and sweating. I passed the guardhouse and parked, then raced to get to the bathroom on time. I puked for a while, then unloaded my gear. Cecil didn't say anything, but from the greenish luminescence to his face, I could tell he felt the same.

Cowboy Mack was already back from North Bay, sitting in *my* fucking desk and reading a Tom Clancy novel. He was wearing another brand-new cowboy hat. There was a picture of his mom on his desk. I couldn't stand to look at him, so I went to Cecil's room to smoke.

Cecil was already unpacked and sat strumming a Fender Strat with a starburst pattern when I came in.

"You miss me already?" Cecil said. "I've barely unpacked."

"I think my roommate screws his mother," I said.

"Yep." He plucked a tune by The Stone Roses.

"Nice guitar. Is that 'Sugar Spun Sister'?"

"Yep," he said. "I've decided to study rock and roll. It's for my mental health."

"Do you have any more butts?"

"Desk drawer. Ashtray's under the sink." Cecil hated himself for smoking, but loved to smoke.

There was a Zippo and a pack of Marlboro Lights in the drawer. Cecil lived very much by the motto "A place for everything and everything in its place." His penchant for order and cleanliness bordered on fanaticism. One time, during Christmas exams, I dropped by for a study break and found him bleaching his walls.

I smoked for a while, listening to him play, grateful that I didn't have to hang out with Mack the Whack. Cecil had his own room, which was a luxury for a first-year. After a while he put the guitar down and lit a smoke for himself. We'd probably have at least one more cigarette apiece, but he put the lighter and the pack back in his drawer anyway.

"I noticed you got that old feeling when we came through the gates," Cecil said. "This shit hole's going to drive us around the bend, I swear to God."

"I threw up," I said. He nodded.

"You have to tow the line, Verbal."

"I'm failing four courses. The squad com told me I'm hanging on by a thread."

"You have to watch it, man."

"Yeah," I said.

"I'm serious Verbal. They'll boot you out of here if you seem like a lost cause. What the fuck are you doing here if you're just going to get hoofed?"

"I know," I said. "I don't want to talk about it."

We smoked for a while. Cecil's cigarette dangled like punctuation from his lower lip, an exclamation mark to all things terse and unhappy. I couldn't stand sitting still anymore so I got up and started poking around his room, sifting through his CDs.

"You're like a fishbowl, Verbal. Always shit moving inside."

"Hmm." I put The Inbreds' *Kombinator* in the player and got another cigarette from his drawer. Cecil was already cleaning the ashtray.

I wanted to get out of that place so bad I couldn't stand it. I turned the stereo off and threw the van keys in his lap.

"That's what I like about you Verbal. You know, but you don't have to say."

"Yeah? Well I'll say it anyway: You want to go play thirsty-boy?"

"How's my drinking, Mama!" he said. In the van he pulled out a big stash of BC weed and rolled a fat one.

"I haven't smoked since Gertie left," I said. He lit the joint with the van lighter and passed it to me.

"I christen you Herbal," Cecil said. "We burn this down for your sister, Herbal."

On weekends I started living inside my van, trying to ignore my uniform. The old headaches were back, so when they were bad, I drank. And when it wasn't the bottle, it was the leaf.

I scraped through first year, barely. I wrote supplemental exams in Calculus, Physics, Chemistry.

"You passed by a cunt hair," Cecil said. We had to spend the summer at RMC for Second Language Training, but passed the bulk of our time buying Labatt 50 on tap at the Toucan.

There was windsurfing when I wanted it. There was mountain biking, too. And there was soccer in the early mornings and rugby in the evening. There was always swimming—jumping off the pier into the brown silt of Lake Ontario. One day I swallowed too much water while trying to windsurf, and the next day my tongue was black. I ran to MIR, imagining I had the plague.

"You've been swimming in Navy Bay," the military doctor said.

"Yes," I said.

"Don't swim there," he said. "You'll be lucky if you can have kids."

So I stopped windsurfing, and started smoking a pack a day.

Canada Day found me in Ottawa, fumbling towards happiness with eyes dilated from magic mushrooms. Won-ton and Icky arrived in Won-ton's Jeep to drive me and Ruth to various parties. Won-ton donned a big Canadian Flag, wrapped around his neck like a cape. He had twitchy hands—they shook non-stop. Icky handed me a big bag of shrooms, for free. I forgot I was in the military; everything was so far gone, it was lovely.

At our first cocktail party I gobbled more shrooms and disappeared without a word to lock myself in the master bathroom. The shower was definitely a woman's shower—soothing pink coral everywhere and fluffy, clean towels. What started me laughing as I stripped naked in front of the mirror were these huge, pastel plastic flowers all over the bathroom. The overhead fan moved them softly on small breezes, so they looked alive. They spoke:

"Smile," they said. Smile! "Come on, get clean, get happy!" they sang. I hopped in the shower, talking to the flowers, knowing it wasn't real, but scrubbed down with every available girlie product. When I was done I smelled delicious, and I thought there was no way this trip could go sour. But over the course of the evening I took more and more, and in the end you always get what you paid for.

Before we left for Icky's I plucked a yucca tree in the piano room, leaving a mound of green leaves in the centre of the floor.

How could Ruth be so distant when I smelled so clean and happy? I giggled with the flowers in my mind—less tangible but more real.

We raced along the canal in the Jeep, flags whipping around our heads. We are really strangers. I can see that Won-ton is so proud of his Jeep with the roof off, the stereo loud. We think we're having a good time, I thought, but we are all of us only ignorant, and suffering.

Ruth was trying to bring me down, but I didn't care because for once I was not thinking about making my bed or shining my shoes or ironing Vs into my goddamn wool pants. I scream and holler, and Ruth stares. Ruth knows everything, and has ever since I couldn't get it up to make it with her, since she grimaced at my skid-marked gitch on the floor, smelled my sour underarms, watched me vomit beside her bed. Ruth knows I'm ripe, going off. Right on the edge.

Sometimes I think I'll make it up to her. Sometimes I think I'm too late.

We left Icky's almost as soon as we got there because it's small and cramped but mostly because Icky had all jets burning. He rolled a fatty to slow down the speed he snorted because the shrooms hadn't kicked in yet. I stole weed from Won-ton's friend Hoppy Bloom because I was sick to death of hash. I ended by blowing a gagger with some stranger who was all alone on his doorstep for Canada Day, just watching the misfits pass.

Somewhere along the line, I hook up with Cecil in the crowd of hundreds of thousands. We don't find it odd to bump into one another. I'm jealous because he's drunk and confident: Cecil seems like he's got a plan. I have no plan. I am rudderless, without a compass. I smoke more cigarettes, and Cecil comments on my yellow fingers.

I culminate in downtown crowds, thousands, millions up close, the dirt and the smell and the shadows are penetrating my happy shower.

From the sky: a rolling sea, confused "O Canada," a sea of drunk reds and dirty whites. Cecil says amazing things to me— things that are true and pertinent, but I don't remember any of them. I remember back into the night, hours ago, eons ago, and that there was a fight.

Inside the crowd we walk, a gaggle of us holding hands, following Won-ton back to Hoppy Bloom's for shroom tea and Mexican Pizza. Won-ton drinks a glass of skim milk.

"What true Mexican ever ate pizza in his life?" I ask Cecil. "Where's Ruth?"

"You don't remember? She's gone Verb—you had it out on Parliament Hill."

Blam! Won-ton is hit so hard from the tea, he blacks out and hits the floor in convulsions.

I don't panic. I try to remember the first aid I learned in the Army but all I can do is hold his head with one hand and eat my slice of pizza with the other. I watch him puke milk, and there's blood gushing from his nose.

I'm terrified but I still want to eat my pizza. I tell Cecil that soon I'll do no more drugs, that I'm cleaning up. I'm going to get healthy, I tell him.

I stay awake through the night holding Won-ton's head, waking him up from time to time to ask him if he's in a coma from the impact of bashing his head against the linoleum. It's the least I can do.

A Foolish Whimsy

My lacklustre academic performance continued, and continued, and by my third autumn at the college, I decided I was tired of trying to just keep my head above water, and that it was time for a change. The Dean of Engineering sent me letters through inter-campus mail, and he spoke to my professors on my behalf, though I never asked him to. Nobody cared too much about the state of my academic career until I put in a request for a program transfer to the English Department. Overnight, I became the Dean's pet project.

"I can empathize," the Dean said. "I too can appreciate the desire to study literature. Books are important—literature is nice. I don't mind telling you that I once suffered from the same whimsy as you—during my college days I even penned a few verses for the school paper. But my post requires me to inform you that by voluntarily transferring out of the RMC Engineering program, you are passing up on some very important—even lucrative—opportunities."

In the end, I left his office without his signature of approval, which I required in order to transfer out. I was only failing three courses and he was determined to bring me back to the flock. He called me back to his office a week later.

"The answer for you is to get involved," he said. "I spoke with your professors. I suggest you take an active role in the upcoming bridge-building competition. It is precisely the type of atmosphere you need to kindle the creative spirit within you. Yes! I said creative spirit—and so it is! The highest level of creativity you can aspire to is right under your nose—in this very department! You will bear witness. On graduation day, when you march through the Arch with an iron ring on your finger, you will have me to thank."

I needed another way out. By midterm I was failing four courses, which was cause enough for alarm, and then put in a transfer to Math and Physics. This was less insulting to the Dean than the complete about-face that an English Department transfer would require, so he finally assented.

The problem with Math and Physics was that I had all the same courses as in Engineering, plus an extra course in Quantum Theory and a feel-good course in Astronomy. I was issued my own telescope, but I didn't even stick around the program long enough to take it out of the box.

I applied for another transfer to Applied Science, which was approved after some minor wrangling, and found myself with considerably less of a workload. I adjusted by doing considerably less work. By the time I applied to the Dean of Science for a transfer to English, he was so fed up with my performance that he didn't even hide his glee to see me go.

"I think that's the best place for *you*." He said *you* like he was saying *your kind*. And so it was, after almost a year of effort and consistent failure, I was given a general timetable for a course of study in English Literature. It had been almost two years since I had read a real book.

80 Minutes

The greasy scrum half was feeding the scrum all day. If Carleton U players weren't such cheaters, and if the ref wasn't half-blind, we'd have put the Ravens away in the first half.

Dad and Ailish showed up just before kickoff and were on the sidelines watching me. We were stuck wobbling over ten metres of real estate in midfield, and I wasn't sure where I should be.

I look at the sidelines. One side of Dad's face hangs down, loose, and he can't use the muscles. He says he's not worried—the doctor said it may have been a small stroke or a type of palsy. Looking at him, cockeyed like that, it seems that any minute the earth will open up and reveal secrets to me; there is something I am on the verge of understanding, I am sure of it.

"What is wrong with me?" The sound of my own voice even scared me. Then I remembered what I hadn't remembered in so long—what it was like to be a kid. Did I need medication? Was I going crazy? I remembered that I used to be a smart kid, and happy, and that, as a kid, I would have pitied a guy in my position. I would have thought that a guy like me was badly off. There was no more distinguishing me from the classic military prick. In my head and my heart I felt different, but essentially I wasn't. This is something I wanted to tell somebody—but who? Christ knows if I told anybody at RMC I'd be up the hill in the base shrink's office before you could say "Prozac."

After we got off the tour bus, I warmed up with the backs on Carlton's rugby pitch, and put on the old #10 jersey. My nerves had been frayed ever since the flagpole, like I could jump out of my skin if someone looked at me sideways. I'd been having panic attacks non-stop.

I questioned how I looked in my rugby gear. I had turned my collar inside the neck of my jersey to look unique and tough, yet my hands were trembling. When we started talking about strategies, I was frozen with fear—afraid to take leadership and call out a play. I felt like an imposter, that I didn't belong on the team. I asked myself then if I even liked rugby, and to my surprise I didn't know. I started playing rugby because it was a tough sport. I started playing rugby because my old man played rugby—but as far as I know, I may not even enjoy it.

I resolved to make some changes in my attitude and my behaviour. I wanted to be a force for good rather than feeling like a conduit for evil.

After the first time I got hit, I was able to concentrate a little better on the game. It's hard for me to say what Les, the coach, was thinking at that point. I'd been riding the pine a lot. I think Les put me in because I told him my old man was going to show. He probably had second thoughts when I duffed the kickoff, and it went shy of their backfield.

The moment I saw that I buggered the kick all to hell, I sprinted to their forty. I haven't got a bad set of wheels, and at that point I was more afraid of what Les was thinking than of the opposing team. The poor winger never knew what hit him. We weren't five minutes into play, and they had to call an ambulance onto the field to take the guy to the Queensway-Carleton. He was conscious but his hip was dislocated, apparently. It was a clean hit; nobody could say it was a bad tackle. But the funny thing is, I was happy he got hurt. Like his injury was a feather in my cap. I was tired of watching rugby from the sidelines. Fuck him, I thought.

And then with a pang of terror, I realized I was being that guy I didn't want to be. Again. Not even five minutes after I resolved to change. I fought the urge to go ask the paramedic if I could go to the hospital too.

"I'm going crazy," I said.

"Keep it up," said our 8-man. "That was an awesome hit."

The next play was iffy, at best. Their fly half faked a switch to the inside centre, but it was a lousy fake—he totally telegraphed it. Or maybe it was just that I could read everyone's true intentions with my new insight. The point is I didn't buy it for a second, and played the ball, not my man. He swept right and tossed it back to the fullback, who probably didn't hear the call properly because he was standing still. Maybe he was scared, I don't know. He saw me coming, and I saw his eyes and I knew he was thinking about the winger's broken hip. I barely touched him before he went down like a sack of hammers. I rolled right over him, and went down to pick up the ball.

At that moment, I was thinking how there was a new lesson in this for me—how perception can change everything. I was acutely aware of certain facts: (a) I was too timid and not practised enough to make tackles successfully, (b) that I observed myself going in too high for the tackle against the fullback, and (c) that because the opposing team thought I was a heavy-hitter due to the winger's broken hip, I was becoming a better tackler.

We were alone—me and this fullback who hit the ground so hard—for at least four seconds, and I knew I could score if only this wanker would release the fucking ball. But no, he was curled up in the fetal position, hanging on. So I punched him. Made a fist and cranked him twice, hard, on the jaw. His eyes went blank and—open sesame—the ball was mine.

I barely made it two steps before the ref blew the whistle. He called the fullback on failure to release, then turned around and called a penalty for retaliation on me. We lost twenty yards of good enemy ground.

"Jesus Christ what's wrong with me!" I cried. Only moments after I'd made a second, more determined resolve to live my life in a noble fashion—there I went punching some guy in the face. I thought I was going to break down right there on the field, which would be the worst thing to do, especially considering my old man was on the sidelines.

"Let's go Kempt!" I heard Les shout. I looked around and yelled something at our backs. Like I said, Carleton's #9 was feeding the scrum all game, and the ref must have been smoking crack not to see it. I decided I would kick the little fucker's teeth in if I had half a chance. We played on, and I ran around the field like a madman, screaming and yelling and hitting people.

When there was less than ten minutes left in the game, I scanned the sidelines to find Ailish. She was playing with some other kids. I expected her to be clutching Dad's hand and staring at me intently, almost imploringly. Dad wasn't watching the game either—he was talking to some old geezer.

I took my mouth guard out, wiped it on my shorts and stuck it in my pocket. My mouth was dry, but I spit anyway.

"I'm never drinking or doing drugs again," I said. "I'm never using girls for sex when I'm drunk, ever again," I said.

"Are you okay?" said Proctav, our scrum half.

This is a dull game, I thought. Nobody's even watching it. Then I thought about how dull the last three years had been. My classes were dull, my roommate was dull, parades were dull, inspections were dull. Being drunk was dull. Sober was dull. The only thing left was rugby, but even here nobody seemed to be paying attention. I don't know why everybody had to pay attention in my mind, but I knew that if it wasn't for rugby, I'd be on parade right now sweating in my scarlets.

Their scrum half faked the put-in once or twice. He was the team showboat—what do you expect from a white guy with dreadlocks?

"Play the ball you fucking hippie cocksucker!" I yelled. The ref gave me a warning look. I couldn't believe it myself.

Of course the scrum half fed the ball again—why change now? And the ref refused to see it. Our hooker, Haunch, was swearing like a trooper, so I knew there were punches being thrown in the scrum. Miraculously, Haunch stole the ball, which was fed back slowly, perfectly. The 8-man guarded it while Proctav guided the scrum forward expertly, checking it from rolling too far. Proctav bought us twenty yards and time to set up an offence. We were just over midfield and rolling, and our 8-man, Big Jilm, looked hungry for it, like any moment he was going to pick up and break off.

"Tabernac-hostie les boys!" I said. Any French swear word means I'm calling for the ball short side. Big Jilm faked the pickup and drew their scrum half offside, taking him out of play. Proctav reached in and grabbed the ball, and in the same fluid motion pitched it to me as he leapt through the air, to avoid a tackle from their inside flanker. I didn't even have to move my hands to catch the ball—that's how good Proctav's passes are.

But something went wrong because as soon as I had the ball, their inside centre was on top of me and I was moving way too slow to get out of his reach. Without thinking I popped it up high, a clean up-and-under right between their backs and the fullback.

I straight-armed the inside centre to keep him from bowling me over. I followed the ball, zeroing in on the fullback who was moving up for the catch. He called the mark too late. He called it with a yelp as my shoulder hit his stomach, and the air rushed out of his lungs—I could *hear* it rushing out, and he was down.

He released immediately: I had possession and lots of time— just the green green grass of home between me and my first try, ever. I slid into the end zone and touched the Mitre leather down smack between the pipes.

I closed my eyes hugging the ball and smelled the freshly cut grass of Carleton's pitch. I thought of how lucky I was to be alive, and that from here on in I'd live clean and good. I lay there until Proctav came and shook me. He told me to get up, that they needed the ball.

The Dark Side

The Department of English was tucked away on top of the Currie Building, and when I walked into my first class—Twentieth Century British Literature—I thought that I had interrupted something private. I felt like I had exposed some kind of secret.

The classroom consisted of couches and easy chairs and coffee tables. The room was carpeted, overstuffed bookshelves lined the walls and there was a television in the corner. There were five or six students in the room—all male—and they were sprawled out on the furniture holding steaming mugs of tea and a copy each of Joseph Conrad's *Victory*.

The teacher looked like he'd just stepped out of 1969. "Love-child" is the only word to describe him; my only thought was how this guy had ever secured employment at a military college. Why wasn't he teaching at, say, Trent? I had assumed up until now that all professors at the college wore suits or skirts—this guy wore old drawstring khakis and a worn fisherman's knit sweater. On top of that, his hair was past his shoulders. It was a shocker, sure—but it was my fellow cadets who floored me.

They didn't look like cadets at all. I recognized them from around campus—cadets who generally kept to themselves, and whose hair always seemed just a bit longer than the limits of regulation length. All of them in that room—every single one—had removed his shoes. Some had their stocking feet up on the couch and some wore slippers. Slippers! They had also removed their battle blouses, which wasn't so bad, but they had removed their ties as well. They were wearing civilian sweaters or cardigans. It looked like a goddamn Mister Rogers convention. I can't say why, but my first reaction was anger, and it alarmed me. I felt like marching right over to Mackenzie Building to report them all. Sure, I'd asked to study English—but this type of behaviour defied any rational explanation. What kind of cadets were these? I had already started mentally composing a memorandum to the Director of Cadets when the prof introduced himself.

"Hi, I'm Jerry. You must be Herbert."

"Officer-cadet Kempt," I said. "Transferring in."

"Well, welcome to the dark side, Officer-cadet Kempt. We're just finishing up with Conrad. Would you like a cup of chai?"

Jerry never gave a lecture. There wasn't even a blackboard in the room. Nobody seemed surprised by this—the format was more of a round-table discussion. I sat down in one of the vacant comfy chairs and loosened my tie. I thought of taking my shoes off, but then didn't want to give the impression that I was trying to fit in.

"We were just wrapping up with Axel Heyst in Joseph Conrad's *Victory*," Jerry repeated. "It is almost as if the father-son relationship defines his experience on the island—and the concept of 'island' is significant—and he accepts rather than questions the events which lead him to what he *knows* will be his demise. The tension between the family members reflects the danger of son becoming father—this is what we see when Luke is in peril of joining the dark side of the Force. Each son takes a lesson from Darth Vader, as does each father."

Right when Jerry said that is when I had the sickening urge to jump up and punch him in the mouth. I was thinking that I should probably transfer to the History Department when one of the cadets spoke up.

"The archetypal relationship is almost laid out for us on a silver platter. Of 'the barbed hook, baited with the illusion of progress,' Heyst says 'And I, the son of my father, have been caught too, like the silliest fish of them all.'"

"Exactly," Jerry said. "We—none of us—can escape our parents. Especially our fathers."

"Jesus Christ," I said. I was sweating bullets.

"Exactly!" Jerry screamed, pointing his finger in the air. "Him too!"

The discussion continued, and I heard some of it through waves of nausea. I had to keep reminding myself that they were talking about a book—a book I hadn't even read. *It's just a book,* I kept thinking. On the sly, I checked my pulse—putting two fingers against my carotid artery. I worried that my heart might stop beating any minute. I wasn't even sure what they were talking about, but I had this deep feeling that if I paid too much attention I'd pass out.

"If Axel Heyst's actions are unchecked by any sort of self-consciousness, the suffering of an overly self-conscious mind is implied. Heyst's memory reminds him sharply of his failed attempt for guidance. His father advises him to 'cultivate that form of contempt which is called pity,' and that, if Heyst is anything, he is 'as pitiful as all the rest.' This pity is something his father cultivated in himself, and it is what prompts him to leave Axel with the final words, 'Look on—make no sound.' This queer deathbed advice can be marked as the signal for Heyst's withdrawal from society; the image, or voice, of his father leaves him alienated and strongly distrustful of his surroundings. This striking admission of alienation is what prompts him to live in isolation, in the present—almost like a dark Buddha—with a deep regard for his father's conception of truth."

After class I called a cab to the Toucan and waited at the guardhouse, smoking butts. I had just enough cash for several pitchers, enough to do the trick.

Stranger

A trick I learned in the Army: if you want to stop thinking about food or smokes or booze, think about sex. Another trick I learned in the army: if you want to stop thinking about sex, think about food and smoke and drinking more. It's a simple plan that has helped me avoid many unpleasant feelings. These things occupy my senses, dull the ragged edges of being that peep up from time to time to tell me my life is passing me by. Getting involved in my body seems to take me out of my mind—at least for a little while.

In England, for instance, during an RMC rugby trip to Sandhurst, Big Jilm got caught pissing on the Proctav's calves in the shower. Proctav turned to piss on Big Jilm and hit the hooker, Haunch, with his stream. Haunch turned toward Proctav, put his hand under his own ass, and squeezed out a dark log.

"Haunch! No! You've gone too far!" Jilm yelled. I bolted out of the shower just in time to avoid the shit-flinging. Haunch was also the guy who bought an inflatable, fuckable sheep in Soho. He went on to get decorated for bravery after a tour as a platoon commander on active UN service in Bosnia.

We're always proving ourselves to ourselves, even when we're sick of it. Being a soldier in peacetime is a strange job. Even if it kills us, we'll prove ourselves to ourselves, to each other, to our dead fathers—even if it kills us. And along the way, we'll simplify death—we'll reduce it until we're comfortable with it—even if it means holding a turd in our hands.

Stocker once gave me the opportunity to prove myself during a Brock Squadron mess dinner. Some fat Air Force general was the guest of honour, decked out lavishly in his medals, his beautiful trophy wife within arm's reach. A good sport, the old fatty joined us for a game of crud after dinner and played balls out. I suppose he still had something to prove, too.

During the dinner proper, when it was forbidden to leave the table until the port had been passed and the guest of honour led the wave to the heads, Stocker scrawled something on a napkin and passed it to me.

KEMPT! SITUATION: Factions of Brass are guarding the head table from November Flight infiltration of the Guest of Honour. MISSION: Using stealth and whatever tactics you deem necessary, you will infiltrate the base of the Head Table and tie Dan Ackroyd's shoe laces together. EXECUTION: the DCdts and the DSM hold fortified positions to the L flank of G.O.H. the Commandant and his wife hold a strong position on his R flank. You will stalk beneath the table without drawing attention to yourself until you have reached Ackroyd's Guccis, at which point you will untie his laces and tie them together without revealing your position. SUPPORT: Weiland, Wommersley, Gaze, Mann are attached as support. Services include friendly Gungas of the kitchen staff.

He may have meant it as a joke, but I had done it. Sweating under the table, crawling an inch at a time in my scarlets, I'd made it to the General and back without being detected. Knowing that my seat, as custom dictated, would be removed while I was gone, I managed to have Billy and Josh hide it between them under the table. In fact, I'd accomplished the mission with stealth and bravado, and I'd even afforded myself a long gaze up the skirt of the Commandant's wife, catching a breathless view of cream see-through silk over a Brazilian manicured and perfumed pussy. I'd had so much wine by that point, that I honestly considered diving in there to eat her out, convinced that she wouldn't move, wouldn't say anything, that she'd just let me go down on her in a gracious, heartfelt act of anonymous cunnilingus.

Thankfully I stuck to my mission, but when I got back, Stocker was half-gassed, pouring himself another port, puffing away on a cheap cigar. He ignored the outcome of my mission entirely. The whole thing, as far as Stocker was concerned, was forgotten after he'd written the note.

In anger, I later stole into Stocker's room when he was passed out with his boots still on. I unscrewed the cover to the heater, and left an open carton of milk in there before covering it up again. A few weeks later, all of N Flight could hear Stocker screaming and swearing about the stench in his room. He was forever burning incense and scented candles after that, but it lasted about a month before the smell subsided, though it never fully went away.

Even Cecil got caught up in the proving madness—proving to himself that he wasn't part of the game. While he hated RMC, Cecil wanted to get into the Ritz Club so bad that he accompanied the rugby team as a tour manager on a trip to Newfoundland, just because he'd heard that the Ritz would be recruiting a few members in St. John's for their secret society. Some guys got together in capes and masks and at midnight blindfolded Cecil and told him that if he drank his piss he would be in the club. Cecil pissed in a bottle and drank it, then he was told that he was too stupid to be in the Ritz Club because he was a piss drinker. He claims that he didn't actually drink the piss—he just allowed it to sit on his lips. Fuckin' Cecil—what a nutcase.

And then there was me: soldier, rugby player, son, brother, lover, fighter, drinker. These titles defined my relationships with other people, but it was getting harder and harder to discern which ones I believed in. I woke up that morning with the buttons ripped off my uniform, blood on my tunic, my fists skinned and swollen, and my pants soaked with my own piss. The last thing I remembered was talking to Mom on a pay phone from Lino's Restaurant when I was already half-cut. I remembered her telling me about the Colonel and how it was worse than they thought. He had a fucked-up face and something wrong in the brain. He'd be going under the knife any minute.

I had to return home but lately I'd been on the piss, or hungover and having panic attacks, or on parade. I was afraid to get on the highway. Anything could happen.

Seeking Amnesia

Because of who my father was, my squad com had the authority to grant me two weeks of compassionate leave from the college. At home I sat through each day in the basement, captain of the Colonel's old tweed easy chair. The drinking chair. The worn cherry wood coffee table became a receptacle for stray ashes, wineglasses, spilled tea. I had the trots bad, and so five times a day I'd sit on the toilet and feel myself disintegrate. I didn't talk much. Ailish, who was growing up to be a bit of a wiseass, started calling me Verbal, too.

Mom wanted me to visit the Colonel with her. She wanted me to get outside, get some fresh air.

"I think you're drinking too much," she said. Her voice was firm but her hands were trembling when she said it.

"I think you worry too much," I said. She asked me to go to church and pray for my father and my family. By family I knew she meant Gertie.

I drove Dad's old Datsun to the OC Transpo Park-and-Ride at Baseline Station. I didn't think I could navigate downtown traffic with the anxiety attacks. The panic was almost all day long by that point. It had me living on guard, constantly at the position of attention—even at night, when I woke gasping for air. Drinking would help it along for a while, smooth it out through the night, but first thing in the morning my stomach would be sour, my blood dry fire, my thoughts black.

Nobody spoke on the bus. It was a quiet ride. When I saw the Rideau Centre I rose to ring for my stop. It was hot on the bus and I was soaked through my shirt with sweat. I was sure I felt my heart palpitate. I stuck two fingers up against my carotid to make sure I had a pulse. I descended the steps at the rear, waiting for the doors to hiss and swish open. I stepped over a salt slush-hole on the curb and, wary of my footing on the icy sidewalk, I crunched my way through the market and down Bruyère Street towards the main doors of the health centre.

At the information desk, a dark-skinned nurse who smelled like coconut butter told me where my dad's room was. She smiled when she spoke, and her voice was warm, and her eyes helpful. She was very professional in her white smock, and her white blouse underneath. She had a tight figure and thin, muscular legs. It terrified me to realize she was much more than a piece of tail. It occurred to me that she went home after shifts. Some nights she would make popcorn and watch cable TV, and some nights she would hold her man and make love to him, and they would make decisions about their life in the bed they shared.

I saw that she was a woman who had been a little girl, and maybe she had liked horses and peaches or dolls and clothes. Maybe she liked lakes but was afraid to swim in them. She had preferences, and she made decisions, but she never stopped growing old. And I saw that someday she would retire, and her legs would wrinkle and her skin get tough, and she would grow old and grey. She would nap with a quilt, and someday she would die.

The walk through the corridor was strangely familiar, though I'd never been inside Elizabeth Bruyère Hospital. The floor was highly polished and smelled of antiseptic, lemon-fresh death. I was parched, and bought an orange juice from a vending machine in the hallway, and took the elevator to Dad's floor. I found Dad's room easy enough. There were murmurs and whispers and soft sucking noises coming from other rooms. Some rooms had a large apparatus in them—monitor and breathing machine, IV poles and bags of fluid.

My dad was unconscious in his bed. The cancer had forced them to scoop out part of his brain during surgery. Mom had been told that the tumour was so twisted and large that it was impossible to relieve any pressure in the Colonel's skull with-out taking a chunk of his mind. The surgeon had explained that it had already taken over ninety percent of his left hemisphere.

He'd been at my rugby game just ten days ago. Dad's face, bloated and pasty, was dripping with sweat before he ever complained of pain. I don't think he'd ever seen me play a sport before that day.

"Take it easy, old man," I had told him. His face was droopy: one side hung down, dog-tired. His right eye looked lazy and didn't move at the same time as his left. He smiled at me, but only the left side of his mouth curved up, making his face look like he was snarling.

The doctors surmised that he'd had the tumour for eleven years.

He was asleep, with some sickly sweet drug washing through his heart. I checked his chart: morphine. Morphine would be all right in a pinch. The room was climate-controlled, anti-infectious. No dust on the sill. I tried to open it, thinking fresh air couldn't do any harm, but it was bolted shut.

I sat in the chair reserved for those who come to watch others die. It was still warm. Mom must have just left for the cafeteria, maybe the chapel.

The shaved patch on Dad's scalp was growing in already. This phenomenon of growing hair on a dying man seemed absurd. His face was jaundiced and swollen to twice the size it should've been. He looked like no man I knew. Still, I knew he was my father. Staples circumnavigated the crown of his head. His breathing was unsteady, heavy and strained.

After some time I was thirsty. The orange juice was cheap and shopworn, rotting in my guts like the SunPac battery acid we used to get at kye.

"Dad," I said.

He didn't stir. I couldn't look at his face. I felt a dark bubble of weight growing from the lump in my stomach and my jaw went numb. The bubble pushed against the wall of my chest, shortened my breath. It heaved inside me, against my lungs. I gave a large yawn. I was exhausted and needed a real drink.

I bent over, my head nearly cast in my lap and I felt for his hand, held on to his thick fingers. I tried to conjure up images of good old times, of happy times. I wanted to cry for him—I thought it would be proper to cry for him. But I couldn't cry and then didn't really want to, so after a while I stopped trying.

I pulled out the flask Dad had given me and took a drink. I had planned to save it until outside, but I needed a taste. I took a few more snorts and then held it out.

"You want some, Kernel?" I said. "I took it from your cabinet. It's the strong stuff."

He didn't move. I listened to him breathing. There was a wet scratching noise from his lungs each time he exhaled.

"Jesus," I said. "The wheels are falling off this chariot in a hurry, eh?"

I left Dad without looking at him again, as if the pain on his face might be infectious.

Oily Night

At the end of the corridor I realized the elevator was on the other side of the building. But I found the stairs down a narrow hallway. The door was twice as wide as any door I'd ever seen. I pushed against it. It was heavy and opened slowly, without a noise. I rested for a while to let my eyes adjust to the dim light in the stairwell. The door clicked behind me with a swoosh of damp, musty air.

My steps echoed as I descended: a hollow tap and then a granular, concrete scrape. Shh-shh, shh-shh, shh-shh, as if something was warning me that this was no place to be making noise. I quickened my pace, trying to remember how many floors I'd gone up from ground level. The lighting seemed dimmer with each successive floor, and I suddenly sensed that there was someone following me. I imagined there was a tall form, soft-shoed, black-clad, ready to reach out and grab the collar of my jean jacket and throw me down. I turned around to listen, but there was nothing there. I leapt stairs, jumping down three or four at a time, hanging onto the cold metal of the banister, and finally stumbled through the door marked *M*, which flew open under the weight of my momentum.

"Hey! Watch it, buddy!" A nurse pulled a stretcher down a shiny, blinding hallway. The old woman on the gurney lay still, staring at me vacantly. I'd almost capsized them.

I turned the corner to my left, walking briskly through automatic sliding doors into a room of stale energy. There was a ceiling-mounted small-screen television broadcasting *Jeopardy*. It was grainy and soundless—a pulsing blue eye. I looked at it, trying to pinpoint my senses onto something that could be easily understood. Alex Trebek mouthed a question.

I turned around. I was in the community room for the dying patients. A waiting room, so to speak. The room was packed, but I spotted the exit at the other end. I whirred my way through gnarled fingers, yellow teeth and sullen eyes; I groped past stretchers and acute snapshots of moles, wrinkled skin, willowy tufts of hair soiled with wax. Spittle-lips moved silently, mouthing imperceptible words. A gnarled hand with flaky skin reached out and touched my arm—I flung it off and ran. The room was packed with moaners, heated with the metallic scent of fear, body odour, blood and dying skin.

I kept my eye on the exit as I made my way through the last wheelchairs, and I was out of the hospital and into the oily evening. Anything could happen.

The air was damp and dark. Later, at the wake, I would tell people that I was glad to have seen him one last time—but really it was a visit I could have done without.

Before he died, the Colonel was struggling to relearn the art of speech, retraining his brain after they'd hacked part of it out. He fought like a soldier, and eventually lost to an enemy without a face. The enemy had infiltrated his own cells, attacked him with his own blood, hit at him in guerrilla-sized pockets hiding in his brain, eating his thoughts, his emotions, swallowing his understanding. His face remained shattered, disfigured by the operation, bloated with drugs, water retention, insipid unconsciousness.

"Mom," I said at the wake. "Do you remember the time Gertie and I were picking flowers in a field outside of Wainwright—the day Gertie caught her fingers in the car door?"

"Yes," she said.

"Do you remember what I found? In the bulrushes?"

"No, I don't think so—what?"

"You don't remember? How can you not remember?"

"I'm not sure, what was it? Refresh me—maybe I remember."

"I was walking ahead of you—Gertie and I were walking ahead of you and Dad. And then I took off on my own and got lost in the high grass. Dad only found me when I started screaming. Do you remember?"

"I don't remember you getting lost."

"I was only lost for a few minutes. But I found a skull. A human skull."

Either she didn't remember or didn't want to. But I remembered picking up the skull, and not thinking much about it. I turned it over and stared at it. I felt quite peaceful and curious about it, until it hit me what it meant. It was a calling card of death, and I kept on holding it. I didn't even know I was screaming. I watched Dad run toward me through the tall grass, pick the skull out of my hands and cover my eyes. He held me against his chest while I screamed.

We took a long look at Dad, ready to go under. They did quite a job with his face—I have to give them that. The Colonel had all his medals on. My father's at supper, in full mess kit. Not where he eats but is eaten.

"What did you do with the skull?" Mom said.

"Dad took it. I think he wrapped it in plastic and took it to the police."

"Oh my God—I DO remember!" Mom said, clapping her hands over her mouth. "That was that little native girl who'd been missing for years. I didn't know it was you who found her."

"It was a little girl?" I said.

"She was twelve or thirteen when she was abducted. It was horrible. I do remember."

"I didn't know it was a girl. I had nightmares about it, but it was always a man's skull in my dreams.'

"You used to get nightmares all the time."

I still did. There was a different one—a new one. The dream took place at RMC. There was a grainy black-and-white TV screen, and on the screen the image of a muzzle against someone's temple. In my dream the camera pans out a bit—like watching TV—just enough to see that it's my own face I'm watching on TV. And I'm laughing. I don't want to, but I'm laughing.

The camera pans out a bit more, and then I can see that the Browning 9mm pressed against my temple is in my own hand, and my finger's on the trigger and there's no way I can stop the trigger on the screen from being squeezed. I try to scream, to warn myself, but my face on the TV just laughs. Then the camera pans in real tight for a shot of my throat, and there's a white-hot light coming out of my mouth, onto the screen. But then the screen turns into the windshield of my van; there's a bird flying low over the highway and I'm cruising straight for it. I can't swerve, and the bird's flying directly at me. It smacks right into the grill. The weirdest thing is, I can read the bird's mind. This bird was on her way to a lake. She's got compassion for my van, and she always flies alone. I read her mind, and then it's blank—nothing—and I can tell that this bird is now just feathers, bones, skin and blood all stuck there in the fucking grill.

Go Left

They changed the chimes in the clock tower to play the good old college hymn "Precision": "Heads up and swing along, Hearts light and a ringing song, Life's but a march and it's easy when your spirit's willing…"

III OCdt Kempt

1. Section 129 NDA Conduct to the Prejudice of Good Order and Discipline in that, at or about 02:30hrs 13 September, at the Royal Military College, Kingston, Ontario, did enter the RMC pool after hours contrary to Director of Athletics Facilities SOPs and signs posted in the area.

Finding: guilty

Sentence: a fine of $250.00

I almost got shipped to Fort Drum for the long weekend; they needed bodies to play enemy force for the Yanks, but I never got on the truck. Instead I followed my gut at the last second when I realized at the Armouries that there were too many bodies for the exercise. Caruthers was pedantic, feeling shit-hot now that we were third-years, taking about how keen the Ex would be.

"A good leadership opportunity," he said.

"Shut up, Caruthers."

The Reserve Major walked up. "Any of you gents want the weekend off?"

I was on my feet in double-time with my rucksack hitched up tight, ready to go. Heads-up and swing along. I tried to look every bit the responsible, but grieving, student-cum-soldier. My combat uniform was always clean.

I used Dad as an excuse and got off the hook first, then trucked it back to the college in my slick black Cadillacs. A good soldier's combat boots wear like slippers. I stopped to use the payphone in the basement of Champlain. Icky wasn't home, Won-ton wasn't home. Nobody was at home in Ottawa—it was Friday night.

"I made a mistake coming back here," I said. Maybe Gertie had known something I didn't when she sent me that postcard back in first year.

I walked down the hallway on the second floor of Champlain, and slowed down as I approached my room. I sensed that something was off: my door was left wide open, my bedside light was on, and Rufus Wainwright played on the stereo.

First off, I'm not in the habit of leaving my bedroom door open. And even if I did overlook the door, there's not a chance that I would have left the stereo *and* the light on. I dropped my rucksack in the middle of the floor and took the stairs two at a time to check with Cecil, to make sure he was the one in my room. One had to be careful at RMC—CDs and books went missing all the time. The place was crawling with crooks.

Halfway down the stairwell I ran smack into some dude in a yak-wool coat, long hair and a beard—none other than Icky Kotlarsky. He had the devil's own grin on his face, hair down past his shoulders and a case of Stock Ale hoisted on his shoulder. He looked very at-ease, considering how physically and mentally out-of-place he was.

I was suddenly self-conscious about my uniform, about the whole appearance of the college. A first-year squeezed past us. He was trying to *march* up the stairs, for crying out loud.

"Good day, Mr. Kempt!" he belted out.

"Hi Recruit," I said. "You don't have to march up the stairs. Just check your arms at your sides and double-time it up."

"Yes, Mr. Kempt! Thank you for improving my slack and idle body!"

Icky, still grinning, looked me up and down.

"Going somewhere, Mr. Kempt?"

I looked at Icky's torn and faded cords, his leather hiking

boots beaten to shit and untied as usual, the yellow bandana around his head. Looking at him was exciting and frightful—like remembering there was something I had to do. But I couldn't remember exactly what.

"Not going anywhere… not at the moment."

III OCdt Kempt

1. Section 97 NDA Drunkenness in that he, on 3 November at the Royal Military College, Kingston, Ontario, was drunk.

2. Section 97 NDA Drunkenness in that he, on 4 November at the Royal Military College, Kingston, Ontario, was drunk.

Finding: guilty

Sentence: a fine of $500.00

I had a new plot twist in my recurring dream. I dreamt that I was lined up with a group of nameless, faceless people, though I could sense that all these people were my true friends. We stood staring at a large TV screen on which was displayed the muzzle of a Browning 9mm pressed against someone's temple. This time it was Dad's 9mm. The screen cut to the internal mechanisms of the weapon and I witnessed the firing pin snap forward in slow motion until it hit the firing cap of the chambered round; in acute detail I watched the ensuing chemical explosion, which forced the steel ball to be rocketed through the barrel on a blanket of gas. The screen cut to an external view just in time to show the steel ball rip through hair, skin, flesh, skull and finally the brain of my friend's head. Each skull was displayed on the screen in a similar manner, in grainy black and white. One by one they were all gunned down, but I couldn't see any faces.

Ultimately it was my turn and at first I was aware of nothing except the sensation of hot steel against my temple. This time, however, the view panned out to display my whole face, which was very disconcerting as I was smiling coldly to myself through the TV. I was annoyed with the picture because I was imminently aware of this vacuum housing brain and blood and water, this organic material trying to make sense of what I could see on the screen. The grainy image of my face repeated the word "Death," and what scared me was not knowing whether this notion would still exist once the trigger was pulled. The image laughed as the view pulled back further—wide-angle fish-eye lens—revealing what I always knew to be true: that the pistol was in my own hand.

III OCdt Kempt

1. Section 129 NDA Conduct to the Prejudice of Good Order and Discipline in that, on 23 January, at the Royal Military College, Kingston, Ontario, was parked in the LaSalle parking lot, contrary to the College Parking Policy.

2. Section 129 NDA Act Conduct to the Prejudice of Good Order and Discipline in that he had a "Staff" parking sticker installed on his windshield which is contrary to the College Parking Policy.

Finding: guilty of both charges

Sentence: a fine of $450.00

Just weeks before summer training in Gagetown, I latched on to a desperate philosophy. I tried to believe that my problems were forging me into what I needed to be. I forgot about my steely resolve to get clean, and I reassured myself that the panic and the heartache and the hangovers and the hives and the hemorrhoids were all part of my destiny. I thought they would, if nothing else, make me write one hell of a poem. I would suffer nobly through it all, and someday I would get what was coming to me.

III OCdt Kempt

1. Section 97 NDA Drunkenness in that he, on 18 February at the Royal Military College, Kingston, Ontario, was drunk.

2. Section 97 NDA Drunkenness in that he, on 19 Feb at the Royal Military College, Kingston, Ontario, was drunk.

3. Section 129 NDA Conduct to the Prejudice of Good Order and Discipline in that, at or about 02:30hrs 19 February, at the Royal

Military College, Kingston, Ontario, did enter the RMC pool after hours contrary to Director of Athletics Facilities SOPs and signs posted in the area.

Finding: guilty of all charges

Sentence: a Reprimand and a fine of $775.00

Woke up at Lollapalooza in Barrie, dialled Ruth long distance and told her things. I called her to attention, made my case. I called her to come back to me. I couldn't help thinking of touching her, how I'd once been able to simply reach over and hold her in my arms, to take her in hand and mouth.

"Would you just get over me?" she said. "It's for the best, Herbert."

"There's something I need to tell you."

"You're drunk."

"Are you fucking someone else?" I said. Ruth hung up, so I called her back to tell her things.

"I love you. I imagine you fellating football teams."

"Herbert: I'm cancelling my calling card and my credit card. Stop using them!"

"But I need to tell you about the heron!"

She hung up. I called back again and again, but the phone was off the hook.

The heron happened a week prior, when I went AWOL and took my van to the cottage, went driving after good memories. I had a hope that Gertie would be hiding out there, which was foolish and founded only on a memory triggered by listening to the 1812 Overture. She wasn't there and I drank alone.

After giving my liver whatfor I sat on the dock, unable to banish Ruth and the Colonel and the Army, feeling any minute like I'd crumble into thousands of clay pellets, that I'd sift through the cracks and into the lake. I could imagine myself disintegrating into fish feed. It was humid and the air was heavy and electric and oppressive.

I had more wine, more Wild Turkey. I had more Jagermeister until there was nothing left but Coors Light, and I drank that, too. I absolved myself with nicotine, but couldn't inhale the instinct for self-preservation.

I fiddled with Dad's fishing rod, wishing I knew how to use it. I was comatose on my ass, sleeping awake in the tense moonlight. It wasn't morning yet, but soon it would be. It was still dark enough for the bats swirling above my head. Then I heard the crack, felt the jolt, then felt nothing.

Click. I was out. Free. I was in the sky, and sober, above my body, staring down at my bloody nose and the last flash of lightning hitting the lake then *click*—I was back inside myself, a drunken sailor docked without a ship. My watch stopped.

"4:44," it said. It sounded like it was said out loud. Maybe it was I who said it.

I said a prayer to Ruth, to Ailish, to Gertie, to Mom, to God. I said a prayer, My Father: Send me an omen, something to prove that everything will be all right. I couldn't remember any real prayers, so I sang The Beta Band song:

"Take me in and dry the rain, I will be all right," I sang.

And I cast a long one with Dad's best rod, my nose still bleeding from the lightning on the lake.

This long one I cast was weighted to go deep, a silver fin and a fat worm dancing on the hook. I sat, awaiting the divine strike, the God-sent rainbow trout that would tell me I will be all right, I will be all right, I will be okay. I reeled it in slowly, patient for my miracle, and snagged it in the weeds because my line was too heavy. I was ready to chuck the rod into the fucking lake until I remembered that the miracle would most likely happen on the third try. Not the first. One is the loneliest number. I tossed the line out again and reeled it in quickly.

I had to change the worm because I reeled it in so fast it fell off. Either that or it rubbed off against a deadhead. I didn't know if I should count this cast as the official Third Cast, or if all three casts had to be made with the same worm. I threw the line in again. I waited, waited a bit more, and reeled it in slow.

Nothing.

"Eloi, Eloi, lama sabachthani," I said. Then I realized that there should be four casts, on account of my watch stopping at 4:44. So I cast again.

Nothing.

Nothing.

Nothing. I put a fresh worm on the hook; it coiled, writhing in its own slime, cutting itself more and more on the hook. I lined out again, a really long cast, only it snagged deep and snapped after a few tugs. Worm and hook and silver fin were gone and I broke the fucking rod in two and chucked it into the bitch bastard lake, regretting it instantly because I knew it was the Colonel's favourite and that Ailish liked casting with it, though she only weighted the line with sinkers—she never put a hook on.

The rod floated, the pieces just bobbing there, drifting slowly back to shore. I sat down on the dock and wiped my nose on my shirt, ready for bed or another smoke until I finally understood: the Other Side! I was to cast on the Other Side.

I didn't have a rod, but who the hell needs a rod for a miracle? I rolled up the sleeves of my fleece.

"Send me that omen now," I said, and plunged my arms in deep, eager to grip the fish that would be waiting quietly, patiently, for my hand.

There was nothing there, though. Not even a lousy minnow, or tadpole. I reached further, with both arms in up to my shoulders; there was enough light to see my drunken reflection until the blood from my nose rippled the water, obscuring it. This happened just as my right hand touched bottom and was sliced open by a clamshell.

Then I heard a low, rising whoosh, whoosh, whoosh. I looked around and couldn't see anything until the giant blue heron was above me. She had approached noiselessly until she was on top of me with a wingspan greater than the length of my body. The heron curved, circling, circling, circling then suddenly with a decided flutter of her great wings she landed with a majestically small splash. She was five feet away. I could almost reach out and touch her—and she stood at least four feet out of the water with her long neck craned and dark eyes gazing solemnly, confirming something.

Hey Verbal.

"You came," I said.

I live here, Verbal. You came.

The heron lifted off as noiselessly as she had arrived, gliding only a breath away from the shimmering surface of lake. Only then did I remember my Homer, how Telemachus had seen the bird flying high and to the left.

"Go left!" I screamed. "GO LEFT, GODDAMN YOU!" and the heron soared high above the adjacent forest and curved out wide to the left and then disappeared behind the treeline.

Undone

Sitting on a rocky outcrop at Fort Henry Hill, I pulled my toque off and ran a hand through my damp hair. It was still regulation but I was letting it grow out a bit, and it felt good. To be alone on Heartbreak Hill was pleasant. I took note of the birdsongs. There were many birds, but they were all of the small, grey-brown variety. I'd seen this type of bird hundreds of times.

I'd been dry for a week or so, and was starting to think I might have been smarter as a young boy.

It seemed odd that the birds would be *there*. They came in tiny swarms, flying above me and chirping madly, then disappearing, only to return moments later. There wasn't a tree in sight.

"Are you omens?" I said. "Are *all* of you omens?"

I lay back and stared up at the pastel orange of morning sky. I couldn't see the bay, or the campus below. Just the sky above, and the birds playing in it. I marvelled at how they egged each other on and excited each other. I closed my eyes and remembered the heron as if I was remembering a promise made long ago. With my eyes closed I could hear the last remnants of ice cracking at the edges of Lake Ontario. The lake never looked dirty in the spring or in my mind.

From the amphitheatre below, I listened to the RMC machine flicker and cough to life. I sat up and watched the lights of the Stone Frigate illuminate one by one for reveille, just as the morning star cleared the horizon. The smell of breakfast wafted from the mess kitchens, surfed a breeze to my nose. It reminded me of my first days in training. Bacon, sausage, pancakes. Some neon-pink fruit-flavoured drink. Endless mornings of burning up and down a hill not unlike the one I sat on.

257

Something had happened; it was still happening.

I hadn't minded blackening my boots every morning, or hoisting a log in forced camaraderie. The miserable toil and weariness of it all had promised me a liberating sense of accomplishment, if only I could stay among the finishers.

It was about making it across the line, again and again.

I had once kept the company of those who knew what it felt to be strong, to learn how far I could push myself. But somewhere along the line the sweat started to smell acrid, the issue olive drab turned musty.

I looked at Fort Champlain from the hill, and I could smell the pungent odour of shoe polish and panic from years ago. There's no life like it.

I'd been eighteen when I signed that piece of paper.

Something—a sense of self-preservation perhaps—told me that it wasn't over yet. They hadn't touched my core.

I mouthed the words over and over: Dismissal Without Disgrace.

That was my option. The Commandant had had me in for a sit-down, still doing favours for the honour of my dead father.

"You're out, Kempt. You're out now, if that's what you want. No harm done. Dismissal Without Disgrace. I know it's been hard on you, but every soldier has to toe the line. We must adapt and overcome, Kempt. There's no denying these charges against you, but the fines will be forgiven if you want to take the release.

"If you're going to stay, and I offer this in the knowledge of where you hail from, the fines will be paid in full. You will be allowed to continue your education and your training, provided you place among the top ten candidates in your Phase Two Infantry Training.

"You do your summer training, you come back here, and you make the call. I'm not going to tell you what I think your old man would say, because that wouldn't be fair, but I will tell you that despite all your shit-disturbing at this college, I think you've got real potential. I think you have your father's strength. Dismissed, Kempt."

It's true I had become sloppy. I'd started thinking too much. My mediocre marks inched constantly towards failure. My headaches were worse; I had difficulty concentrating. I'd gone off the track, couldn't read the signposts.

I watched the first cadets mill about the edges of the parade square and make their way to the mess. I could pack my rucksack and leave today. I had that choice—I was aware suddenly that it was mine to make.

I stood up and put my toque back on, swung a leg over the saddle of my mountain bike. I pedalled to the gatehouse then coasted easily down the paved decline, picking up speed. I veered off suddenly onto a steep dirt trail, narrowly missing the fence. When I hit the bottom I kicked it across the rugby pitch, pumping madly.

Life's but a march, and it's easy when your spirit's willing.

I still wondered about those birds, that I should know what kind of birds they were, that I wanted to know.

Ducimus

By the time they shipped me for summer training, I told myself I was ready to eat smoke. At the base in Gagetown, New Brunswick, there was an official plaque that said "Home of the Army."

I arrived on base one day before infantry training started. I hooked up with Doogie, the only black cadet from RMC. I mention his blackness as a matter of political interest, because although he was the only black man at the College, his picture was on every recruiting poster across the country. That's Canada for you.

The barracks in Gagetown were the most single-purpose buildings I could imagine. There was no extra detail, not one. Not one more nail than needed to build your basic barracks. There were four bunks to each room, and Doogie and I made sure that we moved in early enough not to be shacked up with any crybaby fuck-pots.

Doogie and I picked a room at the end of one hall. One of the beds was heaped with kit, another early arrival. We unloaded our duffle bags and rucksacks, and were waiting for CMTT to arrive with a shipment of boxes carrying the rest of our gear when a blond soldier sauntered into the room. He was dressed in PT gear that fit him perfectly, and though he was a touch shorter than either of us, his body was imposing. He had the kind of body Dad would have called a "brick shithouse." It seemed impervious to pain. He wore a faded grey ARMY t-shirt and running shorts, and it seemed to me that I'd seen his face before. Soaked with sweat, he extended a meaty palm. Attached to his hand was an arm thickly braided with muscle.

"Lebris," he said. "Call me JP."

"Doogie," said Doogie. They shook.

"Hi. I'm Kempt," I said. JP crushed my fingers, then went to his bed where he stripped down.

"Hey boys, check this out," JP said, flashing his neatly shaved bag.

"Jesus," said Doogie. "You put a fucking razor to your balls?"

"It's all about maintenance. The chicks lap it up, man. They love it."

"I don't know if I could put a blade that close to my nuts, man."

"Nothing to it—feel 'em, boys."

Genuinely interested, Doogie and I reached over and touched his sack.

"Maintenance, eh?"

"It's key, boys. Makes them cream. I have to grab a fucking shower," he said, and threw a towel around his waist. "We might as well head into Freddy for some decent food and a few pints before they start dishing us cock. Tonight is last call for pussy."

We were here for training and we were gearing up. Already my language was terse and vulgar. JP tells us to feel his balls and we do. There's nothing weird in it. The rugby boys piss on each other in the shower. We stake claims in the sexual, the oral, the scatological. Since Dad died, I see how our minds are on hold, our thoughts deindividualized; only our bodies belong to us, and then so infrequently there is no room for social convention. We must stake our claim between the runs, the drill, the push-ups. We stake claims in our bodies, and feel comforted, grounded, brotherly.

I braced myself for the cold mornings of gut-wrenching PT, for the hard-ass room inspections, for the never-ending field exercises—the hard rations, the sleep deprivation, the trenches, the forced marches, the advances-to-contact, and the navigation exercises, where I'd be alone for hours in the dark wilderness.

I said to myself that I was ready to train against the invisible Fantasian Forces, to get green acne from camouflage paint, to dry-shave in the grey light of pre-dawn, to chew instant coffee and peel scabs off my feet with dried-blood socks, to pepper my diction with curse words. If I couldn't clean up my act, I could toughen it up.

"Shit," I said to Doogie. "I am fuckin' more than ready for the cock these fuckin' cunts are gonna dish out."

"Fuckrights, Verbman. We lead."

When faced with these prospects, I welcomed them. I was anxious to let my hands do the same work as Dad's. Mom once said that we had the same strong, lean hands, the same graceful but powerful motions.

I no longer hated the weak for being weak; I simply dismissed them. I would patiently ignore them until they failed out or quit. I wanted those mornings to come, mornings on the MLVWs, to smell diesel and dust. I yearned for the sunrises I'd watch from a trench after days of no sleep and hamburger feet.

That summer I smelled death: the melon-quash, the pumpkin-smash, the rotting fruit-stand caravan. The fragmentation I'd been feeling all year contracted, just a bit, but enough to know that the task which lay ahead needed me to centre myself, to focus.

I had no response but to get stronger, harder, leaner. I think I knew then that somewhere that summer I'd find the Colonel lurking about.

Coach

There was a designated smoking area on the range. I took a few deep cuts from a Player's Filter before our break was over, checking self-consciously every minute to ensure my rifle was still with me. Do I have my rifle? Did I make safe? These are questions I was never sure about.

Though I'd fired my rifle probably a thousand times, and though I'd carried it all summer through the swamps of Gagetown, it felt strangely light. It was an awkward extension when I held it with both hands. I could *almost* forget about it when it was slung over my shoulder and stretched diagonally across my back, as if it was nothing more than a bookbag.

But then there were the other officers in training, my brothers shod in the olive drab of combat, with their black C7s always touching some part of their body. Like a piece of one of those puzzles you just can't put down, no matter how much it frustrates you.

"Your rifle is part of you," they told us. "Take care of your rifle and it will take care of you."

And sometimes I wished it *was* a bookbag, and that Gertie's journal was inside. I would forget myself some days, but now and then I remembered that I was here to learn effective killing.

Where is my rifle? Did I make safe?

I let myself think about nothing while smoking with the others. Captain Wilde walked up to us.

"Time to quit this gagglefuck and get to work," he said. I ground out my cigarette with the heel of my combat boot and caught a whiff of the Captain. He smelled like Old Spice, fresh coffee and wine-tipped Colts. That smell had a sense of purpose to it, like proof that Captain Wilde was The Coach. It was a comforting and familiar scent to have on the range with a platoon of live weapons.

Tucked neatly in his left breast pocket was a notebook and pencil. Not your ordinary pencil—the gourmet click-action all-weather kind. His face was bronzed from all the hours he clocked on the range, he had a perfect haircut, and his eyes seemed to affirm that he never got tired. Looking at him you just knew he ran about 12 km every day and pumped iron five times a week. The binoculars around his neck were the best on the market. He tapped a folder (presumably holding our shooting records) against his palm.

"Put me in Coach," I said. I was ready to shoot. Hell, I could be the Coach myself, I was so ready.

As a coach, be alert, painstaking and very patient. Avoid hustle. Give praise when it is due. Avoid over-coaching and useless chatter. The firer can deal with only a few faults at a time. Sort out the basics and progress from there. Keep the critiques short. Rest the firer during critique.

I lay on the grass in the prone position, my turn for one-on-one coaching, and Coach lay beside me. I only had to glance at Captain Wilde's cap badge, the PPCLI on his shoulder, and the Airborne Wings on his chest to understand these symbols as concrete emblems of pride and courage and heroism. It was evident that he was offering me the key to these things, perhaps the very keys I had thus far missed. I felt, in his presence, the suggestion that I too could express myself through the same symbols. For too long I'd been hard on the Army, not understanding it at its basic, crucial level. I'd been too harsh—too judgmental, but I could make it up to a man like Captain Wilde. He was a simple man, and he represented strength.

The goal of coaching is to improve the soldier's shooting techniques and knowledge to such a degree that they have the confidence and ability to use their weapons effectively in battle.

Captain Wilde lay on my open side, and watched. He inspected my ammo and I was now ready to plug five rounds into target number three, a silhouette of an attacking soldier, at one hundred metres.

Breathe in.

Breathe out.

Breathe in.

Let out half a breath, focus, squeeze—

"Stop."

I took my finger off the trigger and looked at Coach.

"What's wrong with your sights?" he said.

I looked at my sights. Not sure. The front aiming post looked fine to me—it was straight up-and-down, anyway. The rear sight was—

"I have the rear sight on the large aperture, sir."

"Correct. That is for close-range and night shooting. Adjust your sight, Kempt."

I clicked the safety catch and adjusted the sight to the small aperture, then disengaged the safety and took aim again. Now Captain Wilde's breath smelled of cinnamon Dentyne. The old man used to chew cinnamon Dentyne. Maybe the Army gets a discount. I wouldn't have minded a stick myself—all I could taste was stale Player's Filter.

The butt of the rifle felt good in my shoulder, but the sleeve of my combat shirt seemed super tight around my left arm (which was extended so my left hand had a firm grasp on the muzzle guard). I smelled gun oil.

Breathe in.

I adjusted my weight on the sandbags and breathed out.

Breathe in.

Half a breath. Hold it. Squeeze.

PAP. The recoil was slight but I flinched anyway. I looked at Coach but he was spying the target with his field glasses plastered to his eyes. I aimed again and squeezed another round off, determined not to flinch. I wanted to feel the rifle as an extension of myself, but it felt awkward, as if I was pissing out of someone else's penis. Coach was there to watch me piss, to see if my aim was true, if my stream could make it all into the bowl.

I had three more shots to fire before we checked my grouping, and I aimed again at the Fantasian soldier's chest. *Always shoot at the centre of mass.* The Fantasian soldier's helmet looked suspiciously German, circa World War II.

I fired three more rounds, and although I couldn't see where they'd landed, I felt that each one was subsequently worse. The last one I squeezed off blindly, just to get it over with.

"Clear your weapon," Coach said. I removed the magazine, cocked the action and looked down the barrel.

"Clear."

"Okay. You rushed it a bit. You've got a wide grouping."

"Yes." I said, wondering how the hell he could see a bullet hole at one hundred metres out. I waited for the people in the butts to pull the targets and score them. Captain Wilde must have known I couldn't see my own wide grouping.

"You've hit wide on both sides of the target. This means you lack determination in firing, and you were probably varying your aiming and holding."

Hard to believe I lacked determination. In sniper talk that must be like being impotent.

"Pick up the rifle and take aim, Kempt."

I did.

"Okay: feel this here? Where your shirt is stretched across your back? Well your shirt's too small. For now you can take it off and shoot in your singlet, but you'll have to go to clothing stores ASAP and get some bigger combat shirts. What's this—a small?"

"Yes sir," I said.

"Get a medium at least. Next thing: once you take aim, try not to change your firing position—this will help you tighten your grouping. I could see where your rounds were going."

"How can you see bullets?" I asked. I was learning how to shoot from Superman, apparently.

"Not the bullets, the air displaced by the bullets. It's called 'swirl.'"

"Oh, right," I said. "Swirl."

"Your breathing is good, I don't think that's a problem for you. Focus on these points and I'll have you qualifying in no time.

"Now I'm going to fire five rounds. I want you to use the binoculars to watch for swirl so you can tell where each shot lands. After the first three rounds, look at me and study my breathing and posture. Make sure, when using the glasses, that you place the top of the eyepieces into your eyelids and push your eyelids open—so you don't blink when I'm firing."

I never caught the swirl, but every minute action, every part of Captain Wilde's body was behind each round that he fired into the target. No unnecessary movement, micro movements for exact intention and purpose.

For me, no time turned into three hours on the range and about half a million rounds. But I qualified. My rifle was slowly becoming an extension of my body. Then we moved onto the next objective. And the next. We were always looking for the crest of the next hill. Me and Doogie and JP and the boys stared out at the dreamy horizon, anticipating the day we'd be on the top of that hill. It was déjà vu. The next hill, the next posting, the next course, the next tour. Perhaps with the next promotion we'd be standing at that spot on the horizon and looking down into the valley. But, try as I might, I could never see an end to the climbing.

On the range I fancied I had Coach potential, finally holding the rifle in my arms as if it belonged there. I wanted Captain Wilde, with his Airborne tattoo, to throw me just a crust. I wanted something in my skin, too; I wanted an indelible marking of conviction, a permanent sign of strength.

Later, sitting in the concrete reinforced butts, listening to the crack-thump of bullets whizzing over my head and into the target, I imagined that the Fantasian soldier wore the snide expression of Mr. Stocker. Stocker, who's already taken about ten rounds, is still grinning when I pull him down, patch him, and throw him back up for the firing squad. Then I grow tired of that—tired of having to look at his face—so I turn my attention to the battalion of mosquitoes settling on my arms and hands (where I refuse to wear DEET since it melted my plastic watch band and made my tongue numb whenever I inadvertently touched my mouth) and preoccupy myself with hundreds of small deaths and the sight of my own blood.

And I guess then I knew. I knew there, in the damp butt-mare armpit of New Brunswick called Gagetown, that I had a choice about losing my final grip. I'd learned the feeling of displaced absurdity.

This is what I knew: it was inspiring to see the illumination from paraflares popping in the night sky over a defensive position. It was nice to put a tube on my shoulder, press a button, and watch a tiny rocket shoot out and impale itself through the armour of an old tank. It was nice to ride in choppers and yell and cuss and spit and sweat. But still I felt sick right through the middle of my guts, and imagined I was being slowly poisoned from the inside out.

I wanted my Dad back.

Some man. Sitting in the butts I wept like an old man, swaying to and fro to the music of live rounds and wishing for Daddy. But I was so goddamn tired. I wanted him to hold me even for a split second—that would be enough. That would be enough for anything. I could soldier on and take the next hill and a hundred after it with just an ounce of his strength.

Then it came. It came the night they dropped me in some remote section of the vast and unfamiliar training area. They dropped me, solo, at 23:00 and I had less than seven hours to reach a dozen or so navigation points. I had no flashlight: just a map, a compass, and the moonlight.

If I didn't reach the last point by dawn, I would fail. It was impossible to reach the last point unless I covered each of the previous points successively, since I could only obtain the next set of coordinates by making my way through the darkness to a small plaque which gave me my next bearing. It was needle in a haystack type work if you couldn't trust your compass.

"Always trust your compass," JP had said. I never considered how difficult that could be until I was picking my way through brambles at midnight.

I missed my first point and wandered aimlessly through the bush for a full two hours until I happened upon it accidentally. To make up for lost time I sprinted between the rest of my points.

At 04:00 I was only halfway through, and there it happened. I ran into a wall of stink, a powerful musky smell that made me shiver. The hairs stood up on the back of my neck. It was just a smell, and it was a smell I didn't recognize, but something about that smell was encoded in my DNA, and my DNA did not like it one fucking bit.

When I made the bear out in the darkness, I was almost on top of it. Reaching for my rifle, I had intended on scaring it off by firing blanks. Something stopped me.

I stood there, thought of Dad. What would he do?

I called out to the bear. I called out.

The beast, a mid-weight black bear, just grunted at me, sniffed my blood through my skin, and shuffled off.

I stood there and listened as it crashed its way through the trees. I listened long after it left. I listened to the invisible worlds of insect life that moved on at their conscious, tireless pace. I listened and I thought that my meeting with the bear, in the tiny space of time that had spanned less than a minute, was imprinted on me forever. It had more significance than the past three years. It stuck out truthfully as one of the tangible occurrences in my life; few things could match its delicious reality.

I knew that I would forever be saturated with that musky smell, that pregnant moment in the darkness of the Gagetown woods.

I couldn't describe how or why, but I knew then where my dead father was.

Surrender

Whether I deserved it or not, I came out of Gagetown ranked third. I was no JP Lebris, first place his entire life, nor was I Doogie, sliding just below radar in the number-two spot. I think Goethe said it best: "Be bold, and mighty forces will come to your aid."

I flew back to Mirabel in a Dash-8 (the smaller planes keep it real) and Mom and Ailish met me at the train station in Ottawa.

"You look fit, Verbal," Ailish said. "You've got a nice tan."

"Combat tan," I said. "Too bad I can't wear jeans on the beach."

"We got a postcard from Gertie," Mom said.

"You're kidding me. Where from?"

"Spain. She was on the last leg of El Camino de Santiago," Mom said.

"What's that?"

"Some kind of pilgrimage, a long hike apparently."

"Any return address?"

"No."

"Well, it's good to know she's alive."

I still had three weeks of leave before I had to be back in Kingston, but I knew I'd have to sacrifice some of that time for rugby camp if I wanted to play A-side this year. But I had a week, anyway—and a week of Round Lake sunshine can do wonders. Mom drove the Datsun up early, and Ailish and I followed a day later in my van. There was a sense of kinship in coming home to the van.

"Can we stop at the grave, Verbie?" Ailish said.

"You want to?"

"Do you?"

"Yeah. I think I do."

At the funeral I had thought that when I returned to his grave I'd undertake an involved ritual to say my goodbyes. I planned different scenarios in my head, some of which included gathering a bunch of bulrushes for his headstone, pouring a bottle of whiskey on his plot of land, reciting Thomas Gray's "Elegy Written in a Country Churchyard" and blaring Neil Young's "Old Man" out of the back of the van. But we just stopped by on our way up to the cottage, just dropped in to pay a visit. I was empty-handed, Ailish had a package wrapped in brown paper.

"Well," said Ailish.

"Well, well," I said.

"Do you want to say something, Verbie? I mean, in private?"

"Should I say something?"

"I don't know. I thought you would."

"I thought so too, but nothing comes to mind," I said.

"Maybe you could just say goodbye," she said.

"Maybe," I said, remembering the bear. "But I think I already did."

"You want to sit down?"

"Are we supposed to? I mean, isn't it disrespectful?"

"I don't think Dad would mind," she said.

"No. You're probably right." We sat.

"Verbal, do you think I'm more mature?"

"Than me? Definitely," I said. Ailish laughed.

"No—than before."

"You've always been mature. You tried to hide it with baby talk remember? Even when you were a baby you were too mature."

She plucked some grass and played with it. Pensive. Young woman soon. I wished she could skip the heartache and the growing up she'd have to do like all the rest of us.

"Listen Ailish: being mature is overrated. Just be yourself. You are perfect as you are. Don't go changing for me or Mom or even him," I said. "Right Colonel? See? His silence speaks volumes."

"I don't remember what Gertie's face looks like. It's sad and it scares me."

"You've got her nose," I said. "And you've got her smarts, too. Thank God you don't have her attitude."

"She has Dad's eyes, right?"

"And Mom's mouth. Dad's hair."

We sat for a while, then I said, "You leaving that here?"

She looked at the package in her hands.

"Oh, no. It's for you," she said. She handed it over.

"What is it?"

"Open it," she said. I opened the wrapping. "I found it in the attic," she said. "I thought you might be looking for it."

It was the journal—the journal Gertie had sent me eons ago. I'd forgotten all about it. It seemed surreal that I'd once had grand plans of writing a poem.

"Thanks," I said.

As soon as we turned onto the grass-covered dirt road, the van started bouncing up and down over the rocks, and all the smells of the lake and forest of my youth came back in a rush. Gagetown and soldiering receded. As soon as I set foot in the cottage, with its stale smell of sun and sand and woodsmoke, the city dripped away from me. I hadn't been sober at Round Lake in so long I'd forgotten what it smelled like—I'd forgotten why we used to go up there. Memories were bundled up with smells, and so many of them involved Gertie that I half expected to see her when I came out of the lake after a swim, or took Ailish down to the candy shack. I found an old book of mine there: *Zen and the Art of Motorcycle Maintenance.* I'd read a page or two and put it down when I knew I hadn't retained so much as a single clause. It felt good not to care whether I understood it or not. The book was for naps, not for proving something to myself.

"Wow," said Ailish when we were swimming. "When did you get that?"

I looked down at the tattoo on my shoulder. "I got this in Gagetown."

"What is it?"

"What does it look like?"

"Well I know it's a bird, but what does it mean?"

"It's a heron. It doesn't mean anything. It's just a reminder."

I slept outside—in the gazebo if the sky threatened rain, but mostly in the hammock on the beach. Ailish and I stuck close; our days were for catching frogs and minnows and fishing from the canoe, and our nights were for bonfires and s'mores and ghost stories. We drank cream soda and lemonade and ate around the clock.

"I'm always hungrier at the cottage," Ailish said.

"Me too."

"You've both got hollow legs," Mom said. Mom played crazy eights and Liverpool with us, and we taught Ailish how to play euchre even though we didn't have a fourth.

Brother Down

I drop kick the white leather ball through the uprights, chase it down and kick it back again. I feel at home here on the inner field, despite its proximity to the parade square. I've got a good sweat worked up—I've got the field to myself. Soon I'll head down to the tape room to get pumped up for our big match with Queen's. I've got good, clean strides. I haven't touched a drop in months. My conditioning is good, my lungs getting pinker by the day. No more tobacco, no more sucking it up to get to the breakdown. I can get there with breath to spare.

And I'm at ease—I don't have to decide to stay or go until tomorrow. All I have to do today is play some good solid rugby.

Down in the dressing room I breathe deeply of the sweat and the tiger balm and the impending competition. We huddle up, arms around each other, rocking and swaying as Les appeals to our courage and our strength. We can't play this game by ourselves, Les says. It takes fifteen men, and we've got to use all fifteen of them. We hold each other, building energy against the pre-game jitters, each of us hungry for the first hit. Hands in. We shout in unison.

"In the sack the pig will grunt!"

We rush the field in a tight group, the Queen's players already dispersed in their positions, waiting for the coin toss. The stands are packed and the dorm windows are packed. Cecil works the crowd, taunts the visiting team's bench.

"Fuck 'em up Verbal!" he screams. Cecil is the greatest sports fan.

I don't pay attention to the crowd, knowing Ailish is supposed to be here with Mom. I don't bother looking for them in the crowd. My focus is the field, my guns are aimed at my opposing #10.

We lose the toss and kickoff, then with a growl we steal the first scrum.

I called for it blind side, then pivoted and turned, knowing without looking exactly where the ball would be. I knew where it would be before anyone saw the scrum half pitch it out. Rugby camp has paid off with this one pass. I pivoted and ran and there it was in my hands—a gift, the most natural thing. I faked it to Gaze, who was playing fullback, and running like a freight train to draw them blind side.

I stutter-step back outside and dish it off my hip to Gunny, the inside centre who's running straight upfield. He handles the ball like it's a newborn, and I loop outside of him with all the speed I've got. I call for it and he throws it blindly, though it's a perfect pass just before he collides with the Queen's inside centre, taking him out. I called straight hands, which means I should keep feeding it out to the wing, but at the last second I sell a dummy pass to the outside centre and step back inside.

I'm not being greedy. I'm just reading the terrain. I read the gaps like I've put them there myself. The bodies in front of me are standing still, too slow to recalibrate because I've built up momentum by now. I give a few straight arms, sidestep a low tackle, and I'm clean and free. I run with everything I've got. I've got forty long yards to their goal line, and I've left my support, so I'm going it alone. Their fullback was caught out when we moved to go blind, and I've got nothing but fresh, green grass in front of me.

"Hey dumbass!"

The voice chills me; I run with goosebumps, cold sweat.

"Nice moves, Brother!" Gertie screams from the sidelines. I see her off to my left, standing with Ailish and Mom. She's tanned and lithe and she's got a mischievous grin. She's a woman now. One glance tells me she's seen things, she's got stories, there are new chapters for us to write.

Synapses are firing. Half of them tell me to go score and half of them tell me to run straight to her and squeeze her like mad. She senses this, I guess, because the next thing I know she has rushed the field and is gunning straight for me as I'm kicking it to the goal line.

It's ridiculous watching her run in flip-flops. She's got good wheels though, and if she keeps up the speed she'll cut me off right at the goal line.

"Hello Sunshine," she screams. "It's been a while!" I nearly drop the ball, watching my left flank. She's got a good bearing on me; her flip-flops flap off her feet and sail away in a wide soft arc behind her. She picks up speed in her bare feet and I can hear her breathing now. It dawns on me that her intention is to take me down. I give it all I've got, but with her angle it looks like a tight squeeze to the goal. A rush and a push and I'm just about there as she dives, arms out, and grapples me in a high tackle on the five-yard line. I hang onto the ball and the ref blows to signal the try as we thunder in under the goal posts together, belly laughing.

Gertie's got me pinned; she kneels on my chest, wrestles the ball out of my arms, and bonks me a good one with it, right on my pumpkin. Wide-eyed, I have to wait a moment to catch my breath.

She drops the ball and takes my head in her hands. She stops laughing abruptly and stares hard, panting.

"What?" I say. "What is it?" She's got this weird look about her—something oddly familiar in her eyes. She looks spooked, and opens her tense mouth, but nothing comes out. She's got a few wrinkles and a deep tan. She looks tired, like she has lived a hard life, and I understand that I don't really know this woman.

"Gertie," I say. "Gertie?"

Then I see what it is she's looking at. There he is, right in the centre of her iris, in the flush of her face. In looking at her I can see it's the Colonel she sees. Suddenly she looks uncomfortable, and rolls off me. She doesn't say anything and nor do I. We still have to catch our breath. But it comes.

Acknowledgements

In 1979, when I was six-and-a-half years old, my grade one teacher, Mrs. B, asked each student in turn a frightening question. Eventually she came to me and asked what I was going to be when I grew up. I blurted out a response which eludes me now, only to buy time. When I got home that day I stewed; I may have even developed a fever—I was prone to hot flashes. I was under the impression that once I made a decision I'd be locked in for life, and so I was understandably wary of making a mistake. After dinner I couldn't take the pressure anymore, and so I asked my parents for advice. They probably don't even remember doing this, but they sat me down on our green wool floral-print chesterfield and explained to me rationally and seriously that I could do anything I pleased with my life—it didn't matter one whit to them if I chose to pick through garbage for a living, as long as I was honest, happy, and respectful of others. That is all they asked of me.

That one remark, and the place from which it originated, has had such a positive impact, on so many occasions, in my life. It has been a license to adjust my perception whenever necessary. For this important tool, I am grateful to my Mom and Dad.

I thank my family—my wife, Karie, to whom this book is dedicated, and who has gifted me the time to write, and my children, Jackson and Samia.

I also have to thank the following people: my sisters, Angie, Marie, Andrea, Sheri and Krista; Gonzalo Alvarez; Terry Baine; Rick and Lynn Barré; Phil Barré; Dr. Sylvia Berg; Andy Black; Yanick Bloomfield; Paula Bois; Dr. Stephen Bonnycastle; Peter Burgess; David Caplan; Chris Cianfranni; Michael Connolly; Phil Cowie; Liam Cox; Cliff Dann; Les Davidson; the Dawe brothers, and their parents; the Dewars; Austin Douglas; Jon Evans; cousin Bob, whom I followed through the Arch, and

Uncle Harry and Aunt Bertha; S.N. Goenka; Will Graydon; Mark Grenville Sr.; Mark Grenville Jr.; Chris Grenville and Three Tarts Bake Shop; Craig Gunn; Pete Heelis; Tony Hustoft; Big Jilm Irvine; Mark "The Mouth Harp" Jarman; Eric Jol; Troy Kelly; Knock on Wood Communications, specifically Whitney Zelmer; Jason Labonté; Glen Lantang; Toro Lee; Paul Lopez; Roger Lupien; Lasse Lutick; Pee-wee MacIntyre; Alison Mann; the McClure family, the McKies; Jim McKnight; Duncan McNaughton; clan Milne; Julia Mitchell; John Morrice; Art and Shirley Nugent, who teach the art of giving; Amy Nugent, who helps me with the art of living; David (a.k.a. Gravy, a.k.a. Nancy) Nugent, for inspiration, creative spirit, and laughter; all my cousins, who are my good friends, and who play the most entertaining games of euchre, dominos, and Liverpool; George Parades; Dr. George Parker; Sam Roberts, for his distinctive brand of rock and roll; Bill Travis; the University of New Brunswick; half-assed Johnny Vass; Susan Venables at Nectar, for the fine teas; Justin Wall; Bill Weiss; Darryl Whetter; Mr. Wilson; and Jordon Zadorozny, for all the demos that I listen to when I write.

Special thanks to my editor and publisher, Silas White.